ANNE TYLER

Anne Tyler was born in Minneapolis, Minnesota, in 1941 and grew up in Raleigh, North Carolina. She is the Pulitzer Prize-winning author of *Breathing Lessons* and many other bestselling novels, including *The Accidental Tourist, Dinner at the Homesick Restaurant, Saint Maybe, Ladder of Years, A Patchwork Planet, Back When We Were Grownups, The Amateur Marriage, Digging to America* and *The Beginner's Goodbye*. In 2012 she received the *Sunday Times* Award for literary excellence, which recognises a lifetimes's achievement in books. In 2015 *A Spool of Blue Thread* was a *Sunday Times* bestseller and shortlisted for both the Baileys Women's Prize for Fiction and the Man Booker Prize.

ANNE TYLER

If Morning Ever Comes

VINTAGE

22

Vintage
20 Vauxhall Bridge Road,
London SW1V 2SA

Vintage is part of the Penguin Random House group of companies
whose addresses can be found at global.penguinrandomhouse.com

Penguin
Random House
UK

This edition reissued in Vintage in 2016
First published in Vintage in 1991
First published in Great Britain by Chatto & Windus in 1965

penguin.co.uk/vintage

A CIP catalogue record for this book is available
from the British Library

ISBN 9780099539100

Printed and bound by Clays Ltd, St Ives Plc

Penguin Random House is committed to a sustainable future
for our business, our readers and our planet. This book is made
from Forest Stewardship Council® certified paper.

I

WHEN BEN JOE Hawkes left home he gave his sister
Susannah one used guitar, six shelves of *National
Geographic,* a battered microscope, and a foot-high hourglass. All of these things he began to miss as soon as he hit
New York. He considered writing home and asking for them
– Susannah probably hadn't even listened when he gave them
to her – but he figured she might laugh at him. His family was
the kind that thought only children during their first summer
at Scout camp should miss anything. So he kept quiet about
what he missed and just dropped Susannah a postcard, with a
picture on it of the UN building by night, asking if she had
learned to play the guitar yet. And six weeks later he got a
card back, but not the picture kind, postmarked Sandhill,
N.C., and badly rained-on. He turned the card over and
learned, from Susannah's jet-black, jerky script, that she had
just changed to a job with the Sandhill School Library and
was getting rich and could have her hair done every week
now. She signed it "So long – S," and then there was a P.S.
saying she was going to start learning to play the guitar
tomorrow. Ben Joe read this over two or three times, although
what she had said was perfectly clear: she had only just now
remembered that the guitar existed. Probably she had got up
in the midst of doing something else to drag it from his closet
and twang the slack strings, but having discovered that she
wasn't born knowing how to play and might have to work at
it awhile she had dropped it again and drifted on to something
else that came to mind. Ben Joe thought about starting up a
whole *string* of cards – asking on the next one, for instance,
whether that hourglass was still keeping time okay – until she

1

got snappy with him and packed everything up and sent it to New York. But Susannah was flighty, like almost all his sisters, and rarely finished anything she started reading even if it was as short as a postcard; he didn't think she would notice that he might be missing something. So he stopped the postcards and just wrote his regular letters after that, addressed to the family as a whole, asking about the health of his mother and all his sisters and saying he thought of them often.

By then it was November. He had left home late in August, just after his twenty-fifth birthday, to start law school at Columbia, and although he was doing well, even with three years of empty space behind him since college, he didn't like Columbia. On campus the wind up from the river cut clean through him no matter what he wore, and his classmates were all quick and sleek and left him nothing to say to them. They looked like the men who modeled Italian wool jackets in men's magazines; he plodded along beside them, thin and shivering, and tried to think about warm things. Nor did he like law; it was all memory work. The only reason he had chosen it was that it was at least practical, whereas the other ideas he had had were not, and practicality was a good thing when you headed up a family of six women. So all through September, October, and most of November he sat through Columbia's law classes and jiggled one foot across his knee and peeled his fingernails off.

On this particular Thursday the wind was so cold that Ben Joe became personally angry at it. He stepped out of the law building, pulling his collar up over his ears, and the wind suddenly hit him full in the face and left him gasping. That decided him; he changed direction and headed toward the apartment. Lately he had taken to spending the really cold days in bed with a murder mystery, and he was beginning to think he should have done that this morning.

On Broadway he stayed close to the buildings, hoping that there would be less wind there. He passed the brass nameplate on one of the concrete walls and for an instant saw his face reflected there, made yellow by the brass, with his mouth open and his jaw clenched and his teeth gnashed against the

2

cold. If it had been any other day he would have smiled, and maybe stopped to peer into the brass until the passers-by wondered what he was doing, but not today. Today he only hunched his gray topcoat around him more securely and kept going.

His apartment was five blocks from the campus, in a tiny dark old building with unbelievably high, sculptured ceilings. Opening the front door of it took all the strength he had. And all the way up the three flights of stairs he could smell what every family had eaten for the last day and a half – mainly bacon and burnt beans, he gathered. Ordinarily the smells made him feel a little sick, but today they seemed warm and comforting. He climbed more quickly, making each wooden step creak beneath his feet. By the time he was at his own door and digging through his pockets for the keys he was whistling under his breath, even though his face was stiff with cold.

"That you?" his roommate called from the kitchen.

"It's me."

He took the key out of the door and slammed the door shut behind him. Inside it was almost as cold as it was in the street; all it needed was the wind. The living room was taller than it was wide, and very dark, with high-backed stuffed furniture and long, narrow windows that rattled when a gust of wind blew. The mantel and the coffee tables were bare and dusty. There were none of the flower pots and photographs and china do-dads that he was used to from the houseful of women in which he had been raised, but a huge clutter of other objects lay around – newspapers, tossed-off jackets, textbooks, playing cards. In the middle of the dark wooden floor was a square scatter rug colored like a chessboard, and ridiculously tiny plastic chess pieces sat upon it in a middle-of-the-game confusion.

Ben Joe stripped his topcoat and his suit jacket off and threw them onto an easy chair. He untied his tie and stuffed it into the pocket of the jacket. From the daybed he picked up a crazy quilt from home and began swaddling himself in it, covering even his head and huddling himself tightly inside it.

"For Pete's sake," his roommate said from the kitchen doorway.

3

"Well, I'm cold."

He backed up to the daybed and sat down. The bed was a wide one; he worked himself back until he was leaning against the wall and his legs were folded Indian fashion in front of him, and then he frowned.

"Forgot to take off my shoes," he said.

He patiently undid the quilt and untied his shoes. They fell to the floor with two dull thuds. With his cold feet pressed beneath the warmth of his legs, he reached again for the quilt and began pulling it around him.

"Hey, Jeremy," he said, "grab this corner, will you?"

His roommate left the doorway and came over, carrying a cup of coffee in one hand. "I've never seen the like," he said. "You wait till it's really winter. Which one?"

"The one in my left hand. There. Thanks."

He leaned back against the wall again and Jeremy drifted over to the window, slurping up his coffee as he went. He was younger than Ben Joe – twenty-one at the most, and an undergraduate – but Ben Joe liked him better than most of the other people he had met here. Maybe because he didn't have that sleek look either. He was from Maine, and wore sneakers and dungarees and dirty red Brewster jackets to class. His hair was so black it was startling; it gave him a wild look even when he smiled.

"I thought you had *two* classes on Thursdays," Jeremy said.

"I did. But I only went to the one. I got cold."

"Oh, pooh." He sat down on the edge of the window sill and swung one sneaker back and forth. "In Maine," he said, "we'd be swimming in this weather."

"In Sandhill we'd be sending for federal aid."

"Oh, now, don't you give me that."

He stood up and began tugging at the window. It screeched open; a gust of wind blew the newspaper's society section into Ben Joe's lap.

"Will you shut that *window*!" Ben Joe said.

"In a minute, in a minute. I'm trying to see what the thermometer says. Thirty-four. Thirty-four! Not even freezing."

4

"It's the wind," Ben Joe said.

The window slid shut again, leaving the apartment suddenly silent.

"Want to walk with me to the drugstore, Ben Joe?"

"Not me."

"I got to get a toothbrush."

"Nope."

Jeremy sighed and headed for the bedroom, twirling his empty coffee cup by the handle.

"Last night," he said as he walked, "I figured out the prettiest-sounding word in the English language. I did. And now I can't remember it."

"Hmm," Ben Joe said. He reached behind him to flick on the wall switch and smoothed out the newspaper in his lap. It was last Sunday's, but he hadn't got desperate enough to read the society section till now. It crackled dully on his knees, looking gray and smudgy under the flat light from the ceiling.

"I mean," Jeremy said from the bedroom, "usually you can think of a word that's *one* of the prettiest-sounding. But no, sir, this was *the* word. *Really* the word. I meant to tell this comp professor about it, that I see in the cafeteria. And then I woke up this morning and it was gone. It had an s in it, I think. An *s*."

"*That* should narrow it down," Ben Joe said. He grinned and tipped his head back so that it was resting against the wall.

"You want a date tonight, Ben Joe?"

"Who with?"

"This real cute freshman, has red hair and brown eyes, which is my favorite combination, and comes from, um—"

"Too young."

He opened the society section and folded it back, letting his arms emerge partway from the blanket.

"Thank you anyway," he called as an afterthought.

"Oh, that's okay." Jeremy was standing in the doorway now, with one end of a pillow in his teeth. "I've decided to clean the bedroom," he said. The words came out muffled but still intelligible. "I haven't changed my sheets in three weeks." He shook out a pillowcase, held it below the pillow, and

5

opened his mouth to let the pillow drop into the case. Then he tossed the pillow toward his bed and vanished from sight again.

Ben Joe started reading the society section, holding it upside-down in front of him. He had started learning to read when he was three, but his parents wanted him to wait until school age; they made him stand facing them when they read him bedtime stories, so that the book was turned the wrong way around. It wasn't until too late that they realized he was reading upside-down. Usually he read the right way now unless he was bored, and then upside-down words came to his mind more clearly. He held the newspaper at arm's length and frowned, studying an upside-down description of a golden anniversary where the couple had had another wedding performed all over again.

"What's this mess of lima beans doing on the floor of the closet?" Jeremy called.

"Oh, leave them. I'll take care of them."

"I know, but what are they *doing* there?"

"I forget. Hey, Jeremy, if you were having your golden anniversary would you have another wedding performed all over again?"

"Hell, no. I wouldn't have the first one."

On the next page there were ads to run through, detailed little line drawings of silver patterns and china patterns and ring sets. He yawned and then set to picking out a ring set, ending up with a large, oddly shaped diamond and a wedding band that was fine except for a line of dots at each edge that bothered him. Then he chose a silver pattern and a very expensive china pattern, platinum-rimmed, but he was already beginning to be tired of the game and abruptly he turned the paper right-side up, picked out a bride for himself that he considered most likely to meet all his requirements, and, with that finished, pushed the society news to the floor and stood up.

"Where's last Sunday's crossword?" he called.

"I already did it."

"You did it the week before, too."

"Well, I waited till *Wednesday,* for God's sake."

Ben Joe went into the bedroom. Jeremy was sitting on the floor with one of the bureau drawers beside him; he was slowly going through a stack of postcards and throwing some out but keeping most of them. The rest of the room was in chaos; Ben Joe's bed was unmade, Jeremy's was made but covered with the things he had decided to throw out, and there was a heap of dirty sheets on the floor between the two beds.

"Worse than it was before," Ben Joe said.

"I know. That's the trouble with cleaning up."

Ben Joe leaned his elbows on the dresser and looked into the mirror with his chin in his hands. The mirror was wavy and speckled, but he could at least recognize himself: his thin, flat-planed face, which almost never needed shaving and took on a sort of yellow look in the wintertime; his level gray eyes, so narrow that they looked as if he were constantly suspecting people; and his hair, dark yellow and hanging in shocks over his forehead. It was getting shaggy at the back and sides; he looked like an orphan. And walked like one, letting his shoulders hitch forward and burying his hands deeply in his pockets so that his arms could remain stiff and his elbows could dig into his sides. One of his sisters had once told him, meaning it kindly, that he was homely, all right, but *trustworthy*-looking; if people could do what they liked to strangers on the street, they would stop him and reach up to pat the top of his head. He sighed and straightened up and began moving around the room, kicking dust balls with his stockinged feet.

"I thought you were going out for a toothbrush," he said to Jeremy.

"I am. Soon as I finish this drawer. A red one."

"A red what?"

"*Tooth*brush." Jeremy threw a stack of postcards in the direction of the wastebasket. "I always buy a red toothbrush for the wintertime."

"Oh." Ben Joe sat down on the edge of his bed and frowned at the sheets on the floor. After a minute he said, "You ever seen one of those toothbrushes with a bird on the end? The kind that gives a soft little whistle when you blow on it?"

7

"Sure. That's for kids, to make them want to brush their teeth."

"Well, I know it." He lay back crosswise on the bed and stared at the ceiling. "My sister had one of those once," he said. "My older sister, Joanne. She's away now. But she had a little pink toothbrush with a bird on the end, and it wasn't when she was a little girl, either. It was when she was in high school and had taken to wearing red dresses and gold hoop earrings and flinging that black hair of hers around. One night I was writing this philosophy paper. I came out of my room for a drink of water and I felt like hell – my mind all confused and tired but still popping off like a machine gun. And out of the bathroom just then came Joanne, not in red but in a little quilty white bathrobe, and sort of dreamily blowing the bird on her toothbrush. She didn't see me. But it was so damned *comforting*. I went to bed and slept like a rock, no more machine guns in my head."

He lay quiet for a minute, following the sculptured molding around the ceiling with his eyes.

"What was I saying?"

"About toothbrushes."

"Oh. Well, that was all."

He turned and rose up on one elbow to see what Jeremy was doing. Jeremy was reading all the postcards he had saved.

"Hey, Ben Joe," he said.

"Hmm."

"You want to hear something funny?"

"What."

"It's from this buddy of mine that goes to college out west, with a picture of this gorge, real deep down with a river at the bottom. Says, 'This gorge is habit-forming. Threw a bowling ball down it to hear how it sounded and it sounded so good I moved on to bigger and better things and last night me and some buddies threw a piano down it.' A *piano*. What do you guess it looked like when it hit? Ben Joe?"

Ben Joe looked up.

"Ah, you're not listening," said Jeremy. He put the postcard back in the drawer and moved on to the next one.

8

Ben Joe sat up, running his fingers through his hair. "What time is it?" he asked.

"I don't know. Eleven or so."

He reached over and pulled open the top drawer of his own bureau. At the right was a stack of letters; he pulled the top one out, looked at it to make sure it had been signed by his sister Jenny (she was the official family letter writer), and then lay back down, holding the letter over his head, right-side up, to read it:

Dear Ben Joe:

We received yours of the 12th. Yes, of course we are well. I don't know why you keep asking us, since you know as well as we do that the last time any of us was in the hospital was five years ago when Susannah had all four wisdom teeth pulled at once. Mama says to tell you you worry too much. We are getting along beautifully & hope you are too.

Financially things are going smoothly. Next month both of the twins are getting raises at the bank, but Lisa is getting $6 more a month than Jane, which make family relationships kind of tense. Tessie is taking drawing lessons after school now for $2 a lesson, which I think we can afford, & the only extra expense this month has been the eaves pipe falling down from the roof outside Tessie's & my window due to Tessie's standing on it. Tessie didn't, tho. Fall, I mean. I'll never know why.

I wish you would write a letter to the family suggesting that we go back to a policy of my doing the grocery shopping. Specially since it was me you left in charge of the money. Gram has been doing it lately & the results are disaster. She gets anything she feels like, minced clams & pickled artichoke hearts & pig's feet & when I ask where are the meat & potatoes she says it's time we had a little change around here. She's ruining us.

Enclosed is next month's check for your expenses, etc. I hope you will remember to send a receipt this time as it makes my bookkeeping neater.

Sincerely,

Enc.   Jennifer.

Ben Joe folded the letter and sat up again. "I wish someone besides Jenny would do the letter writing in my family," he said.

"Why?"

"I don't know." He began walking around the room with his hands in his pockets. "You never know what's going *on*, exactly. Just about the dratted eaves pipes and stuff."

"The what?" Jeremy sat back and stared, and when Ben Joe didn't answer, he said, "Oh, now, are you getting started on your family again? What you worried about?"

Ben Joe stopped in front of the window and looked out. There was a venetian blind between him and the outdoors; the buildings across from him were divided into dozens of horizontal strips.

"Someone's lost a red balloon," he said. "They must've lost it out a window, it's flying so high."

"Maybe it's a gas balloon."

"Maybe. What bothers me is, sometimes I think my family doesn't know *when* to get upset – the most amazing things happen and they forget to even tell me. I try to keep quiet, but all the time I'm thinking, 'I wonder what's going on back there. I wonder if maybe I shouldn't just chuck everything and go on back and see for myself, set my mind at rest if nothing . . .'"

He was sitting on Jeremy's bed now, and reaching for the phone.

"You going to call home?" Jeremy asked.

"I reckon."

"You want me to get out?"

"Nah, that's all right— Operator, I want Sandhill, North Carolina, two four oh—"

"You got a Southern accent," she said. She was snappy and cross, with a New York twang to her voice. "I can't tell if you said 'four' or 'five'; you don't—"

"I haven't got one, either. I said 'two, four, oh—'"

"Yes you do. You said 'Ah.' 'Ah haven't got—'"

"I did not. My mother's a Northerner, even."

"Number, please."

"Two four oh, six seven five four. If I had an accent I'd say 'foh.' No 'r.' But I said the 'r.'"

"And *your* number, please."

"Academy four, six five five nine."

10

"Station to station?"

"Yes'm."

The telephone had a familiar plastic smell; the receiver was warm and already a little damp in his hand. He hated using the telephone. The thought of speaking to someone, and listening to him, without seeing him was as panicky as not being able to breathe. How could he tell anything about a person if he couldn't see him? Sometimes he thought something must be wrong with his ears; what he heard told him almost nothing. And usually he read too much harshness into a voice. He could hang up a telephone receiver and feel hurt and bewildered for days and then find out, weeks later when he asked what he had done to annoy them, that they were just talking above the noise from a TV set. So now, to make it easier for himself, he tried to picture exactly what was going on at the other end. He pictured the house in Sandhill at eleven o'clock on a Thursday morning, with the autumn sun shining palely through the long bay windows in the living room. His sisters would all be at work, he guessed, except for Tessie, who was still in grade school. Or was it her lunch hour? No, too early. That left only his mother, and maybe even she would be gone; she worked part time at a book store. The phone rang twice. He waited, tensed against the pillows.

"Hello?" his mother said. He could tell her from his sisters, although their voices were almost the same, by that way she had of seeming to expect the worst when she answered the telephone.

"Hi," he said.

"I beg your pardon?"

"It's me. Ben Joe."

"Ben Joe! What's wrong?"

"Nothing's wrong. I called to see how you were."

"Didn't you get our last letter?"

"Well, yes. I guess I did. The one about the eaves pipe falling down?"

"I think that was it. Did you get it?"

"*Yes*, I got it."

"Oh. I thought maybe you were worried because you hadn't heard from us."

11

"No, I heard."

"Well, that's nice."

Ben Joe waited, frowning into the receiver, twining the coils of the telephone cord around his index finger. He tried desperately to picture what she looked like right now, but all he came up with was her hair, dust-colored with the curls at the side of her face pressed flat by the receiver. That was no help. Give him anything – eyes, mouth, just a stretch of cheek, even – and he could tell something, but not *hair*, for goodness' sake. He tried again.

"Well," he said, "how *is* everyone?"

"Oh, fine."

"That's good. I'm glad to hear it."

"It's too bad you called while the girls were away. Joanne's the only one here now. They'd have liked to talk to you."

"Susannah, you mean."

"What?"

"You mean, *Susannah*'s the only one here."

"No, Susannah's switched to a full-time job now. I thought Jenny told you. She's working at the school library. I don't know why that should be tiring, but apparently it is. She comes home all cross and snappy, and last night she had a date with the Lowry boy and ended up shoving his face into a cone of buttered popcorn at the Royal Crown theater. I forget what movie they were showing."

"Never mind," said Ben Joe. "What I'm asking is, *who* is it that's the only one home but you?"

"Joanne. I told you."

"Joanne?"

"Well, yes."

"Mom," Ben Joe said, "*Joanne's* been gone for seven *years.*"

"Oh. I thought Jenny wrote you about that."

"Wrote me about *what*?" He was up off the bed now; Jeremy looked over at him curiously.

"I think maybe you *didn't* get our last letter," his mother said. "Come to think of it, it was the next-to-the-last letter about the eaves pipe falling down. The last one should get there today or so. Have you gotten today's mail yet?"

"No."

"Why, what time is it?"

"Mom," Ben Joe said, "is Joanne home or isn't she?"

"*Yes*, she's home."

"Well, then, why? And when did she get there? Why didn't you—"

"She left," his mother said vaguely.

"Just now? Didn't she know I was on the phone?"

"No, I mean she left Kansas."

"Obviously she left."

"She took the baby and ran away from her husband."

"*What?*"

Ben Joe sat down again on the edge of Jeremy's bed. Jeremy took a sidelong glance at him and then got up and left the room.

"Ben Joe, is there a bad connection on your end? Can't you hear me?"

"I can hear you."

"Well, don't be so dramatic, then. What's done is done, and it's none of our affair."

Ben Joe closed his eyes, briefly; he wondered how many times in his life he had heard his mother say that.

"Are you there, Ben Joe?"

"Yes'm. How is she?"

"Oh, fine. And the baby's a darling. Very well behaved."

"Has she changed much? Joanne, I mean. What's she like now?"

"Oh, the same as ever."

"Can I talk to her?"

"She's asleep. She stayed up last night to watch the late show."

Ben Joe took a breath, hesitated, and then said, "I'm coming home, Mom."

"Ben Joe—"

"It won't hurt to cut a few classes. I want to just see how everything is."

"Everything's *fine*."

"I know, but I want to set my mind at rest. I've been worrying."

13

"You're always worrying."

"I'll see you tomorrow, Mom."

"Ben *Joe*—"

Ben Joe hung up, neatly and quietly. There was that giddy feeling in his head that always came from talking for any period of time with his mother, or even sometimes with his sisters; he felt confused and uncertain, as if he and his family were a set of square dancers coming to clap the palms of their hands to each others', only their hands missed by inches and encountered nothing. It was only after he had gone over the conversation in his mind, arranging it in a logical order and trying to convince himself that everything was really all right, that he felt better. He stepped to the door and said, "Jeremy?"

"Yeah, Ben Joe." Jeremy came in, looking quickly at Ben Joe's face. "Trouble?"

"I'm going home for a few days. If the university calls, you tell them I'll be back, will you?"

"Sure."

"I'll take that night train. Be there by morning." He pulled his suitcase out from under the bed and then sat down, staring at it blankly.

"You see what I mean," he said. He spread his arms helplessly, looking up at Jeremy, who was leaning against the wall with his hands in the pockets of his dungarees and his face worried. "You get these cheerful little financial statements, and meanwhile what's going on? Joanne's run away from her husband and come home, after seven years of only phone calls and letters from her—"

"Joanne," Jeremy said. "She the one with the red dress and bangles?"

"Yep. Her. On the way out to get your toothbrush, will you pick up today's mail? I bet they tell about it in a P.S., that's what."

"You going to try and make her go back to her husband?"

"No, just going to see her."

"Well, I'll go get the mail," said Jeremy.

"Okay."

Ben Joe crossed back to his bureau. The drawer was still open; he pulled out a large leather jewelry box and flipped the

14

lid up. Inside were all the odds and ends that he never knew what to do with. He searched through two-cent postage stamps and Canadian nickels and old scraps of addresses and worn-out snapshots and eventually he came across the torn-off flap of an envelope with train times scrawled across it. He picked out the night train to North Carolina. Then, whispering the time to himself as he walked, he went to his closet to choose the clothes he would wear home.

2

HIS CAR ON the train was only half full; rushing through the darkness it made a hollow, rattling sound. It was cramped and peeling inside, with dirty plush seats and a painted tin roof. At the front hung a huge black-and-white photograph of some people on a beach in Florida, to show that this was the southbound train. Maybe once the photograph had been shiny and exciting, so that passengers gazing at it had counted the hours until they could see the real thing. But now the plastic sheet over it had grown scratched and dull, and the people in it – dozens of tiny people in homely old bathing suits, caught forever in the act of skipping hand in hand toward gray waves or sitting close together under gray-and-white umbrellas – seemed as sad and silent as the flat, still palm trees above them. For a while Ben Joe gave himself up to just staring at it, until the strange feeling it gave him was gone and it was only a photograph again. Then he turned away and looked at the people who shared this car with him.

Mostly they were upright, energetic Negro housewives, sitting like wide shade trees over their clusters of children. Around their feet were diaper bags and paper sacks and picnic baskets; above their heads, in the baggage racks, was an abundance of feathered hats and woolen scarves and sturdy, dark-colored coats. Like Ben Joe, who had a sheepskin-lined jacket folded across his lap, they had come prepared for the time when the hot, stuffy car would suddenly turn too cold for sleeping. They clucked to their children constantly and passed them hot lemonade and pieces of Kleenex, dug up from the bottoms of grocery sacks whenever they heard someone sniff, whether it was their own child or not.

"Here your pacifier, Bertie."

"You let Sadie at the window now; you been at it a sufficient time."

A thin blond man in a pea jacket passed through, carrying a box of toys with "80 cts" printed on it in purple nail polish. He came even with the children just across the aisle from Ben Joe and from the box he pulled out a toy – a rubber donkey with a cord and squeeze-bulb attached to it. The children reached for it, their hands like four little black spiders.

"Want it?" the man asked.

The children looked at their mother. She was a comfortable, smiling woman sitting in the seat ahead of them with a friend. When she heard the man's voice she turned and looked at the children and smiled more broadly, and then frowned and gently shook her head.

"Watch," the man said.

He pressed the bulb and the donkey bucked, tossed his head, kicked up his heels. Then the little rubber knees buckled in the wrong places and the donkey was lying down in the man's hand, limp and ridiculous-looking.

"Only eighty cents," the man said.

The children watched, round-eyed. With one hand the little girl began stroking the back of her mother's head, patting the curls of her hair with soft, tiny pats.

"How much you say?" the mother asked. She turned only halfway, so that she seemed to be asking the woman beside her.

"Eighty cents, ma'am. Eighty little pieces of copper."

"*No* sir," the mother said. She turned to the children and said, "No sir. You wait, chirren, we'll get us something in Efram. In Efram, we'll see."

"Eighty cents," the man said.

"*No* sir." She reached out to straighten the collar of the smaller child, the girl, and then gave her a soft pat on the shoulder and smiled at her.

"How about you?" the man said to Ben Joe.

"No."

"No kiddies at home?"

"No."

"Ah, well."

The man moved on. At the back of the car it began to be noisier; that was where the men sat. Some of them were apparently the women's husbands, and others – the younger, more carelessly dressed ones, slouching in their seats and tipping hip flasks – belonged to no one. They offered swigs to the married men now and their conversation became gayer and louder. Up front, the women clicked their tongues at each other.

"Lemuel Barnes, I coming back there after you if you don't hush!" one called.

"You watch it now, you men, you watch it!"

That was the woman ahead of Ben Joe, a young, plump woman with a baby whose head rested on its mother's shoulder like a little brown mushroom button. She was sitting alone, but she had been talking steadily ever since she boarded the train, calling to her husband at the rear and soothing her baby and carrying on conversations with the other women passengers. Now she stood up and faced the rear, with the baby still over her shoulder, and shouted in a piercing voice:

"You all going to wake the baby, Brandon, you hear? Going to wake up Clara Sue. You want me come back and check on you?"

She started into the aisle, obviously not meaning to go through with it, and stopped when Brandon shouted back, "Aw, Matilda, this Jackie boy the one. *He* stirring all the trouble up."

The other women chuckled.

"That Jackie, he become a pest afore we even got out of the station."

"Brought him *two* bottles. Say no one bottle'd do him."

"Need a wife to keep him still, that boy."

"*Hoo*, Lord."

Matilda smiled down at them and sat down slowly. "Going to make that Brandon come up *here* he don't behave," she said loudly to the window. "I *mean* it, now."

Ben Joe tried smiling at the children across the aisle, stretching his mouth farther than it wanted to go, but the children stared soberly back at him with little worried frowns.

18

Ahead of them, their mother opened a paper sack and handed back two pieces of fried chicken. The children accepted them automatically, their eyes still fixed on Ben Joe.

"When I get home," their mother said to the woman beside her, "I going to have me a mess of collard greens."

"You got you a good idea there," Matilda called.

The woman turned back and nodded gravely. "They don't feed you right in New York," she said. "Don't know how a person keep himself alive, in New York."

"Ain't *that* the truth."

They were quiet a minute, picturing home. For a minute Ben Joe pictured it with them, knowing almost for a certainty exactly what their homes were like. Who could be that definite about where *he* came from? A hundred years ago, maybe, you could look at a Carolina white man and know what he would have for supper that night, in what kind of house and with what sort of family sitting around him. But not any more – not in his case, at least. He felt suddenly pale and plain, going back to a big pale frame house that no one could tell was his. He looked at his reflection in the black windowpane and frowned, seeing only the flat planes of his cheeks and the worried hollows of his eyes.

"The way they does their chicken in New York," called Matilda, "they puts it in the oven stark nekkid and let it lay awhile. *I seen* it done that way. With a cut-up *frying* chicken I seen it."

"That's so, I know. That's so."

"Ticket, please."

Ben Joe looked up at the conductor, standing stolidly beside him and smiling down over a huge stomach. He handed him his ticket, already a little frayed, and the conductor tore off one section of it.

"Won't have to change," he said. He gave the rest of the ticket back and swayed on to the next passenger.

Someone sat down beside him, so suddenly that Ben Joe was almost frightened for a minute by the jounce in the springs. He turned from the window and found himself no more than three inches from the pointy nose of a curly-haired boy, who was leaning so closely toward him in order to see his face that he was practically lying on his side against Ben Joe.

"*Pardon* me," the boy said. He sat up straight again, folded his coat in his lap, and stared ahead of him at Matilda's baby.

Ben Joe settled back more firmly on his side of the seat and examined the boy's face. He would judge him to be about fifteen, but a New York fifteen; he was very self-assured and his face, except for that one moment of inquisitiveness, was tightly closed and smooth. When he became aware of Ben Joe's stare, he turned toward him again and said, explaining himself, "Just wanted to see what you looked like. See you didn't talk a lot or weren't drunk or nothing."

"I don't talk and I'm not drunk," Ben Joe snapped.

"Okay, okay. But I was sitting with this old man, see, and he was talking all the time. Made me nervous. *All* these guys make me nervous."

"That's *your* problem," Ben Joe said.

"The old man's dying."

Ben Joe looked around, alarmed. "Which one?" he asked.

"White fellow, sitting way back. Can't see him from here."

"Why didn't you tell me before? What—"

"Re*lax*. He's only dying slowly, of old age."

"But—"

"He's *okay*, see."

Ben Joe sat back and stared out the window. The rushing sound of the train and the deep blackness outside made everything seem dreamy and unreal. It was hard to believe that the train was going anywhere at all; it was only standing still and swaying slightly, against a moving screen of darkness and the occasional pinpoints of lights. He told himself that he was finally going home, after all that worrying about his family and wanting desperately to see them again. He told himself what was even more real than that: that when he got there he would immediately feel sad and confused again, the way he always did. But no, Joanne was back. Joanne could change things; just by smiling that smile of hers she could make everything seem safe and in its right place. He closed his eyes, picturing home. He pictured his house as another kind of train, lighted also, floating through darkness. But with the sound of his own train in his ears he couldn't hear their voices;

he stood outside his family's windows and watched their movements without hearing a single sound.

His mother would be moving rapidly around the house, pursing her lips tight and flouncing her hair because Ben Joe *couldn't* come home, she wouldn't have it, and then going off to put clean sheets on his bed. His grandmother would be standing on a counter in the kitchen to see what Ben Joe might like from her special private stock of food on the top shelf. And in the ruffly, perfumey closed circles of their worlds, his sisters would hear Ben Joe was returning and then forget again until his return was an actuality and they could get briefly excited over it. Joanne would laugh. She would look at her feet, propped bare on their father's leather hassock, and laugh easily for no reason at all.

(Only would she? It was seven years now since he'd seen Joanne; why couldn't he ever realize the happening of a thing? Surely she'd be different now – calmer and more even-tempered. Or did she wear a low-necked, swinging red dress when she took the baby for a stroll? And toss her hair and flash that teasing smile when she ironed her husband's shirt for him?)

"Plate of okra!" Matilda shouted. "That's what *my* mind fixed on!"

"Be right good. I declare if it wouldn't be."

Ben Joe reached into his shirt pocket. From behind a crumpled pack of cigarettes and an old lighter of his mother's he pulled out this morning's letter, already dingy at the creases. He held it up under the tiny bulb that was supposed to be a reading lamp and read, once more:

Dear Ben Joe:

We received yours of the 21st & are glad to hear you are well. It is too bad that the Asian flu shots gave you Asian flu. Also we are sorry to hear that you are cold.

The big news of course is that Joanne is home. She left her husband altho it's not clear why and of course the first thing Mama asked was was he unfaithful, they all are, & Joanne just laughed at her. The baby is as cute as she can be & is going to be spoiled rotten.

Tessie is going to have to have braces, which will be quite

an expense. Gram is going to knit you a sweater for the cold but has forgotten the measurement from the tip of your shoulder to your wrist & would like you to tell her. Also what is your favorite color & if it's still purple forget it, because whenever she knits you a purple sweater she gets to seeing polka dots in front of her eyes before she goes to bed at night.

Ben Joe, you did not write telling Gram not to shop any more. Last night we had crabmeat and black olives in our Monday-night casserole. She also thinks I am not handling the money right & so yesterday she went over the bank books and decided the bank had credited us with $112 too much so she quick withdrew it and put it in another bank before they could find out. I had to go & change banks back again this noon.

Let us hear from you & don't worry.

Sincerely,
Jennifer.

Ben Joe put the letter back in his shirt pocket. He pulled the lever under the arm of his chair and pushed against the back of the seat to make it slant more. There was no point in staying awake worrying about things.

Someone sat down in the curly-haired boy's lap. The boy awoke with a start and said, "Hey! What you—" and began fighting, flailing his arms out and heaving his body and hitting mainly Ben Joe. Whoever sat in the boy's lap was big and solid and quiet, in a heavy tweed overcoat, calmly tipping a bottle to his mouth.

"*Brandon!*" Matilda shrieked. She stood up and, with one hand still holding the baby to her shoulder, reached out and grabbed a handful of Brandon's hair and shook him by it, hard. "You no-count you, Brandon—"

"I'm just *set*ting, Matilda," said Brandon.

"You setting on some*body*, Brandon."

Brandon turned around and looked beneath him.

"Oh, hey," he said.

"You are *sitting* on me," said the boy. He was breathing hard, and looked as if he might start crying.

"I surely am sorry, sir. I didn't see you at all, sir, I come to say hey to this yellow-haired gentleman—"

"Get yourself *offen* him, Brandon."

22

Brandon rose, confused, and bent over Ben Joe's rumpled seatmate. "I surely do hope I didn't hurt you none," he said. "I surely am sorry. I surely am."

"For*get* it," the boy said. He straightened his jacket and then settled down further in his seat and closed his eyes, determinedly.

"Aren't you *ashamed* of yourself, Brandon."

"Yes'm."

"He ain't *never* like this," she said to Ben Joe. "It's that Jackie egg him on. Brandon has always been a real pillar to me, a real— Come up here and set, Brandon."

"Yes'm, just a minute. I want to speak some with this *yellow*-haired—"

He sat down heavily on the arm of Ben Joe's seat, but taking care not to touch the boy, and leaned across to look at Ben Joe.

"Believe you Ben Joe Hawkes," he said. He switched the bottle to his left hand and shook Ben Joe's hand several times, up and down. His breath smelled of gin, but other than his first mistake he didn't act like a drunken man. His face was sharp and alert, and although he seemed very young there were the beginnings of lines at each corner of his mouth, downward-pulling lines that made him look as if he were in pain. "I'm Brandon Hayes. This here my wife, Matilda. Matilda, this Dr. Hawkes's boy. Dr. *Phillip* Hawkes – him."

"That so?" Matilda said. She turned to Ben Joe, still uncertain, and when Ben Joe nodded, she look relieved. "Looks like you know a *little*, Brandon, I will say. I remember about him having a boy, though I ain't met you ever." She switched the baby to her other shoulder and sat down again, sideways, so that she could see them over the back of the seat. "Your daddy fixed Brandon here's leg," she said. "Was broke in two places, back when he a boy and me just a girl in the same Sunday school class with him. I remember."

"It's true," Brandon said. He settled down more comfortably on the arm of the chair. "Way I saw you, you were in the office with him, wanting him to come home for supper. You mustn't of been but twelve or so but I remembered. I good at faces, yes sir. Been eight years since I even *seen* Sandhill, but there's many I remember though they mightn't remember me. How your daddy now?"

"Well . . ." Ben Joe said, startled. "He, uh, he's dead. Died some six years back."

Brandon looked down at his knees and shook his head, silently. His wife made a sad little cooing sound.

"I do say," Brandon said finally. "Well, I do say. I surely am sorry to hear it. We been gone so long, they don't write the news like they should . . . I surely am sorry."

"How he go?" Matilda asked.

"Heart attack."

"Law, law." She shook her head too, echoing Brandon. "Well, I know it was a dignified passing. Wan't it?'

Ben Joe, taken off guard, didn't answer.

"Oh, I sure it was *very* dignified, Matilda," Brandon said soothingly.

In the cramped space between the wall and the curly-haired boy, Ben Joe carefully crossed his foot over his knee and twisted one shoelace, staring down at it.

"*Well*, now," said Matilda, suddenly becoming very brisk. "How about your mama?"

"Oh, she's fine."

"And there more of you, ain't there? A passle of sisters? I recollect that. How they?"

"Oh, they're fine, too. The oldest one's got a baby of her own now."

"Well, glory. She marry a Sandhill boy?"

"No. She left Sandhill a little before Dad died, and got a job, and then a few years back she called to say she was married to this boy from Georgia. Haven't seen her since, or the boy, either. They live in Kansas. But she's at home now."

"Well, I know you be glad to see her. I bet your mamma went to Kansas when the baby come, hey?"

"No."

"That daddy of yours a fine man," Brandon said. "Fine man."

'Well," said Matilda, "your mama had enough to do with chirren of her own, I reckon, Maybe just couldn't *make* it all the way to Kansas."

"That's a nice-looking baby *you* got," said Ben Joe.

"Well, thank you. Name's Clara Sue. *I knew* it'd be a girl. I got fatter and fatter in the behind all the time I carrying her."

"Now, Matilda, he don't want to hear about that."

"Well, I just mentioning. You want to sleep, Mr. Ben Joe, and I know Brandon he wild to get back to that gin."

"It was good seeing you," Ben Joe said. He and Brandon stood up and shook hands, and then Brandon left and Matilda turned around to face forward again.

When he was settled back in his seat, Ben Joe leaned his head against the windowpane and closed his eyes, trying to ignore the vibration of the pane against his skin. He wished he knew what state they were passing through. The last of New Jersey, maybe. He felt unsure of his age; in New York he was small and free and too young, and in Sandhill he was old and tied down and enormous, but what age was he here?

With his eyes closed, the division between sleeping and waking became blurred and airy. He saw the sunlit front porch of his house in Sandhill floating up toward him through the darkness behind his eyelids. His father came out of the house, humming a tune beneath his breath, and began crossing the yard to the front gate.

"You come pick me up when it's suppertime, Ben Joe," he said, speaking to the empty air. "I'll be in my office."

The sun shone on his lined face, and on the top of his white hair. From somewhere far off, Ben Joe shouted, "But I'm not there! I'm over here!"

His father made a shoulder-patting motion in space. "We'll walk home together," he said.

Ben Joe began running, trying to be beside his father before he reached the gate, but he was too late. When he got there his father was gone, and his mother had come out on the porch holding a glass of lemonade that flashed piercingly in the sun.

"You've been dreaming about your father," she said.

But Ben Joe said, "No. No, I didn't. I never did."

He awoke, and found that the sill of the train window had pressed a wide deep line into his cheekbone.

3

IT WAS STILL very early in the morning when Ben Joe reached Sandhill. The wooden station house seemed deserted and the parking lot behind it was white and empty, with the pale sunlight glinting on the flecks of mica in the gravel. Beyond that was a thin row of trees and then, after that, Main Street, running parallel to the railroad tracks and lined with the little stores that made up the downtown section of Sandhill. From where Ben Joe was standing, beside the tracks, all he could see of Sandhill was smoking chimneys and white steeples. The town looked small and clean and perfect, as if it were one of those miniature plastic towns sitting beside a child's electric railroad.

The only other passengers to get off at Sandhill were Brandon's family and a tiny old snuff-chewing white man whom Ben Joe had not seen before. They all stood by the tracks in a group, motionless, soaking in the early morning sunshine and listening to the train fading away behind them. When the air was completely silent again Brandon said, "Sure do feel different from New York."

"Sure do," the old man said.

They turned to look at him.

"Softer, I guess," he said. "I don't know."

They nodded and turned away again. Ben Joe felt as if they might almost be a family, the five of them, standing so close together and so watchful. The sleepiness and the sudden silence seemed to have left an odd gentleness, in himself and in the others, that made him reluctant to leave the station.

"Can't see much of a change from *here*," Brandon said. "See they ain't fixed the clock on the Sand-Bottom Baptists' steeple tower yet."

26

He was holding the baby now, and in his other hand was a large striped cardboard suitcase. Beside him his wife clutched a diaper bag to her stomach. In the sunlight they both looked much younger; Brandon was bundled into a woolly-collared maroon windbreaker that a little boy might wear, and his wife had a thin brown topper on, girlishly awkward and too short-sleeved, and a simple blue dress that had faded a little. Beside them stood the little old man, also faded but still very clean and polished-looking, as if some brisk daughter-in-law had scrubbed him like an apple with a clean white cloth before she packed him on the train. He had a funny way of breathing – short and fast, with a tiny kitten's mew at the end of each intake. Ben Joe wondered if he were the one that the curly-haired boy had said was dying.

"Anyone know where Setdown Street is?" the old man was asking.

"I do," said Ben Joe.

"I want to find it. Be mighty obliged."

"I'll show you."

A dusty black Chevrolet pulled into the parking lot. It seemed stuffed with laughing brown faces, piled three deep, and even before it had come to a complete stop, the doors had popped open and a whole wealth of brightly dressed Negroes had begun pouring out. Brandon gave a joyous hoot of laughter that was almost a shout and said, "*Hey*, man, hey, Matilda, look who *here*!" and the baby woke up and blinked her round berry eyes at Ben Joe.

"You waking Clara Sue," Matilda said.

"It's *all* of them done come, man, all of them!"

"Mr. Ben Joe," said Matilda, turning halfway to him while she seemed still to be looking toward the Chevrolet, "won't your family planning on meeting you? Because we'n take you in the Chevy, you know. That Brandon's brother driving."

"Well, I reckon my family's not even up yet," Ben Joe said. "But the walk'll do me good. Thanks anyway."

"You, sir?" she said to the old man.

"Oh, I'll be going with him. Iffen it's not too far." He

27

looked up at Ben Joe, questioning him, and Ben Joe shook his head.

"Well, good to see you," Matilda said. She turned to catch up with Brandon and her baby. Across the chilly air the voices of their relatives rang cheerfully; they were grinning and standing awkwardly in a cluster now beside their open-doored car, as if they wanted to give Brandon and Matilda time to get used to them again before they descended on them all at once. And Brandon and Matilda seemed in no hurry. They walked slowly and with careful dignity, proud to have such a large turnout for them. Over Brandon's shoulder the baby waved both fists helplessly.

"Might as well start," said the old man.

"I guess."

"Sure it's not far?"

"Sure."

The old man picked up a large, very new suitcase and Ben Joe led the way, with his own lightweight suitcase swinging easily in his hand. "Ought to be just far enough to get you hungry for breakfast," he called back over his shoulder.

"Good to hear that. Been traveling too long for *my* preference."

They cut through the station, through the large, hot waiting room with its rows and rows of naked, dark wooden benches. Ben Joe could never figure out why Sandhill had provided space for so many passengers. The waiting room was divided in two by a slender post, with half the room reserved for white people and the other half for Negroes. Since times had changed, the wooden letters saying "White" and "Colored" had been removed, but the letters had left cleaner places on the wall that spelled out the same words still. A fat, red-haired lady sat in the ticket booth between the two halves of the waiting room; she frowned at the old man and Ben Joe and tapped a pencil against her teeth.

As soon as they were outside, going up the short gravel driveway that cut through the trees onto Main Street, the old man became talkative.

"You shouldn't of mentioned breakfast, boy," he said. "Lord, I'm hungry. Wonder what they'll feed me."

"Who?" Ben Joe asked.

"Oh, them. And you know them colored folks off the same train as us? Know what they're doing now? Setting down to the table with their relations, partaking of buckwheat cakes and hot buttered syrup and them little link sausages. Makes me hungry just thinking of it."

His breath was squeaking more now; the nostrils of his small, bent nose widened and fluttered as he drew in bigger and bigger amounts of air.

"My son got me this suitcase special, just for the trip. It was real expensive. I said, 'Sam,' I said, '*you* don't need to spend all that money on me, son,' but Sam he said, 'It's the least I can do.' 'It's the least I can do,' he tells me. He wanted to come take the trip with me, but I could see he was busy and all. I wouldn't allow it. Law, I am eighty-four years old now and *capable*, it's what I keep telling him. Capable. Though I will admit the train was something bumpy, and I feared that it would jounce all my insides out of place. I got this fear, someday my intestines will get tied in a bow by accident, like shoelaces. You ever thought of that?"

"Not that I can remember," Ben Joe said. He was getting worried now; the old man's voice had become a mere wheezing sound, and he was so out of breath that Ben Joe's own throat grew tight and breathless in sympathy.

"Well, I have. Often I have. I don't know if you ever knew my son Sam. He's a businessman, like on Wall Street, except that he happens to be in Connecticut instead. Got a real nice family, too. Course I think he could of made a better choice in wives, but then Sally's right pretty and I reckon I can see his point in picking her. Just a mite bossy, in all. And then her family's Jehovah's Witnesses. Now, I got no quarrel to pick with *any* religion, excepting may be a few, but I heard somewheres that Jehovah's Witnesses they turn off all the lights and get under the chairs and tables and look for God. They do. Ain't found Him yet, neither. Course Sally she's reformed now, but *still* and all, still and all . . ."

On Main Street he became suddenly silent. He walked along almost on tiptoe, looking around him with a white, astonished face. Sometimes he would whisper, "Oh, my, look at that!" and purse his mouth and widen his eyes at some ordinary little store front. Ben Joe couldn't understand him. What was so odd about Sandhill? Main Street was wide and white and almost bare of cars; a few shopkeepers whistled cheerfully as they swept in front of their stores, and a pretty girl Ben Joe had never seen before passed by, smiling. Except for the new hotel, there wasn't a single building over three stories high in the whole town. Above the squat little shops the owners' families lived, and their flowered curtains hung cozily behind narrow dark windows.

At the third block they turned left and started uphill on a small, well-shaded street. Main Street was the only commercial district in the town; as soon as they turned off it they were among large family houses with enormous old pecan trees towering over them. The old man had stopped exclaiming now, but he was still tiptoeing and wide-eyed. Although his baggy coat seemed paper thin and the morning was very cool, the surface of his face was shiny with perspiration. With a small grunt he switched his suitcase to his other hand and it banged against the side of his knee.

"I'll trade you suitcases for a while," Ben Joe said.

"No no. No no. You know, when I was a boy we'd of been plumb through town by now."

"Sir?"

"Town's *grown* some, I said."

"Oh. You mean you've been here before?"

"Born here, I was. But I ain't seen it since I was eighteen years old and that's a fact. Went off to help my uncle make bed linens in Connecticut. Though at the time I never wanted to. I wanted to go to Africa."

"*Africa?*"

"Africa." He stopped and set down his suitcase in order to wipe his forehead with a carefully folded handkerchief from his breast pocket. "Wadn't but two streets that was paved then," he said. "Main and Dower. Dower's *my* name. It was named after my daddy, who moved out west soon after I went north on account of the humidity here being bad for

30

my mother's ankle bones. But there wadn't no street called Setdown then. Got no idea where *that* is."

"Well, it's not far," Ben Joe said. "You got relatives living there?"

"Nope. Nope."

"Where you going?"

"Home for the aged."

"Oh."

Ben Joe stood in silence for a minute, not knowing what to say next. Finally he cleared his throat and said, "Well, that's where it is, all right."

"Course it is. Going to die there."

"Well. Well, um, I trust that'll be a long time from now."

"Don't trust too hard," the old man said. He seemed irritated by Ben Joe's embarrassment; he picked up his suitcase with a jerk and they continued on up the hill. As they walked, Ben Joe kept looking over at him sideways.

"Don't you corner your eyes like that," Mr. Dower said. "Not at me you don't."

"Well, I was just thinking."

"Don't have to corner your eyes just to be thinking, do you?"

"I've been away some time myself," Ben Joe said. "Some time for *me*, anyway. Going on four months. It seemed longer, though, and I sort of left planning not to return."

"Then what you *here* for?" Mr. Dower snapped.

"Well, I don't know," Ben Joe said. "I just can't seem to *get* anywhere. Nowhere permanent."

"*I* can. Can and did. Went away permanent and now I've come back to die permanent."

"How can you have gone away permanent if you've come back?" Ben Joe asked.

"Because what I left ain't here to come back to, that's why. Therefore my going away can be counted as permanent."

"That's what they all say," said Ben Joe. "But they're fooling themselves."

"Well." Mr. Dower stopped again to wipe his forehead. "How much farther, boy?"

"Not far. Right at the end of this block."

31

"Long blocks you've got. Long blocks. This here," the old man said, pointing to an old stone house, "is where Jonah Barnlott lived, that married my sister. Like to broke my family's heart doing it, too. He was a no-count boy, that Jonah. Became a doctor, finally, down in Georgia, but never had any patients to speak of. Was inflicted with athlete's foot, he was, and decided shoes were what gave it to him, so he loafed about his office playing patience in a white uniform and pure-T bare feet, which scared all his patients away. My sister left him, finally, and got remarried to a lawyer. Lawyers're better. Not so concerned with bodily matters. So now it's Saul Bowen lives in that house. I reckon you know *him*."

"No, sir."

"Not know Saul Bowen? Fat old guy who goes around town all day eating pudding from a dish?"

"No, sir."

"Well, no," Mr. Dower said after a minute. "I guess not. I guess not."

They were silent for the rest of the block. The old man's shoes made a shuffling, scratchy noise on the sidewalk and the mewing of his breath was loud and unsteady, so that Ben Joe became frightened.

"Sir," he said at the corner, "it's just one block down from here, on the left. But I'd be happy to walk you the rest of the way."

"I can make it. I can make it."

"Well, it's a big yellow house with a sign in front. You sure you're all right?"

"I am *dying*," said the old man. "But otherwise I'm fine and I'd appreciate to walk by myself for a spell."

"Well. Good-by, Mr. Dower."

"Bye, boy."

The old man started down Setdown Street, his suitcase banging his knees at every step. For a minute Ben Joe watched after him, but the shabby little figure was pushing doggedly on with no help from him and there was nothing more he could do. Finally he turned and started walking again, on toward his own home.

The houses in this area were big and comfortable, although most of them were poorly cared-for. On some of the lawns the trees were so old and thick that there was a little whitening of frost on the grass beneath their limbs, even now that most of their leaves were gone. Ben Joe began shivering. He walked more quickly, past the wide, deserted porches and down the echoing sidewalk. Then he was on the corner, and across the street was his own house.

A long, low wire gate stood in front of it, although the fence that went with it had been torn down years ago when the last of the children had left the toddler stage. The lawn behind it had been allowed to grow wild and weedy, half as high as a wheat field and dotted here and there with little wiry shrubs and seedy, late-fall flowers. And the sidewalk from the gate to the front porch was cracked and broken; little clumps of grass grew in it. Towering above such an unkempt expanse of grass, the house took on a half-deserted look in spite of the lace curtains that hung primly in all the windows. It was an enormous white frame house, in need of a little touch-up with a paint brush, and it could easily be the ugliest house in town. Round stained-glass windows popped up in unexpected places; the front bay window was too tall and narrow, and the little turret, with its ridiculously curlicued weather vane, looked as if it must be stuffed with bats and cobwebs. People said – although Ben Joe never believed them – that the first time his mother had seen the house she had laughed so hard that she got hiccups and a neighbor had had to bring her a glass of peppermint water. And all the while that Ben Joe was growing up, little boys used to ask him jealously if his room was in the turret. He always said yes, although the truth was that nobody lived there; it was just a huge hollow space above the stairwell. The only thing that saved the house from looking haunted was the front porch, big and square and friendly. A shiny green metal glider sat there, and in the summertime the whole porch railing was littered with bathing suits and Coke bottles and the lounging figures of whatever boys his sisters were dating at the time. In front of the door, Ben Joe could just make out a rolled-up newspaper. That brought him to life again; he crossed the yard cheerfully, stopped on the porch to pick up the paper, and opened the front door.

Inside, there was the mossy brown smell that he had been raised with, that seemed to be part and parcel of the house and was a wonderful smell if you were glad to be home and an unbearable smell if you were not. And mingled with it were the more temporary, tangible smells – bacon, coffee, hot radiators, newly ironed dresses, bath powder. He was standing in the narrow hallway and looking into the living room, which was stuffed with durable old ugly furniture that had stood the growing up of seven children. On the walls hung staid oil paintings of ships at sea and summer landscapes. The coffee tables were littered with things that had been there as long as Ben Joe could remember – little china figurines, enameled flower pots, conch shells. Periodically his mother tried to move them, but Gram always put them back again. On the floor was an interrupted Monopoly game, a pair of fluffy slippers, a beer can, and a pink baby sweater that reminded him of Tessie. It must belong to Joanne's baby now. He set down the suitcase and the newspaper and crossed into the living room to pick the sweater up between two fingers. It seemed to him that every girl in the family had worn that. But had it really been that tiny?

In the kitchen a voice said, "I'll tell you what. I'll tell you what, Jane. Every time I even pick *up* a glass of frozen orange juice, it makes me think of vitamin pills. Does it you?"

Someone answered. It could have been any one of them; they all had that low, clear voice of their mother's. And then the first voice again: "I'd rather squeeze oranges in my bare hands than drink my orange juice frozen."

Ben Joe smiled and headed through the hallway toward the voices, with the sweater still in one hand. At the open doorway to the kitchen he stopped and looked in at the five girls sitting around the table. "Anybody home?" he asked.

They all turned at the same moment to look at him, and then their chairs were scraped back and five cheeks were pressed briefly to his and questions hurled around his head.

"What you doing here, Ben Joe?"

34

"What you think Mama's going to say?"

"How'd you get *in*, is what I want to know."

"Sure, a burglar could've walked in. We'd never even heard him."

"Would anyone be a burglar before breakfast? And what's to steal?"

"Where's your luggage, Ben Joe?"

He stood smiling, unable to get a word in edgewise. They were circled around him, looking soft and happy in their pastel bathrobes, and if they had been still a minute he would have said he was glad to see them, even if it *would* embarrass them, but they didn't give him a chance. Lisa reached for the baby sweater in his hand and held it up above her head for the others to see and laugh at.

"Why, Ben Joe, you bring us a sweater? Isn't that nice, except I don't reckon it'll *fit* us too well."

"He's been away so long, forgotten how big we'd have grown."

"Aren't you exhausted?"

"I am at that," said Ben Joe. "Feels like my head's come unscrewed at the neck."

"I'll get you some coffee," Jenny said. She was the next-to-youngest – it was only last spring that she'd graduated from high school – but, of all of them, she was the most down-to-earth. She went to the cupboard and took down the huge earthenware mug that Ben Joe always used. "Mama didn't know if you meant it about coming home," she said, "and says she hopes you *didn't*, but she changed your bed, anyway."

"I'm going to it, too, soon as I've had my breakfast. Hello there, Tessie. You're so little still I damn near overlooked you. Maybe it's you this sweater's for."

"Not me it's not," said Tessie. "It's too little for Carol, even."

"Who's Carol?"

"Carol's our *niece*."

"Oh. Where's Joanne?"

"In bed. So's Carol."

"I forgot about her being named Carol," Ben Joe said.

"One more girl to remember. Hoo boy." He took off his jacket and turned to hang it on the back of his chair. "Ma gone to work already?"

"Yup. This man's bringing a truckload of books real early."

The mug was set before him, full of steaming coffee. Tessie passed him a plate of cinnamon buns and said, "You notice anything different about me?"

"Well . . ." Ben Joe said. He frowned at her, and she frowned steadily back. Of all the Hawkes children, she and Ben Joe were the only blond ones. The others had dark hair, which they wore short and curly, and their eyes were so black it was hard to tell where they were looking. They were almost round-eyed, too, whereas Ben Joe and Tessie had their father's too-narrow eyes. And there was something tricky about their coloring. At one moment they could seem very pale and at the next their skin would be almost olive-toned. But all of the girls, even Tessie, had little pointed faces and small, careful features, a little too sharp; all of them wore quick, watchful expressions and their oval-nailed hands were thin and restless. People said they were the prettiest girls in town, and the ficklest. Thinking of that, Ben Joe smiled at them, and Tessie tugged at his arm impatiently and said, "Not them, *me*."

"You." He turned back to her. "You've gone and gotten married on us."

"Oh, Ben *Joe*." Her giggle was like Joanne's, light and chuckly. "I'm only ten years *old*," she said. "Don't you see *anything* different?"

"Nope."

"I've had my ears pierced!"

"Aha," said Ben Joe. He took her face in his hands and turned it first one way and then the other, examining the tiny gold rings in her ears. "What for?"

"Oh, just because. Joanne and Susannah and the twins have pierced ears. Why not me?"

"Did it hurt?"

"Yup."

"Did you cry?"

"Nope. Well, tears came out, but I went on smiling."

"Good girl," Ben Joe said. "Better run along and get ready for school, now. You'll be late."

"You'll all be late," Susannah said.

The others got up and left; the pinks and blues of their bathrobes clustered together for a minute at the doorway and then vanished into the hall. Ben Joe could hear their soft slippers padding up the stairs, and somewhere a door slammed. "What about you?" he asked.

"I've got another half-hour."

"Is Gram up?"

"Yes. She's up in her room, making a gun belt for Tessie out of an old leather skirt."

He watched Susannah silently for a while, following her quick little movements around the kitchen. She hadn't changed any; she got the coffee grounds half emptied and fled to the orange-juicer and then to sponge the top of the stove off before she remembered the coffee grounds again.

"Have you talked to Joanne?" he asked.

"Oh, sure."

"What'd she say?"

"What about?"

"About leaving Gary."

"Oh." She tossed the insides of the coffee pot into the sink and went dashing across the kitchen after a cream pitcher. "I don't know," she said. "It never came up."

"Oh, for heaven's sake."

"Well, it's none of *my* business."

"She's your sister, isn't she?"

"That still doesn't make it my business."

"What does, then?" Ben Joe asked.

"*Nothing.*" She lifted up one soapy hand and pushed a piece of hair off her forehead with the back of her wrist. "You're the one that's so worried. Why don't *you* talk to her, if you think you know where she'd be happier."

"It's not that I much want her to go *back* to him," Ben Joe said slowly. "Gary's an awful name. Whatever he's like. It reminds me of a G.I. with a crew cut, and 'Mom' tattooed on his chest, and lots of pin-up pictures on his wall."

"Oh, you," Susannah said. "That's beside the point. Go up and get some sleep, Ben Joe. The house'll be bedlam when Carol wakes up."

"Okay. Have a good day at work."

"Thank you."

He stood watching her for a minute, but Susannah had already forgotten him. She was on her hands and knees under the table now, crawling after one of her slippers, and it was as if Ben Joe had never been there.

4

WHEN HE AWOKE, his mother was in the doorway watching him. He was not sure whether she had spoken his name or not; in his sleep he seemed to have heard her voice. But maybe all that had awakened him was the feel of her eyes – wide eyes, as dark as her daughters', but with small lines now at the corners. She was the kind of woman who did not become very wrinkled as she aged but instead acquired only a few lines around her mouth and eyes, and those so deep that they were actual crevices even when her face was calm. She was smiling a little, so that the mouth lines curved and deepened even more, and she stood with one hand on her hip and the other on the doorknob and watched Ben Joe.

"Ben Joe Hawkes," she said finally, "what on *earth* are you doing home?"

Ben Joe sat up in the familiar wooden bed and pushed his hair back from his forehead. "I already told you," he said. "I told you the reason on the phone."

"That was no reason." She shook her head. "Of all the things to do . . . What's going to happen to your school work?"

"I don't have to be there every minute."

"If you make good grades you do. If you're going to be any kind of decent lawyer."

Ben Joe shrugged and pulled his pillow up behind him so that he could sit against it. The sheets smelled crisp and newly ironed; his mother had smoothed them tight on the bed herself and turned the covers down for him, and he could hold that thought securely in his mind even when she scolded him for returning. You had to be a sort of detective with his mother; you had to search out the fresh-made bed, the flowers on the bureau, and the dinner table laid matter-of-factly with your favorite supper, and then you forgot her crisp manners. He wondered, watching her, whether his sisters knew that. Or did they even need to know? Maybe it was only Ben Joe, still watching his mother with those detective eyes even though he was a grown man now and should have stopped bothering.

"Have you had breakfast?" his mother was asking.

"Yes'm. Had it with the girls before they went to work."

"Well, I'm home for lunch now. You want a bite to eat?"

"I guess."

She came further into the room and opened his closet door. From the front rack she took a bathrobe and tossed it to him, not watching where it landed, and then crossed to pull the shade up. He saw that she was still wearing those wide walking skirts with the mid-calf hem that had been popular some fifteen years ago. On her, with her bony height and her swinging walk, they still looked up to date. Her hair was a light, dusty color, once as blond as his and Tessie's. It was short and a little too frizzy around the sharp angles of her face, but she still didn't seem like an old woman. He gave up watching her and, pulling the bathrobe around him, stepped barefoot to the floor.

"You're thinner," she said. She had stopped fiddling with the window shade and was taking stock of him now, with her hands deep in the pockets of her skirt. "You've been cooking for yourself, I'll bet."

"Yes'm. What time is it?"

"About twelve."

"Is Joanne up?"

"Oh, yes. She and Carol are in the den, I think."

"Is she okay?"

"Of *course* she's okay. And it's her own business, Ben Joe – nothing we have any right to touch. I don't want to hear about your meddling in it. Hurry up and get dressed, will you? Lunch is nearly ready."

She swung out of the door and vanished, humming something beneath her breath as she went downstairs. Behind her, Ben Joe sighed and tied his bathrobe around him. It would be a good time to shave; none of the older girls came home for lunch.

When he came downstairs he could smell lunch already – all the varied smells of odds and ends left over in the refrigerator and reheated now in tiny saucepans. Although he was rested now, his stomach still felt shaky from the trip and he made a face as the smell of lunch hit him on the stairs. Gram must be doing the cooking today; she was an old Southerner and floated all her vegetables in grease.

He pushed open the kitchen door and found his grandmother standing by the stove just lifting the lid off a steaming saucepan. She was his father's mother, and close to eighty now, but there was a steely, glinting endurance to her. Joanne used to say her grandmother reminded her of piano wires. She was small and bony; she wore men's black gym shoes that tied around her bare ankles, and her dress, as usual, was a disgrace – a sort of blue denim coat that was fastened with one string at the back of the neck and hung open the rest of the way down the back to expose a black lace slip. (Her underwear was her one luxury; she had seven different colors in her bureau drawer.) As she stirred the leftovers she sang, just as she always did, in a deafening roar that came effortlessly from the bottom of her tiny rib cage:

"I ain't gonna knock on your window no more,
Ain't gonna bang on your door . . ."

"Hello, Gram," Ben Joe said in her ear.

She spun around, just missing him with the saucepan lid. "Ben *Joe*!" she said. "I hear you came in this morning and didn't even say hey to me. That true?"

"You were up in the attic making a gun belt," he said.

He hugged her and she hugged him back, so hard that he could feel her hard, bony chest and the point of her chin just below his shoulder.

"We're having leftovers," she said. "I know what view you hold of leftovers, but you just wait till tonight. You just *see* what manner of things we're preparing."

She replaced the saucepan lid and undid her hair. It was her habit to take three bobby pins from her head, at least twenty times a day, and let her straight white hair fall almost to her shoulders. Then, with the bobby pins clamped tightly in her mouth, she deftly wound her hair around one finger, squashed it on top of her head in a bun, and nailed it there again with the three bobby pins. All this took less than a minute. While she was doing it she kept right on talking, shifting the bobby pins to one corner of her mouth so that they wouldn't interrupt her speech.

"Turkey we're having," she said, "and giblet dressing, and yams— Ben Joe, you got to talk to Jenny about her grocery rut. She's got into a rut about grocery shopping. Buys the same old thing every time. No imagination. Now, Jenny, she is a right good cook and I want to see her get married, real soon. I don't hold with a girl staying and looking after her family and being a little old secretary all her life when she is as home-minded as Jenny is. Got to get a family of her own. But what man'll marry a girl feeds him hamburgers every night? Course she does all *manner* of clever things to dress them up a little, but still and all it's hamburger and the cheap kind of hamburger at that. Ever since you left and put her in charge of the money matters she's been *parsimonious*, is what, taking it too serious. Call people to eat, will you? Your ma's upstairs and the others're in the den."

"Yes'm."

He left the kitchen and headed for the den, which was through the living room and at the other end of the house. It had once been his father's study, and although the medical books on the shelves had long since been disposed of, there was still the extra telephone on the desk, installed when the girls had first become old enough to tie up the lines on the regular phone. Since their father's death the room was used as a TV room, and now the set was blaring so loudly that Ben Joe could hear it way before he crossed the living room. And once he was inside the den the sound hurt his ears. The shades were down and at first it was too dark to see anything but the silhouettes of the people watching and beyond them the screen, bluish and snow-flecked. A fat man was shouting, "Whaddaya say, kiddies? Huh? Whaddaya say?" and behind his voice was a

42

loud, angry humming from the set itself. Ben Joe blinked and looked around.

All he could see of Joanne was the white line that edged her profile from the light of the TV screen on her face. She had her eyes lowered to something in her lap – a piece of cloth. And she was sewing on it, pushing the needle through and then stretching her arm as far out as it would reach in order to pull the thread tight. Joanne was the type of person who used just one enormous length of thread instead of several short practical lengths. On the cane chair in front of her sat Tessie, also just a silvery profile but with a snatch of yellow over her forehead where the light hit her blond hair. And farthest in front, so that her back was toward Ben Joe, sat a small child in a child's rocking chair. Of her Ben Joe could see nothing, except that she was so small (she would have been two only last June) her feet stuck out in front of her on the chair, and she was rocking violently. He could make out her small hands gripping the chair arms tightly; she flung her head first forward and then back, to make the chair rock. From here he could almost swear her hair was red, although that was improbable. He took another step into the room and said, "Has she got *red* hair?"

Joanne started and looked at him.

"Hi, Joanne," he said.

"Ben Joe, come here! No, wait. Come out into the living room. It's dark as night in here."

She rose and pulled him out into the light and kissed him on both cheeks, hard, and hugged him around the waist. The little dress she was sewing was still in one hand, but the needle had slipped off its thread and was lying on the rug at her feet. It was funny how the tiniest thing Joanne did was exactly like her, even now, even after all these years. Any of the other girls would have stuck her needle into the cloth for safekeeping before she went to kiss her brother. "God, you're thin," she said. She was laughing, and her hair was mussed from hugging him. "I can't believe it's really you. Have you gone back to being a vegetarian?"

"No. Mom says it's eating my own cooking that does it."

"Mm-hm. You're older, too. But that's all right. I don't reckon you're *ever* going to get any lines in your face."

43

"That's from having no character," he said absently. He was trying to decide what was different about her; something was making him feel a little shy, as if she were a stranger. Probably the way she dressed was partly responsible for it. In place of the blazing red dress of the old days was a soft yellow sacklike thing that hung loosely from her shoulders. She was still thin, though, with a face just slightly rounder than her sisters'. Almost immediately he decided what the change in her was; she was pretty much the same, with that same warm chuckly laugh, but she had a different way of showing it. A subtler one, he thought. Yet the bangles were still on her arms, and the twinkling, chin-ducking smile still on her face. He smiled back.

"I see you're not old yet," he said.

"Almost I am. Did you have a good trip?"

"I guess so. I came to call you to lunch, by the way. Gram's dishing up."

"I'll get the children."

She pattered back into the den, barefoot, and came out again with Carol in her arms and Tessie trailing behind her, blinking in the sunlight. The TV had been forgotten; accordion music seesawed out noisily from the empty room.

"You met Carol yet?" Joanne asked.

Ben Joe looked at Carol, checking her hair first because he was curious to see whether it was red or not. It was. It was cut, cup-like, around a small, round face that was still so young it could tell Ben Joe nothing. "Can you talk yet?" he asked her.

She smiled, not telling.

"Only when she's in the mood," Joanne said. "She's got to say a word exactly right or she refuses to say it at all. A perfectionist. I don't know where she gets it."

"What about her red hair?"

"What?"

"Where's she get *that*?"

Joanne frowned. "Where you get any kind of hair," she said finally. "Genes."

"Oh."

"I sure am glad to see you, Ben Joe," she said as they crossed the living room. "I am. You don't know how glad."

44

Embarrassed, Ben Joe smiled down at her and said nothing. At the stairway he stopped and yelled up, "Mom!" and then continued on into the kitchen, not looking at Joanne or waiting for his mother's answer. But just before they reached the doorway he said, "Well, I'm happy to see *you*."

"That's good," she said cheerfully.

In the kitchen Gram was bustling around, ladling food onto the plates on the table. Joanne pulled the old high chair up and sat Carol in it. "Don't you go wiggling around," she told her. She gave her a little pat on the knee. It made Ben Joe feel strange, watching Joanne with Carol. He never had really thought about the fact that she was a mother now with a child of her own.

"Where's your mama?" Gram asked.

"Coming."

"Well, her meal's getting cold. Sit down, Joanne. Sit down, Ben Joe. Tessie, you got to hurry now. What happened to your napkin?"

"It's on the screen porch."

"Well, it's not supposed to be. No, don't go get it. More important to get your meal down you hot – stave off germs that way. Ben Joe, honey, aren't you tired to pieces?"

"Not any more I'm not."

"Well, you have a big helping of these here beans. Carol just threw her bib on the floor, Joanne."

She put another scoop of beans on Ben Joe's plate, shaking the spoon vigorously. Seeing her hands, so much older than the rest of her, reminded Ben Joe of the old man from the train. He said, "Gram, did you ever know a man named Dower?"

"Dower." She sat down at her own place, smoothing the front of her apron across her lap. "Lord yes, I did. There was a whole heap of Dowers here at one time, though most have died out or moved on. There was the good Dowers and there was the bad Dowers. The good ones were very great friends of the family once. I near about lived at their house when I was a teeny-iney girl. They're all dead now, I reckon. But the bad ones are living here yet. Wouldn't you know. No relation to the good ones, of course. Living off the county and letting

45

chickens in the kitchen. That kind just hangs on and *hangs* on. I don't know why. They're so spindly-legged and pasty-faced, but they keep on long after stronger men's in their graves."

She stopped to take a breath. Ben Joe's mother came into the kitchen and pulled up a chair for herself. Carol threw her bib on the floor again and said, "Carrot."

"We're going to have to tie a double knot in your bib from now on," Ben Joe's mother told her. She took a raw carrot from the plate on the table and handed it to her. "Gram, what are those little things in the dish over there?"

"Smoked oysters. And that child shouldn't have a carrot."

"Smoked *oysters*?"

"That's what I said. Won't have this grocery rut of Jenny's one day longer. My mind's made up. Ellen, take that carrot away from her."

"Why? She's got teeth."

"But it's a big *thick* carrot."

"Well, we can't mollycoddle her. The rest of the girls had carrots at her age."

"Not while I was around," Gram said. "She'll choke on it." Joanne looked up anxiously and Gram nodded to her.

"On the little pieces of it. She'll choke. I've seen it happen."

"Oh, don't be silly," said Ellen Hawkes.

Joanne reached over and took the carrot away, replacing it with a soda cracker immediately so that Carol didn't have time to start crying. Ben Joe's mother turned back to her meal, resigned. Neither she nor Gram paid much attention to these quibbling arguments of theirs; they were used to them. Gram said Ellen Hawkes was coldhearted and Ellen Hawkes said Gram was soft-cored. The rest of the family was as used to the feud as they were. They went on eating now, cheerfully, and Carol began gnawing at her cracker.

"The reason I asked about the Dowers," Ben Joe said, "is that I met an old man from the train by that name. He said he was born right here in Sandhill."

"That's funny. Good Dower or bad Dower?"

"Well, Gram, I doubt if he'd have said."

"If he was a bad Dower he would have. He would have said he was a good Dower."

Joanne laughed.

"He said there was a street named for his father," Ben Joe said. "I remember that much. He said that when he was here, Main and Dower were the only real streets in town."

Gram looked up, interested now. "That's so," she said. "It's true, that's so."

Carol spilled her milk. It trickled off the high-chair tray and into her lap, and when she felt the coldness of it she squealed.

"I'll get a rag," said Tessie.

She started for the sink, but her mother reached around and grabbed her back by the sash. "You sit right there, young lady. You have to be at school in fifteen minutes."

"It won't take long, Mama."

But Joanne was already up, reaching for paper towels and then lifting Carol out of her high chair to sponge her off. "There, there," she was saying, although Carol was only squealing for the joy of hearing her own voice now and had started pulling out all the bobby pins from Joanne's hair.

"He went off to help his uncle make bed sheets in Connecticut!" Ben Joe shouted above the uproar.

His mother stopped chewing and stared at him.

"Mr. Dower, I'm talking about. And then his family moved away because his mother's ankle bones started hurting—"

"Ben Joe," his mother said, "if all of you children would cast your minds back to when you were small and I told you *never*, on *any* account, to speak to those strange-looking people you seem to keep meeting up with—"

"How old was he when he began in bed sheets?" Gram asked.

"Eighteen, he told me."

"My Lord in heaven!" She laid her fork on the table and stared at him. "Why, that couldn't be anyone but *Jamie* Dower. Jamie Dower, I'll be. My Lord in heaven."

"Was he a good Dower?"

"Good as they come. Shoot, yes. He was six years older'n me, but you'd never believe the crush I had on him. That was the *reason I* practically lived at the Dowers' – following him around all the time. I thought he was Adam, back then."

"*Adam?*" Tessie said. "How was he dressed?"

Her mother pushed her plate closer to her. "Eat your beans, Tessie. Stop that dawdling."

"Where was he going to?" Gram asked.

"Well, um – the home for the aged, is what he told me."

"The home for the aged." She shook her head. "My, my, who'd have believed it? He was a real handsome boy, you know – kind of tall for back then, though nothing to compare with some of those basketball players you see around nowadays. Real fond of stylish clothes, too. What would we have thought, I wonder, had someone told us back then where Jamie Dower would end up?"

"Tessie," said Ellen Hawkes, "I give you to the count of five to drink that milk up. What's that on your front? Beans?"

"Nothing," said Tessie. She finished the last of her milk and wiped the white mustache off her upper lip with the back of her hand.

"That's a funny-looking nothing."

"Well, anyway, I gotta go. Good-by, Mama. Good-by, everybody."

She vanished out the kitchen door, grabbing her jacket as she went. Her mother stared after her and shook her head. "You practically have to *drag* her to school," she said. "Sometimes I think the brains just sort of dribbled away toward the end in this family."

"She's plenty bright," said Gram.

"Well, maybe. But not like Joanne and Ben Joe were – not like them."

"Rubbish," said Gram. She began reaching for the plates and scraping them while she sat at her place. "Too much emphasis on brains in this family. What good's it do? Joanne quit after one year of college and the others, excepting Ben Joe, never went. And Ben Joe – look at him. He just kept trying to figure out what that all-fired mind of his was given him for, and first he thought it was for science and then for art and then for philosophy and now what's he got? Just a mishmash, is all. Just nothing. Won't read a thing now but murder mysteries."

"Neither *one* of you knows what you're talking about," Ben Joe said cheerfully. He had been through all this before;

48

he listened with only half an ear, tipping back in his chair and watching his grandmother scrape plates. "And pooh, what do the girls want to go to college for? I say they're smart choosing not to—"

"Well, sure you do," his mother said. "Sure you do, when all you've got to judge it by is *Sandhill* College. Might as well not have gone at all, as far as I'm concerned—"

"No fault of his," Gram said.

"Well, it's no fault of *mine*."

"If my son'd had his say," Gram said, "Ben Joe'd have gone to Harvard, that's where."

"Your son could've had his say. If he'd come back he could've had his say and welcome *to* it, but what'd he do instead?" She was sitting up straight now, with one hand clasping her fork so tightly that the knuckles were white.

"Who made him like that?" Gram shouted. "Who made his house so cold he chose to go live in another's, tell me that!"

Ben Joe cleared his throat. "Actually," he said, "if I'd made better grades I'd have gotten a scholarship to Harvard. I don't see how it's anyone's fault but my—"

"And who didn't give a hoot when he left?" Gram shouted triumphantly above Ben Joe. "Answer me *that*, now, answer me—"

"That will *do*, Gram," said Ellen Hawkes.

She unclasped her hand from the fork and rose, suddenly calm. "I'll be home by six," she said to Joanne and Ben Joe. They nodded, silently; she pushed her chair in and left. Joanne was staring at the tablecloth as if it were impossible to drag her eyes away from it.

"Cracker," Carol said.

Ben Joe handed her one. She seized it and immediately began crumbling it over her tray.

"I *am* sorry," Gram said after a minute. "There was no call to act like that. I didn't mean to bring it up."

Joanne nodded, still staring at the tablecloth. "I thought you'd have settled that," she said.

"Oh, no. No, just let it slip from being uppermost in my mind, is all. You missed the worst of it. Things went on like before even after you up and left home over it, though you'd

49

think some people might try and change a little. Ah, well, least said soonest . . ."

She sighed and rose to take the stack of dishes to the sink. "Ben Joe, honey," she called over her shoulder, "you reckon Jamie Dower might like a visitor?"

"I don't know why not, Gram."

"You and me'll go, then, sometime this week. I'll start thinking about it."

Joanne rose to help Gram, with her face still pale and too sober. For a while Ben Joe watched them, following their quick, sure movements around the kitchen, but then Carol began blowing cracker crumbs at him and he turned back to her and lifted her out of the high chair.

"Does she get a nap?" he asked Joanne.

"Well, yes. But I'm reading this book that says the same person has got to put her to bed all the time. You better wait and let me do it."

"All right." He headed for the living room, with Carol snuggled in the crook of his arm. "Wouldn't want to make you maladjusted," he told her. She smiled and sucked on a corner of her cracker.

In the living room he sat down in the rocking chair. He pried the soggy mass of cracker from Carol's hand and put it in the ash tray, and then he began absent-mindedly rocking. Carol's head dropped heavily against his chest; her red hair was tickling a point just under his chin. He could feel the small dead weight of her, but he remained unconvinced of her realness and for a long time he just rocked silently, frowning above her head at the faded wallpaper.

5

BY EVENING BEN Joe was beginning to feel the weight of
home settling back on him, making him feel heavy and old
and tired. He had eaten too much for supper; his stomach
ached and he didn't want to admit it to anyone, or to show it
by lying down, for fear that his mother and his grandmother
would be hurt after all that special cooking. So he wandered
aimlessly through the house, searching out something to do or
think about. In the den Tessie and Jenny watched television,
scowling intently at the screen and not looking up when he
came to stand in the doorway. The twins, dressed in different
colors now that they were older but still looking exactly the
same in every other way, were popping popcorn with their
dates in the kitchen, and Susannah and Gram were playing
honeymoon bridge. None of them took any notice of him. He
went upstairs, hoping to find someone up there who would
talk to him, but his mother was using the sewing machine, her
mouth full of pins and her eyes narrowed at the sleeve of a
dress for Tessie. Joanne was giving Carol a bath. He could
hear them even with the door half shut – Carol squealing and
splashing, Joanne calming her with low, soothing noises and
then occasionally laughing along with her.

"Can I come in?" Ben Joe called.

"Carol, you mind if a man comes to watch your bath?"

Carol made a louder splash, probably with the flat of her
hand, and giggled.

"Well, she didn't say no," said Joanne.

Ben Joe pushed the door open and stepped inside. The
room was warm and steamy, and cluttered with towels and
cast-off clothes. Beside the bathtub knelt Joanne, wearing a

terry-cloth bathrobe, with her hair hanging wet and stringy down her neck and her face shiny from her own bath. She had rolled the sleeves of the robe up to her elbows so that she could bathe Carol, who sat in a heap of rubber toys that blocked out almost all sight of bathwater and laughed at Ben Joe.

"Can't be a true Hawkes," said Ben Joe. "No bubble bath."

"Oh, that'll start soon enough."

Ben Joe leaned back against the sink with one foot on a tiny old step stool that read: "For doing some job that's bigger than me." He tested his full weight on the edge of the sink, decided not to risk it, and stood up again.

"I meant to tell you," Joanne said. "Don't feel bad."

"What?"

"Don't you feel bad about what Gram said. About your mind being a mish-mash. It's been in the back of my mind all day to tell you, she didn't mean it. She just said it for the sake of argument."

"I don't feel bad."

"Okay."

She started soaping Carol's hair, expertly, turning the pinkish-red hair dark auburn with her quick, firm fingers. For the first time he noticed that she wasn't wearing a wedding ring. What had she done with it? He pictured her throwing it in Gary's face, but it sounded improbable. Even in her ficklest days, Joanne had never done things that way. No, it would be more like her not even to tell Gary she was going. Or maybe it had been Gary who had left *her*; who knew?

"Where's your wedding ring?" he asked.

"In my jewelry box."

"What on earth for?"

"Well, I don't know. I thought maybe I should wear it so I wouldn't look like an unwed mother, but when I got here Mama said there was no point. She never wears *hers*, she said. It would just keep reminding her."

She took Carol by the chin and the back of the neck and ducked her back into the water swiftly. Before Carol could utter more than one sharp squeak she was upright again, with her hair rinsed and streaming.

"Mom's advice is the *last* I would take," Ben Joe said.

"Now, don't go being mean."

"I'm not. She wants you to say, 'Oh, who cares about *him*?' and then your whole problem is solved. You saw what that did for her."

"Mom's not as coldhearted as Gram keeps telling you, Ben Joe. You know that."

"Oh, I know."

"Besides, this isn't the same kind of thing."

"What kind of thing *is* it?" Ben Joe asked.

Joanne picked out a rubber duck and pushed it toward Carol, who ignored it. Carol was raising and lowering one round knee, watching it emerge sleek and gleaming and then lowering it again when the water had drained off to mere drops on her skin. Joanne watched too, thoughtfully, and Ben Joe watched Joanne.

"I always did like first dates," she said after a minute. "I was good at those. I knew what to wear – not so dressy it made them shy and not so sloppy they thought I didn't give a hoot – and how to act and what to say, and by the time I was ready to come in I'd have them all the way in love with me or know the reason why. But the dates after that are different. Once they loved me, what was I supposed to do *then*? Once I've accomplished that, where else is there to go? So I ended up confining myself to first dates. I got so good at them that I could first-date *any*one – I mean even the people that were on *seventh* dates with me, or even people that weren't dates at all. I could first-date my own *family*, even – just figure out what would make them love me at a certain moment and then do it, easy as that."

She leaned forward suddenly, resting her elbows on the rim of the bathtub and staring into the water at Carol's gleeful face.

"Then I got married," she said.

Ben Joe waited, not pushing her. Joanne stood up and reached for a towel and then just stayed there, holding the towel forgotten in her hands.

"The trouble is," she said, "you have to stop clinking your bracelets and dancing like a maniac after a while. You have

53

to *rest* now and then. Which may have been okay with Gary, but not with me. I didn't know what to do once I had sat down to rest, and so I started being just terrible. Following him around telling him what an awful wife I was. Waking him up in the middle of the night to accuse him of not believing I loved him. He was all sleepy and didn't know *what* was coming off. He'd say sure he believed me and go back to sleep leaving me to lie awake counting the dust specks that floated around in the dark, and making all kinds of plans to get my hair done and have him take me dancing." She frowned at the towel. "Got so I couldn't bear my own self," she said. "I left."

She wrapped the towel around Carol and lifted her out onto the bath mat.

"What'd you come back *here* for?" Ben Joe asked.

She dried Carol silently for a minute. Then she said, "Well, I want Carol to be with some kind of people that know her if I am going to get a job. That's why."

She had finished scrubbing Carol with the towel and now she pulled a white flannel nightgown over the baby's head, saying, "Where's Carol? Oh, I can't find Carol. *Where's* Carol?" until Carol's face poked through the neck of the nightgown, small and round and grinning.

"Besides," Joanne said, tying the ribbon under Carol's chin, "it's not the same place I'm coming back to, really. Not even if I wanted it to be."

"Oh, for God's sake," said Ben Joe.

"What's wrong?"

"You and Mama. You and the girls. And Mr. Dower, even. Of course it's the same place. What would it have gone and changed into? Always pulling up the same silly argument to fool yourselves with—"

"Now, now," said Joanne soothingly. She picked Carol up. "It's *not* the same place really, is it?"

He gave up, helplessly, and followed her out of the bathroom. There was no argument he could give that would convince her; she was too blindly cheerful, giving Carol little pecks on the cheek and talking to her happily as she crossed the hallway. At her mother's door she stopped and looked in.

"Gone downstairs," she said. "Come on, Ben Joe. I want to ask you something."

"What?" he asked suspiciously.

"Come *on*."

He followed her to her own room. It was cluttered with Joanne's odds and ends, and the old white crib had been moved down from the attic to a spot beside Joanne's bed. Other than that, it was almost the same as when she had left it. Huge stuffed animals, won by long-ago boy-friends at state fairs, littered the window seat; perfume bottles and hair ribbons and bobby pins lay scattered on the bureau. She laid Carol carefully in the crib and said, "Where were you when Dad died?"

"Where— Oh, no," Ben Joe said. "No, don't you start that."

"Why not?" She straightened up from kissing Carol good night and turned to face him. "That's not fair, Ben Joe. Nobody'll tell me *anything* about it. I even wrote a letter asking them to tell me. Nobody ever answered."

"Well, you were away," Ben Joe said.

"That doesn't change anything." She spread a blanket over Carol and began tying it down at the corners. "It happened just after Jenny began writing all the family's letters," she said. "Only Jenny didn't write this particular one, I remember. She went through a stage when she wouldn't write or speak the fact that Dad was dead. Susannah told me that. So the twins had to take over the letter writing. Jane and Lisa, they handled everything, although neither one of them will touch a pen ordinarily and you can tell it from their letters. But it was just as well, I guess – their writing the letters, I mean – because I suppose Jenny would just have sent a list of the funeral costs. Or would she, that far back? When did Jenny learn to be so practical? Anyway, there was this note from Lisa saying, 'Dad just passed away last night but felt no pain' – as if anyone could *know* what he felt – and that's all I ever heard. What happened, Ben Joe?"

"What difference does it make?" he asked.

"It makes a lot of difference. Who *won* makes a lot of difference."

"What?"

"Who won. Mama or that other woman."

"Well, that's the—"

"I know." She turned the lamp around so that it wouldn't shine in Carol's eyes and sat down on the foot of the bed. "It's an awful thing to wonder. And none of my business, anyway. But it's important to know, for all kinds of reasons."

He began searching through his crumpled cigarette pack for the last cigarette, not looking at her.

"Here, take mine," she said.

"Not menthol."

"They won't kill you."

She threw the pack at him; it fell on the floor in front of him and he picked it up and leaned back against the bureau.

"Two weeks before he died," Joanne said, "he was at home. I know he was. Jenny put it just beautifully, in this letter she wrote me. She said, 'You'll be happy to know Daddy has got back from his trip' – 'trip'; that's an interesting choice of words – 'and he's living at home now.' Now, where was he when he died? Still at home?"

"At Lili Belle's," Ben Joe said.

"At— Oh." She shook her head. "Lately I've stopped thinking about her by her name," she said. "What with Gram calling her 'Another's House' all the time."

"Well, he didn't *mean* to go and die there," said Ben Joe. "He'd just been drinking a little, is all. Went out to get ice cubes and then forgot which home he was supposed to be going back to. Mom explained that to Lili Belle."

"*Mom* explained it to *Lili* Belle?"

"Well, yes. It was her that Lili Belle called soon as he died. He got to Lili Belle's with a pain in his chest and died a little after. So Lili Belle called Mom, and Mom came to explain how it was our house he'd really intended going back to and not hers; just a mistake. And Lili Belle hadn't really won after all."

"Looks like to me she had."

"But it was by *mistake* he went there."

"Oh, pshaw," Joanne said. She turned to see how Carol was and then faced Ben Joe again. "What about their little boy, his and Lili Belle's? That was named after Daddy? That's

56

more'n *you* were named for. I don't see that *your* name is Phillip. Do you think he would have walked off and left a baby named Phillip for good?"

"That's beside the point. You know, Joanne, sometimes I wonder whose side you're on."

She smiled and ground out her cigarette and stood up. "Don't you lose sleep on it," she said. "Come on, we're keeping Carol awake. I'm going to do my nails and I reckon you have people you'll want to visit."

"I don't know who."

But he straightened up anyway and followed Joanne out of the room. In the hall she gave him a little pat on the arm and then turned toward the bathroom, and he started for the stairs. He stopped at the hall landing, which looked down over the long stairway, and put one hand on the railing.

"You know where the emery boards are?" Joanne called from the bathroom.

He didn't answer; he leaned both elbows on the railing and stared downward, thinking.

"Oh, never mind. I found them."

He was remembering one night six years ago; this spot always reminded him of it. He had been studying in his room and at about ten o'clock he had decided to go downstairs for a beer. With his mind still foggy with facts and dates, he had wandered out into the hallway, had put one hand on the railing and was about to take the first step down, when the noise began. He could hear that noise still, although he always did his best to forget it.

First he thought it sounded like an angry bull wheezing and bellowing in a circle around the house. But it was too reedy and penetrating to be that; he thought then that it must be an auto horn. Kerry Jamison had an auto horn like that. Only Kerry Jamison was a well-bred boy and didn't honk for Ben Joe when he came visiting him. And he certainly didn't drive on the Hawkes's carefully tended lawn.

All over the house the girls had come swarming out of the various rooms, asking what the racket was. Tessie, who was scarcely more than a baby then and should have been asleep for hours, inched her bedroom door open and peeked out to ask Ben Joe if she could come downstairs with the others, because there was a trumpet blowing outside that wouldn't hush for her. She spoke in a whisper; their mother was reading in bed in the room next to Tessie's and would surely say no if she heard what Tessie was asking. But what neither Ben Joe nor Tessie realized at the time was that their mother was answering the telephone in her room, listening to Lili Belle Mosely tell her her husband was dead. Right then she wouldn't have cared if Tessie never went to bed again, but Tessie couldn't know that and she went on in her whispery voice: "Can I, Ben Joe? Say yes. Can I?"

"*No*," said Ben Joe. "I'll go down and shut it up, whatever it is. Get back in bed, Tessie."

"But it's so *scary*, Ben—"

Their mother's door opened. Tessie popped back into her room just as Ellen Hawkes flew out of hers; they were like the two figures in a weather house. Ellen had on a pair of blue cotton pajamas and her hair was rumpled and she was struggling into a khaki raincoat of her husband's as she ran.

"Your father's dead," she said, and rushed down the stairs.

Ben Joe put both hands on the railing and leaned down. His mother had passed the little landing at the curve of the stairs and now she was directly below him, still running down; he could see the top of her head, and the curls lifting a little as she came down hard on each step. "Your father's dead," she repeated to the girls downstairs. Above her voice came the eerie sound from outside, wheezing and bellowing its way around to the front of the house.

Ben Joe let go of the railing and tore down the stairs after his mother. His shirt was open, and the tails of it flew out behind him as he ran. He had no shoes on. On one of the steps his stockinged foot slipped and he almost fell, but he caught himself and kept on going. The girls were waiting for him at the bottom, with stunned white faces. Tessie had come out to stand on the landing where Ben Joe had stood a minute ago and now she looked down at the others and began to cry without knowing why. She had poked her head through the bars because she was not yet tall enough to see over the railing. Her mother, holding on to the newel post at the bottom of the stairs while she struggled into a pair of Susannah's loafers, looked up at Tessie briefly and said, "She'll have got her head caught in those bars again. Better get her out, somebody."

Tessie's head was a tiny yellow circle on the second floor, outlined against the dark cupola that rose above the stairwell. The house seemed enormous, suddenly. The whole world seemed enormous.

"Where are you going?" Ben Joe asked his mother.

"To your father's friend's house," she said, without expression. "I'll be back. Gram's asleep now. Don't wake her. And try and figure some way of getting Tessie's head free without sawing the bars down again, will you?"

Ben Joe nodded. None of it made sense. Everything was harried and nightmarish and yet the same small practical things were going on at the same time. His mother patted his shoulder and then, abruptly, she was off, out the front door and into the darkness of the moonless, early-autumn night. As she crossed the front porch the eerie, wailing sound from outside became louder; as she descended the steps down to the front walk a soldier came into view playing a bagpipe. He was small and serious, with his eyes fixed only on his instrument, and he walked in a straight line across their front lawn and then around to the other side of the house. He and Ellen crossed paths with only inches between them; neither one of them paused or looked toward the other one.

Jenny, standing with the rest of them on the front porch, said, "It's *a bagpipe*."

From out in back of the house came the sound of their mother's car starting, rising above the piercing sound of the bagpipes. A minute later the yellow, dust-filled beams of two headlights backed past them out into the street and then swung sharply around and disappeared.

Susannah stopped staring after the car and turned to Jenny, frowning, trying to sort her thoughts and figure what should be done.

"It's no bagpipe I ever heard," she said finally. "Bagpipes make tunes. This is only making one note."

"Maybe he can't play," Jenny said. She was only twelve

then, a thin, nervous little girl, and she was shivering and seemed to be trying desperately to get a grasp on herself. "I'm sure that's it," she said. "He'll practice this note for a while and then go to the next, and then go—"

"Not in *our* yard he won't," Susannah said. "Run around the back and stop him, Ben Joe."

But there was no need to; the soldier had come around the front again. Apparently he liked having an audience. He emerged from the side of the house at a scurrying little run, with his short legs pumping as fast as they could go, and then as soon as he came into the light from the front porch he slowed to a leisurely stroll in order to parade before them for as long as possible. His chest heaved up and down from the running he had done, and the horrible wailing sound was jerky and breathless now.

"Um . . ." Ben Joe said. He stepped down from the porch and the little soldier stopped. "You think you could do that somewhere else?"

The soldier grinned. He had a small, bony face, with the skin stretched tight and shining across it when he smiled. "No sir," he said. "No sir. Man said no."

"What?"

"Your daddy. 'No,' he says. No."

"I don't—"

"Saw me hitchhiking, your dad did. Told me could I play that thing, I allowed yes I could but not *this* way, with all but one reed gone so there wasn't but one sound. He said anyway, anyway, he said, to play it round his house for a joke and not give up till he come back. When he comes he'll give me a bottle. A free bottle."

He grinned again and put the mouthpiece to his lips, but Ben Joe reached out and took a gentle hold on his arm. "He won't be back," he said. He turned toward Susannah. "Get a bottle of bourbon, Susannah. Bourbon all right with you, friend?"

"Oh yes, oh yes—"

Jenny suddenly came to life. She raced down the front steps and yanked Ben Joe's hand from the soldier's arm. "Leave him be," she said. "You leave him. Let him play." Her face was white and pinched-looking; Ben Joe thought if she shook any harder she would fall down.

"He's getting tired of playing," he told her.

"You leave him."

Susannah came out of the house again, slamming the screen door behind her. "Here," she said.

"Why, thank you, Ma'am. I am much—"

"You play, you," said Jenny to the soldier.

Susannah reached over Jenny's head with the bottle; the soldier held out his hand and Jenny made a grab for the bottle but missed.

"Wait," she said.

'Wouldn't change a thing, making him keep playing," Ben Joe told her gently. "If he played till you had grandchildren, it wouldn't bring back—"

"You wait, you *wait*!"

She was rigid now, not shaking any more but with her hands folded into tense fists and her face wet with tears. When Ben Joe put one hand on her shoulder she spun toward him, not actually fighting him but letting her arm stay rigid, so that her fist swung hard into his stomach and knocked all the wind from him. The soldier clicked his tongue, his eyes round. Ben Joe started coughing and bent over, but he kept hold of Jenny, pinning her arms down at her sides and holding her tight while he and Susannah guided her toward the stairs.

"I told you and *told* you!" she was screaming. "Now you've sent him away and he'll *never* come back—"

The soldier, mistaking her meaning, smiled cheerfully and waved his bottle at her. "*Sure* I'll be back," he called comfortingly. "*Don't* you worry ma'am!"

He set off toward the street, whistling. On the porch, Jane and Lisa took Jenny from Ben Joe while he leaned over the railing and coughed himself hoarse, trying to get his wind again. Susannah whacked him steadily on the back.

"You'll be all right," she said over and over. "You'll be all right. You'll be all right."

She did her best, but she couldn't say it the way Joanne did. And right then he wished for Joanne more than anyone in the world. He thought probably they all did. If she came walking

61

up the steps right now she would fold every single person up close to her and cry, and pat them softly; and they could start crying too and telling her all the secret fears swamping their minds at this minute and then they would realize everything that had happened. If they could only *realize* something, things could start getting better again.

But Joanne didn't come up the steps, and when his coughing fit was through, Ben Joe straightened up and followed Susannah into the house again. Up on the second floor, Tessie was crying.

"You get the twins to give Jenny one of Dad's sleeping pills," Ben Joe told Susannah. "I'll try and get Tessie out of the railings."

Now, six years later, he thought he could still name the two posts where Tessie's head had been caught. All seven children, from Joanne to Tessie, had been stuck in this railing at least once in their lives. But he thought he knew which posts Tessie had been between *that* night, because it was still so clear in his mind. He had soothed Tessie, who had been through this before and was not very frightened, and while he was trying to pull her out he thought about the same thing he always thought when he did this: he must put some screening here, to stop all these ridiculous goings-on. Even if Gram *did* say it would ruin the looks of the railing. Under his hands was the feel of Tessie's head – the thin, soft hair, the tight little bones of her skull. He had turned her face gently, holding her small ears flat against her head, and worked her out from between the bars and scooped her up to carry her back to bed. It was then, standing there with the weight of her against his shoulder, that the first sorrow hit him – just one deep bruise inside that made him catch his breath. He could remember it still. That, and the little flannel nightgown Tessie wore, and the soft sounds of Jenny crying in the room she shared with Tessie . . .

It was so clear still that he could have told Joanne, and by telling her proved that Lili Belle hadn't won. For if his father had *meant* to go to Lili Belle's, he wouldn't have played that bagpipe joke on them. He loved every one of his children; he wouldn't have left them with any unkind tricks. But even though he had thought about telling her, Ben Joe had stopped himself. It was one of those things that wasn't mentioned in this house. Not even he and his other sisters mentioned it.

What else didn't they mention? He looked down the stairs and frowned, wondering what went on behind their cool, bright smiles. What did they think about before they went to sleep at night? He leaned further down, listening. The twins were chattering away in the kitchen; in the living room, someone laughed and Tessie gave a small squeal. He began to feel a sort of admiration for them. It was like watching a man who has been to Africa drink tea in the parlor and make small talk, with all those things known and done behind him that he is not even thinking about. Behind him, Joanne padded back to her bedroom with a pack of emery boards in her hand, but Ben Joe didn't look around. He remained in his own thoughts, with his hand resting absently on the stair railing.

6

WHEN FINALLY HE came downstairs he made another tour of the house, just to see if anyone was free to talk to him yet. He started with his mother, who had joined the others in the living room and was making tiny stitches in a white collar.

"Finish Tessie's dress?" he asked.

"Obviously not, since that's what I'm stitching on."

He stood in the middle of the room, chewing on his thumbnail while he tried to think of another opening.

"Well, how's the book store going?" he asked finally.

"It's all right. What's the matter, Ben Joe, haven't you any plans for tonight?"

"Not offhand."

"You certainly are restless."

He took this as an invitation to sit down and did so at once on the leather hassock beside her. On the couch opposite him Susannah and Gram collected the cards that lay between them and Susannah began shuffling them. The cards made a quick, snapping noise under her fingers.

"Carol sure doesn't look like a Hawkes, does she?" he said.

His mother held the dress up at arm's length and frowned at it. "No, I don't suppose she does," she said finally. She lowered the dress into her lap again and then, feeling that something more seemed to be expected of her, said, "It's really too young to tell yet."

"I wouldn't say that," Gram said. "Has the Hawkes nose, I'll say *that*. Small and pointy. And Joanne's little pointy chin."

There was another silence. Susannah began dealing, slapping down a loud card for Gram and a soft one for herself in a steady rhythm. Ben Joe stood up again and moved aimlessly over to the game.

"I thought we might go see Jamie Dower tonight, Gram," he said. "Car's free."

"Oh, well, I don't think so, Ben Joe. Not tonight."

"Why not?"

"Well . . ." She frowned at the cards in her hand. "I'd rather wait awhile," she said. "He wouldn't have settled his self properly yet."

"What's to settle?"

"Can't be much of a host when you're still feeling like a guest yourself, can you? Give him a couple more days."

"A couple more *days*?" said Ben Joe's mother. "How long are you planning on staying here, Ben Joe?"

"I don't know."

"Well, it seems to me you should be gone by then. Columbia's not going to wait on you forever."

"Oh, well," Ben Joe said. He was wandering back and forth with his hands in his pockets, occasionally kicking gently at a leg of the coffee table as he passed it. "Susannah?" he said.

"Hmm."

"Where's the guitar and the hourglass and all?"

"I'm not sure."

"What you mean, you're not sure?"

She brushed a piece of hair off her forehead with the back of her wrist and then switched a card in her hand from the left end of the fan to the right.

"I asked you if you wanted them," Ben Joe said. "I asked if you would take care of them. 'Yes, Ben Joe. Oh yes, Ben Joe.'" He made his voice into a silly squeak, imitating her. Of all his sisters, Susannah was the only one he was ever rude to – maybe because she was always so cool and brisk that he figured she wouldn't change toward him no matter *what* he did. "I can just see it," he said now. "Bet the whole shebang has just mildewed away to nothing, right?"

"In the *winter*?" Gram said.

"I bid two spades," said Susannah. "Ben Joe, I am sure everything's right where you left it. Except the guitar. The rest of the things I just hadn't assimilated yet."

"Well, where's the guitar, now that you've assimilated that? In the bathtub? Out in the garden holding up a tomato plant?"

"In the *winter*?" Gram said again. "A tomato plant in the winter?"

Ellen Hawkes laughed. When they turned to look at her she stopped and looked down at her sewing again, still smiling.

"I declare," said Gram, "you got no sense of *season*, Ben Joe."

"Where's the guitar?"

"Under the couch in the den."

"Aha, I wasn't far wrong. Right where it belongs."

"Ben Joe," said his mother, "there's no reason to get so excited about a few possessions you've already given away. What's the matter with you tonight?"

"But they're my *favorite* possessions. That I missed all the time I was gone."

"Then you shouldn't have given them away. You're too old to be missing things, anyway. Why don't you stop that pacing and read something?"

He picked the newspaper up from the coffee table and began to read it listlessly as he stood there.

"And *not* upside-*down*!" his mother said.

"Ah, hell."

He threw down the paper and turned toward the den.

"You need someone to take you out walking with a leash around your neck," said Susannah. "Are you going to bid or not, Gram?"

"Pass."

Ben Joe stuck his head inside the doorway of the TV room. "Tessie," he said.

"Sssh."

"Tess, I want to ask you something."

"I'm watching television."

"It's only a cigarette commercial."

"Leave her in peace," said Jenny. "And don't hold that door open, Ben Joe. The noise'll bother the others."

"Don't either one of you want to go to the movies?"

Tessie shook her head, not taking her eyes from the screen.

"It's only what it just about always is," she said. "*Phantom of the Opera.*"

"Why don't you come in and watch TV?" Jenny asked.

"I don't feel like it. I feel all yellow inside."

"Well, close the door, then."

He closed the door and came back into the living room.

"What happened to all those boys you used to go around with?" his mother asked.

"They went *north*, all of them. A long time ago."

"Do you know any girls any more?"

"Them too," he said.

"What?"

"They went north too."

"Oh."

"Gram," said Susannah, "if you keep holding your hand that way I'm going to have to shut my *eyes* not to see what cards you have."

"What about Shelley Domer?" his mother asked.

"Oh, Mom. She was my *first* girl. Her family went off to Savannah seven years ago."

"Gram, wasn't that Shelley Domer we saw the other day?"

"It was," said Gram. "You have another diamond, Susannah. I know you do."

"I don't either. Want to see my hand?"

"What's she doing *here*?" Ben Joe asked.

"I don't know," said his mother. "Their family kept their house here, I think. Kept planning to come back someday."

"You mean she's living in her old home?"

"She wouldn't have been sweeping the front porch of it if she *wasn't*, would she?"

"I'd go see her if you've nothing better to do," Gram said. "Be something to keep you occupied. And you saw right much of her once upon a time."

"Oh, she was all right."

"That all you can find to say about her? *Spades* are trumps, Susannah. Keep your mind on your game. Only thing I ever had against Shelley Domer was her family, to be frank."

"What was wrong with her family, for heaven's sake?"

"Well, I'm not saying they didn't have money. Or weren't

67

nice. But money and niceness neither one isn't all there is. Mrs. Domer still went grocery shopping in shuffly old slippers with pansies sewn on them, and that Shelley, well, she was a sweet child and it was no fault of hers, but many's the time I seen her in a flowered calico skirt and a plaid blouse *together*, like a tenant farmer's girl would wear, and in wintertime overalls under her dress, which is *a sure* sign, a sure sign. As if having those glass-blue, empty-looking eyes like the bad Dowers have wasn't enough—"

"Well, for one who wears black *gym* shoes to the grocery store—" Ellen Hawkes began.

"I can afford to. My family is different, and don't have to worry about being taken for the wrong kind."

Ben Joe's mother bit a thread off the white collar. "Well, I don't see what slippers have to do with it," she said. "Shelley Domer can't help her ancestry, that's for sure. No, all I ever had against her was the way she hung on Ben Joe all the time. None of *my* girls has ever been a boy chaser, I'll say that for them. They've been raised to have pride, and—"

"Pride nothing," Gram snapped. "Nicest thing *about* that girl was her being so sweet on Ben Joe. She used to wait for him every day after school, I remember. Even in wintertime. Till he'd come ambling out at whatever hour he chose to say hey to her."

"That's what I'm—"

"Oh, forget it," said Ben Joe. "I'll go and see her now while you two are arguing." He went to the hall closet and pulled his jacket from a hanger. "Anyone want anything from outside?"

"No, thank you. Have a nice evening."

"Okay."

Outside it was beginning to get cold. There was a little chill around his neck where his collar was open, but he just walked more quickly to make up for it. With his hands in his pockets and his lips pursed in a silent whistle he headed east, down past rows of medium-sized, medium-aged houses that jangled faintly with the TV or radio noises locked inside them. Occasionally he caught glimpses of families moving around behind lace curtains, but no one was out on the sidewalk. A dog rushed past, trailing a leash; nobody attempted to follow him. And at one house an old woman in a man's overcoat rocked on a cold porch glider.

"Hey," she said.

"Hey," said Ben Joe.

"No moon out tonight."

"No."

He turned up Evers and walked more slowly. None of the walk took any thinking. When he was in high school it had become second nature, like going downstairs in the morning for breakfast and then realizing, once he was down there, that the actual descent had been an utter blank in his memory. The first few times he had come here actually shaking, with his hair slicked down and his face thin from the tension of keeping his teeth from chattering. He would have gone to the bathroom six or seven times in the half-hour before, just from nervousness. But gradually it became just an ordinary thing, this walk. Even when there was no definite date planned he would go, just to sit in the living room with Shelley and talk to her. She wasn't very quick-witted and she didn't entertain him with fast talk and bubbles of laughter the way his sisters entertained their dates, but she did listen. No matter what he talked about she would listen, smiling happily at him all the time, and when he was done she would just hug him or tell him how much she liked the way the barber had cut his hair this week, but he knew she had heard what he had to say, anyway. He smiled into the darkness, thinking about that, and cut through a vacant lot to Holland Street and the Domer house.

The lights were turned on inside. The place was the same as always – big and worn and comfortable, with years of dead leaves piled around it. He would have thought Mr. Domer had raked those up by now; Mr. Domer was a small and tidy man. When Ben Joe crossed the front lawn the leaves roared around his ankles. He climbed the long steps to the front door. Years ago, in the summertime, they would stop at this top step when they came in from a date. They would look up to the open window upstairs and there would be the little triangular-faced, white-nightgowned blur of Shelley's sister

Phoebe peering down at them. She must have been about seven, that first year. She had thought, from seeing the cartoons in the *Saturday Evening Post*, that all boys kissed their dates on the girls' doorsteps, and every night she had lain in wait in her bedroom, watching hopefully. How old would she be now? Sixteen or seventeen, he supposed. And gone from that window. There was only the closed glass pane now, and the still white organdy curtains behind it.

He knocked twice. A figure came toward him and peered out the window glass in the door, still only a silhouette behind a mesh curtain. Then she opened the door and let him step in. She seemed stunned for a minute; her mouth was slightly open.

"Ben Joe!" she said. "Is that you?"

"Sure it is. Have I gone and changed all that much?"

"No. No, only it's been such a long . . . Well, hey, anyway."

"Hey."

Shelley stood awkwardly in front of him, beginning to look happy and a little scared. She never had known what to do about greeting people. If she had been one of the girls he had dated after her, she would have come tripping up and shrieked, "For goodness *sake!*" and kissed him loudly on the mouth even if she didn't remember his name. But not Shelley. Shelley stood straight before him, with her hands pleating little bunches of her skirt at the sides, and smiled at him.

"Mom said she saw you sweeping the front porch," he said. "I'm home for a little vacation. I thought I'd stop by and see how you were getting on."

"Oh, well, I'm fine. Just seems funny to see you, I think . . ."

She moved over almost soundlessly to shut the door behind him, and he turned to watch her. There were little changes in her; he could see that even under the dim light in the hallway. Her hair, which used to hang almost to her shoulders in such straight blond ribbons that it had made him think of corn syrup, was bunched scratchily behind her head now and held there by a few pins, much like Gram's bun. Her face was prettier and more clearly defined, but she still gave the impression of a waifish kind of thinness that made her seem more like fifteen than twenty-five. Partly it was because she was pale and without make-up, and her eyes were such a light blue; partly it was because she was wearing old clothes that must have been her mother's and were far too big for her. The skirt was a dingy pink, accordion-pleated and very long; the sweater was an old bulky maroon one that somehow made her shoulder blades stick out more in back than her breasts did in front. But she still moved the same way – almost frightenedly and without a sound, and always in slow motion. Now she slowly opened her hands at her sides, as if she were consciously telling herself to relax, and looked down at her clothes.

"Now, Ben Joe," she said, "I have to go put another dress on. I didn't know I was about to have company. You wait in the living room, hear? I'll be right—"

"But I'm just going to stay a minute," Ben Joe said. "I only came to say hello."

"Well, you just wait."

She turned and darted up the curving stairs, and Ben Joe had to go into the living room alone. He chose a seat at the end of the sofa, nearest the unlit fireplace. The room seemed to him like the huge front room of a long-unused summer house; all the things that were not particularly liked and yet still too good to discard had been left here by the Domers when they moved South. Wicker armchairs and threadbare sofas sat on an absolutely bare wooden floor, and the few decorative items scattered around were worthless – a china spaniel with three puppies chained to her collar by tiny gold chains; a huge framed photograph of a long-ago baseball team; a rosebudded cracked china slipper with earth in it but no plant. Ben Joe shivered. This had been a cheerful room once, back when he was in high school.

He heard Shelley's shoes on the stairs and a minute later she was in the living room, crossing in front of him with a company smile and a white skirt and sweater that fit better than the old ones. She had combed her hair, although he was sorry to see that it was still in a bun, and there was a little lipstick on her mouth.

"I'm going to get you some coffee," she said.

"No, I don't want any."

"It's already made, Ben Joe. You wait here and I'll—"

"No, *please*. I don't want any."

"Well, all right."

She sat down on the edge of a wicker armchair with her hands on her knees.

"Where's Phoebe?" Ben Joe asked.

"Phoebe."

"Phoebe your *sister*."

"Oh," she said. All the breath seemed to have left her; she gasped a little and said, "Phoebe and Mama and Daddy, all of them, they're dead, you mustn't have heard, it only happened a while—"

"Oh, no, I never—"

"They had a wreck."

"I'm sorry," Ben Joe said. He thought of the small white blur in the upstairs window, still almost realer than Shelley herself. He watched Shelley's fingers twisting a pearl button on her sweater. "Nobody told me," he said helplessly.

"I only been back a while now. Not many people know about it."

"Was . . . How old was Phoebe?"

"Seventeen."

"Oh." He fell silent again, and tugged gently at one of the little cotton balls on the sofa upholstery.

"How are *your* sisters?" Shelley asked suddenly.

"They're fine." Almost immediately he felt guilty for that; he thought a minute and then offered: "Joanne's left her husband, though."

"Left him?"

"Yes."

"Well, I declare."

"She's back home now."

"Well."

"Her and her baby."

"I'm going to get you some coffee," Shelley said.

"No, wait. I've got to be—"

"It's *hot* already." She stood up and almost ran to the kitchen, still managing to make it slow motion. Behind her, Ben Joe shifted in his seat uneasily and crossed his legs.

72

"You're hungry too, I bet," she said when she entered the room again.

"No, I'm all right."

"You look right thin to me, Ben Joe. I got this marble cake from the Piggly-Wiggly. Course it's not real home-made, but anway—"

"Shelley, I really don't want it."

"Well, all right, Ben Joe."

She was carrying a chipped tin tray with two cups of coffee on it and a sugar bowl and cream pitcher that didn't match. When she set it on the coffee table everything clinked like the too-loud clinking of tea sets in movies.

"You take yourself lots of sugar," she said. "I declare, you *are* thin." She hovered over him, shadowlike, while he took up his coffee cup. He could smell her perfume now – a light, pink-smelling perfume – and when she bent over the table to hand him the sugar bowl, he could even smell perfume in her hair. Then she moved back to her seat, and he relaxed against the sofa cushions.

"Seems like I have got to get used to you all over again, it's been so long," Shelley said. "Are you feeling talky?"

He had forgotten that. She always asked him that question, to give him a chance before she plunged into her own slow, circuitous small talk. This time he remained silent, choosing to have her carry on the conversation, and smiled at her above his coffee cup because he liked her suddenly for remembering. Shelley waited another minute, sitting back easily in her chair. Once the first awkward moments were over, Shelley could be as relaxed as anyone.

"I don't know if I did right or not," she said finally, "coming back here like this. But my family's passing came so sudden. Left me strap-hanging in empty space, like. And I chose to come to Sandhill. I don't know why, except I was helping to run this nursery school for working mothers' children down in Georgia and so *sick* of it, you've got no idea, and saw no way out. I think I got something against Georgia. I really do. Seems like if there is one thing makes me ill, it's those torn-up circus posters on old barns. You know? And Seven-up signs. Well, Georgia's plumb full of those, though one time this girl I worked with told me she thought it was real snotty of me to say a thing like that. That's what our trouble was down there – the trash thought we were snotty and the snotty thought we were trash. Now, my daddy had to work himself up the hard way, but you know how fine he was, and anyway his mama's folks were Montagues, which should have *some* bearing. And there's nothing wrong with Mama's side of the family, either. But anyway I was lonely there. Didn't seem like there was any group we could really say we belonged to. Back in Sandhill it was better. I always have remembered Sandhill. And I still carry your picture."

She smiled happily at Ben Joe.

"That real goofy-looking one," she said, "that we had taken of you in the Snap-Yourself Photo Booth. Mama used to tease me about keeping it – said I might as well throw it out now. Though she always did like you. When you wrote me that letter, after we'd moved, about you starting to date Gloria Herman I thought Mama would cry. She said Gloria was real fast and loud, though it was my opinion that you knew better than Mama who was good for you. And at least you were right honest, telling me. I said that to Mama, too. And then a month later Susan Harpton wrote to tell how Gloria had moved on to someone new and you'd started dating Pat Locker. It got so I couldn't keep up with you any more. But I wasn't mad. Things like that happen when people get separated from each other."

"Well, it was a long time ago," Ben Joe said.

"It was. I know. Well, don't you worry, Ben Joe, I'm dating a real nice boy now. You'd like him. His name is John Horner and he's starting up a construction firm in Sandhill. You know him?"

"Horner." Ben Joe frowned. "Not offhand," he said.

"Well. You'd like him, though. Course we aren't too serious yet – I only been in town a month or so. But he is the *kindest* man. I don't know if I could marry him, yet."

"Has he asked you?"

"No. But I reckon he will one of these days."

The idea of Shelley's marrying someone else surprised him.

He looked at her as a stranger suddenly, evaluating her. She smiled back at him.

"Course," she said, "I was surprised he even wanted to *date* me. But I figured if maybe he could just endure through the first few dates, till I got easy with him and not so silly and tongue-tied any more, it'd be all right. And he did. He endured."

"Well, I'm glad to hear it."

She nodded, finished with that piece of news, and then frowned into space a minute as if she were fishing in her mind for the next piece.

"Oh, I know," she said finally. "I know. Ben Joe, I was so sorry to hear about your daddy. I wrote you about it and you never answered. But I hope it was a peaceful passing. He was a sweet man, your daddy."

"Thank you," said Ben Joe.

"Susan Harpton told me about it. And about your going to work at the bank after classes and Joanne getting married and all. She said the whole town missed your daddy."

"I did too," said Ben Joe. "Took to riding trains."

"What?"

"Trains. Riding trains. I rode trains all the time. One time I spent a whole month's salary that way. Mom about had a conniption fit – I was almost the family's only support back then."

"Oh," Shelley said. She frowned; she was on uncertain ground now. "Well, anyway, I just wanted to tell you I missed him. And if he lived a little different from most people, I don't think anybody held it against him. Not your daddy. Remember how when he got to drinking he always wanted someone to sing to him? 'Life Is Like a Mountain Railroad,' that's what he liked. Many's the time I've sung it to him."

"And 'Nobody Knows the Trouble I've Seen,'" said Ben Joe.

"That's right." She smiled into her coffee cup and then looked up again, with the next subject decided upon. "I hear you're in law school up north," she said. "Mrs. Murphy told me that. She's the one that's been keeping an eye on the house all these years. She's nice, though I found when I came back that she'd looked through the photograph albums and all Mama's love letters. When your mama and grandma passed by the porch as I was sweeping I called out 'hey' to them, meaning to ask about you, but I had trouble making myself heard, as your grandma was doing some of that singing of hers and your mama was trying real hard to hush her. When your grandma saw me she recognized me right off, though. She shouted out to tell me you weren't married yet, which I already knew, and a minute later your mama remembered me too. Your mama is a little slow in recognizing folks, but I don't hold with what Mrs. Murphy says, that she's on *purpose* slow. This town has always been of the opinion she is coldhearted, but I think it's because your daddy was their fair-haired boy, and they didn't want him hurt. Not that I think she *meant* to hurt him. I reckon she is just a little prideful and thinks pride's the same as dignity so she doesn't try and change herself. Mrs. Murphy said many's the time she herself went to your mama to tell her all she had to do was let herself get to crying and then, as soon as the tears got started good, go to . . . um, where your father lived at and tell him she wanted him back, but your mama always just tossed her hair and said who cared and offered Mrs. Murphy a slice of angel-food cake. It was the doctor's business and no one else's, she would say, though if it wasn't the doctor's *wife's* business too, then what did they get married for?

"Well, anyway, I never did get to ask how you were doing up north, since your mama and grandma were in a hurry. But I know it can be a lonely place. I went up there once to work for the Presbyterian church and stayed for a month, rooming with a girl I'd met who turned out to be a bit touched in the head. Went around in a chiffon gown with a candle in her hand at four a.m. and talked about craning her swanlike neck in the rain. I went home again. I always have been a homebody. I don't know what I'll do without my family. Even Phoebe, and her so mischievous. The last night that Phoebe was . . . was living, the last night I ever saw her, she was in the kitchen with her boy-friend and when—"

"Phoebe had a *boy*-friend?" Ben Joe asked.

"Well, yes, and when I walked in, they were robbing this

loose-change bank of my mama's, shaped like an Indian with a slot in the top of his head where she puts the money in, for odds and ends-like that she wants to buy – they were robbing this bank so they could go to the movies. The boy-friend had just got out his pocketknife to put through the slot and Phoebe was holding out her hand and saying, 'scalpel,' and that's the last I ever saw of her. I'm awful glad to meet up with you again, Ben Joe. All these years I been missing you."

"I'm glad to see *you*," said Ben Joe. He smiled at her in silence for a minute and then looked at his watch and stood up. "I've got to go. I was on the train all last night. Need to catch up on my sleep."

"Oh, don't you hurry."

"I've got to."

He picked up his jacket from the couch and put it on as he followed Shelley to the door. Outside it was raining; the sight surprised them both and they stood there looking at it.

"Don't come out with me," Ben Joe said.

"I won't melt."

"No, stay inside."

"I want to see you safely to the street," Shelley said.

Her face was serious, and she looked worried about him. Without knowing why, Ben Joe said, "Um, this Jack Horner—"

"John Horner."

"*John* Horner. Do you think he'd mind if I came back again?"

"I don't know. I don't— You come see me anyway, Ben Joe. You come anyway."

She was smiling now, looking up at him with the porch light shining clear through those sky-blue eyes of hers. Her face was so close he could bend down and kiss her. He had never kissed her on her doorstep before, despite all Phoebe's hopes; he had kissed her in his mother's old Buick, parked somewhere in the darkness, with that pink smell of her perfume circling him and her arms thin and warm around his neck. Her face hovered under his, still close; she looked up at him. But as he was about to bend toward her he thought that maybe this might commit him again; maybe everything would begin all over again, and time would get even more jumbled up in his head than it was already. So he drew back from the pale oblong of her face and said, "Is Sunday evening all right? About nine?"

"Yes."

"Well."

He stood looking at her for a minute longer, and then straightened his shoulders.

"I'll see you then," he said.

"Good night, Ben Joe."

"Good night."

He turned and started down the long steps, being careful not to slip on the soggy layers of leaves beneath his feet. The rain was no more than an unsteady dripping sound now, with an occasional cool drop landing on his face. Once on the street again, he shoved his hands deep into his trouser pockets and walked very slowly, frowning, sorting his thoughts out. But his thoughts wouldn't sort; he felt as if he was never again going to know the reason for anything he did. The puddles on the sidewalk began soaking into his shoes, and he started running toward home.

7

THE NEXT DAY was Saturday. Ben Joe awoke with a hollow, bored feeling; he dawdled over his breakfast until it was cold and then went back to his room to read a detective novel upside-down on an unmade bed. Halfway through the morning one of the girls knocked on his door and said, "Ben Joe?"

"Mm-hmm."

"It's me. Lisa. Can I come in?"

"I guess so."

She stuck her head in the door and smiled. She was much calmer than her twin; it was the way Ben Joe had first learned to tell them apart. She was wearing a neat blue suit and high heels. "We're going downtown," she said. "Want to come?"

"You have to dress up *that* much just to go downtown?"

"Never can tell who you'll meet." She grinned, and crossed to his bed to hand him a postcard. "Mail," she said. "Who's Jeremy?"

"My roommate. Do you have to read all my mail?"

He looked at the picture on it – the Guggenheim Museum, in an unreal shade of yellowish-white – and then turned the card over and began reading the large, rounded handwriting:

Dear Ben J.,

Hope you are thawing out down there. I borrowed your dinner jacket. That frizzly-haired girl keeps calling wanting to know when you'll be back, and I said Monday or so, right? Pack one of those sisters of yours in a suitcase and bring her along.

Jeremy.

"Which one are you going to pack up?" Lisa asked.

"What?"

"Which sister?"

"Oh. I don't know. Why – you feel like leaving home?"

"I surely do," Lisa said. She sat down with a little bounce on the foot of the bed and looked at her shoes. "I've used up all the boys in this town, that's what."

"What about those two you and Jane were with last night?"

"I'm getting tired of them. I keep thinking maybe I could start new someplace else, in another town."

"Well, I know the feeling," said Ben Joe. He turned the card over again and looked at it, frowning. "I wonder if I've missed any quizzes. Jeremy's right – I've got to get started back there pretty quick."

"Well, do you want to come to town or don't you?"

"No. I guess not."

Lisa stood up and left, and Ben Joe looked after her thoughtfully. "Don't you worry," he said when she reached the door. "New boys're always showing up."

"I know. Yell if you change your mind about coming downtown, Ben Joe."

"Okay."

He stared at the closed door for a few minutes and then got up and padded over to his bureau in his stocking feet. The top drawer looked like Jeremy's had in New York – stuffed with postcards and envelopes and canceled checks. He threw the postcard on top of the heap and then idly leafed through what was underneath. At the bottom was a stack of Shelley's letters from Savannah, neatly rubber-banded together. And a few postcards from the times his father had gone to medical conventions. They were dry and formal; his father had trouble saying things in writing. He stacked everything carelessly together again and was about to close the drawer when he saw something pink lying in the right-hand corner. It was a unique shade of pink – a deep rose that was almost magenta and never should have been used in writing paper – and it was one that had stuck in his mind for some six years now. Even when he saw something nearly that color in a dress or a

80

magazine ad, even now, it made him wince. He pulled the envelope up and made himself examine it. Large, slanted pencil writing ran in a straight line across it, addressed to his father at his office on Main Street. Only his father had never seen it; Ben Joe had taken it from the box when he had gone to bring his father home for supper one day. He had seen the "L.B.M." on the upper left-hand corner and quietly stuffed it in his pocket. Now he stood staring at it without opening it, letting it lie flat in the palm of his hand. When he had stared at it so long that he could see it with his eyes shut, he suddenly slapped it into his shirt pocket, grabbed up his sneakers from the floor in front of the bureau, and slammed out of his room.

"Lisa!" he called.

His grandmother was on the landing, polishing the stair rail and singing only slightly more softly than usual, because she was intent upon her polishing:

"When I was *si-ingle*,
I wandered at my *e-ease*.
Now that I am *ma-arried*,
Got a flat-heeled man to please . . ."

"Gram," Ben Joe said, "has Lisa gone downtown yet?"

She refolded her cloth and smiled at it, still singing, because she was at the loudest part and no one could stop her at a loud part:

"And it's oh, *Lo-o-ord*,
I wish I was but one lone girl again . . ."

"Oh, hell," Ben Joe said. He galloped on down the stairs, two at a time, with his sneakers still in his hands. "*Lisa!*"

"What you want, Ben Joe?"

He stepped over Carol, who was sticking toothpicks upright into the nap in the hall rug. Lisa was in the living room arguing with Jenny and Joanne over the grocery list.

"If she wants all those outlandish things," Jenny was saying, "she can darn well go get them herself, that's what *I* think."

81

Joanne took the list from her and ran her finger down it. "Well," she said finally, "I don't reckon it would *hurt* us any to start drinking burgundy with our meals—"

"But *I'm* the one Ben Joe left in charge of the money. What's the matter with Gram lately? Ben Joe, I want you to look at this."

Ben Joe sat down on the couch and began putting his sneakers on. "I've decided to hitch a ride downtown with you," he said.

"*Look*, will you, Ben Joe? Now Gram's making *me* go out and buy all her silly notions. Burgundy my foot. And her upstairs singing loud on purpose, been singing all morning without taking breath so that no one can interrupt and ask her what she wants with burgundy and oyster crackers and kippered herrings—"

"Oh, she's just tired of the same old things," Ben Joe said. "You going right away? Because if not, I'll just walk instead of—"

"No, we're coming. Come on, Joanne."

Jenny led the way, looking sensible and businesslike in her open trenchcoat. At the front door she took the car keys off a hook on the wall and stuck them in her pocket. "Where's Tessie?" she asked Lisa.

"In the car. Says you and she are going shoe shopping and she's in a hurry to get started."

"Okay. Close the door behind you, Ben Joe."

They crossed through the weedy grass to the driveway beside the house where the car was parked. Inside, on the front seat, Tessie bounced up and down in a short-sleeved plaid dress.

"Where's your jacket?" Jenny asked as she opened the door.

"In the house."

"Well, better go get it."

"Aw, Jenny—"

"Jenny, for Pete's sake," Ben Joe said. "I'm in a hurry."

"Well, I can't help that. Run on and get it, Tessie."

Tessie slammed out of the car, and Jenny turned the motor on to let it warm up. She seemed resigned to all these hindrances; she sat patiently waiting, while Ben Joe, squeezed between Joanne and Lisa, drummed his fingers on his knees and squirmed about irritably. When Tessie came out of the house, dragging her feet slowly as she worked her way into an old corduroy jacket, Ben Joe leaned forward and shouted, "Come *on*, Tessie!"

"What's the matter with *you*?" Jenny asked. She leaned across to open the door for Tessie. "What you suddenly in such an all-fired hurry for?"

"I've got a lot to get done."

"Ten minutes ago you were going to stay home all day," said Lisa.

"Well, not any more."

"Where you going?"

"Just around." He leaned back with his hands between his knees and stared out the window as the car slipped down the driveway into the street. "Got a couple of things I want to attend to," he said. "And Jeremy's postcard reminded me I don't have all year to do them in."

"Better go see your old music teacher," Lisa said. "And Miss Potter, the one that taught you third grade. She asks about you every time she sees me."

"Okay."

"She wants to know if you're a famous poet yet. Says you wrote your first poem in her class."

"*I* don't remember that."

"Well, she does. Says it went, 'My fish, my cat, my little world,' and she's keeping it still for when you get famous."

"My land," Ben Joe said. "Jenny, how far downtown are you going?"

"Just to the A & P."

"And the shoe store," Tessie reminded her.

"And the shoe store. 'Why you want to know?"

"Not past that?" asked Ben Joe.

"Well, no. What *is* past that?"

"Where is it you're going, anyway?" Joanne asked him.

He scowled at her and remained silent, and Joanne turned back to the window. They were still among lawns and houses; Jenny drove so slowly that a man walking at a brisk pace could keep up with her. At one point Joanne said, "Was that the Edmonds' house?"

Ben Joe leaned forward to see where she was pointing. Between two houses was a charred space with only a set of cement steps and a yellow brick fireplace left intact.

"It was," he said. "Burned down the year you left."

"Nobody told me about it."

"You used to date their son, I think." He had come upon them kissing in the den one night; Bobby was hugging her and kissing the hollow in her neck, and Ben Joe had left the room again without a sound.

"I'd forgotten that," Joanne said.

Sometimes he thought his sisters had been born senile.

When they reached the A & P on Main Street, Jenny parked the car. "We'll be in here awhile and then to Barton's for Tessie's shoes," she said. "If you're back in the car by then I'll drive you home. Otherwise you can just walk back whenever you're ready. Hurry, Ben Joe, you're holding Lisa up."

Ben Joe was sitting forward but not getting out. Lisa nudged him impatiently. "*Come* on, Ben Joe. I thought you were the one in such a rush."

"Okay, okay."

He climbed slowly out of the car and then just stood on the sidewalk beside Joanne with his hands in his pockets.

"Well," he said.

Joanne looked at him curiously. Jenny and Tessie were already heading toward the A & P, and Lisa was staring at a sweater in the window next door.

"Maybe I'll go wherever you're going," said Joanne.

"No."

"Well, where is it you're going?"

"Um. To call on Miss Potter, for one thing. You go on and do your shopping. Maybe I'll meet you in Stacy's for a cup of coffee later."

"All right."

She stood there still looking at him with that little half-smile. He wished she weren't so nosy. The others didn't know the meaning of privacy, they were continually bursting into his room unannounced or reading his postcards, but at least they didn't go ferreting around to see what he was thinking about, the way Joanne did. Sometimes he thought she had even *succeeded* in her ferreting – like today, when she remained absolutely motionless and smiled her knowing smile. He scowled back at her.

"So long," he said.

"So long."

When she still stood there, he whirled around abruptly and headed for the drugstore at a businesslike pace. Once inside, he peered out the glass door and saw that her back was to him now; she was calmly waiting for a car to pass before she crossed the street.

The drugstore smelled like his house did when all the girls were getting ready to go out on dates at once. it was spicy and perfumey, with several different kinds of scents that were mingled together and made him want to sneeze. He headed toward the back, where the toilet articles were kept. From the rack on top of the counter he chose a pack of razor blades, taking a long time to compare prices and brand names, and then he turned to the magazine counter and picked out a crossword-puzzle book that was made of dull comic-booklike paper which would depress him before he finished the first puzzle. These he paid for at the cash register; he counted out the exact change to pay a white-haired man he had not seen before.

"Don't bother about a bag," he said.

He dropped the razor blades into his shirt pocket, next to the pink envelope and his cigarettes. The crossword-puzzle book he rolled up carelessly and stuck into his back trouser pocket. Then he looked out toward the street again. This time there was not a sister of his in sight. He smiled good-by to the man at the cash register and headed outside.

Beyond the A & P, which was the last real store on Main Street, the millworkers' houses again. At first they were the big old houses that had been built by well-to-do families but had turned gray and peeling with "Room for Rent" signs on them. Their side yards, once grassy and shaded with oak trees, were now cement squares where Esso stations sat. And beyond these were smaller, grayer houses, most of them duplexes. Dirty-faced children played on the porches in skimpy sweaters; the yards were heaped with old tires and rusty scrap metal. Behind the houses, barely visible above the tar-paper roofs, were the tall smoking chimneys of the textile factory where all these people worked. They made blue denim, day in and day out. It was toward these chimneys that Ben Joe headed. He crossed a vacant lot, knee-high with weeds and brambles, and stumbled over a rusted-out potbellied stove that lay smack in the middle of the field. Then he was on the gravel road that ran down to the muddy little river where the factory was. Opposite the factory was Lili Belle Mosely's house.

He had been here before, many times. The first time was when his father was still alive, living at Lili Belle's as if it were his home and having his patients call him there in the night if they needed him. He had first rented a room there; people said that one night he had finished mending a millworker's arm and was setting out for home when it suddenly hit him that he couldn't bear to go home again, so he had stopped here and rented a room. His wife, hearing about it, clamped her mouth shut and said that was *his* lookout, nothing she could do about it. She said the same when she heard that he had taken to sharing a room with the landlady's daughter; and the same when she heard about little Phillip's being born. But Ben Joe, who never could resign himself to the fact that it was his father's lookout alone, had come to see his father at Lili Belle's one night with his heart pounding and his eyes wide with embarrassment. They had fed him supper – green beans cooked with fat back, hash-brown potatoes in a puddle of Mazola, pork chops coated with grease that turned white when he let the chops cool on his plate. Everyone laughed a lot, and his father ate more than Ben Joe had seen him eat in years. And Ben Joe had not been able to say a word to his father about coming home. He hadn't tried.

As he stood now, facing the long, squat house with its dingy front porch, he could almost see how he must have looked coming out of it. His head down, his face puzzled, his feet dragging. Not just once, but many times, because he had gone back again and again. First he had gone to see his father. Then

86

his father died and left a request that Lili Belle and her son get a little money each month, which Ben Joe's mother could have contested but didn't; she said it wasn't worth her bother. So Ben Joe took Lili Belle her money in person once each month. And once each month his mother said, "Ben Joe, have you mailed off all our bills for this month?" and Ben Joe said, "Yes'm," not ever letting on he had taken it in person. Every month he had taken it, up until he had left for New York and turned the money matters over to Jenny. Now Jenny mailed the money, as she was supposed to, in a business envelope. She wouldn't have that feeling Ben Joe always had, looking at his mother with pure guilt on his face and wondering why he kept on lying to her and visiting a woman whose name was never mentioned in the house. He couldn't have given a reason. When he was a senior in high school, his father came home for an hour one day (after he'd been gone a year) to say that all his life he had been saving the money for Ben Joe to go to Harvard and now there was enough. Ellen Hawkes said that unless he came home she wouldn't take a penny, and he said, well, he didn't see that it would really matter to her if he never came home again. Ellen Hawkes didn't answer that. So Ben Joe went to Sandhill College. But even so, even knowing that Lili Belle was the reason he had to go there, he still came to sit in Lili Belle's house and talk to her about the weather and he still threw little Phillip up in the air and caught him again, laughing.

He crossed the scrubby little yard and climbed up to the porch. The wooden floor boards made a hollow sound under his shoes. At the door he knocked and waited, and then knocked again. One corner of the chintz curtain rose slowly. The door swung open.

"Lili Belle?" he said.

"It's *me*, boy."

It was her old mother standing in the shadows behind the door. Ben Joe had seldom seen her before. She was fat and puffing but very dignified, and she had kept out of sight for sheer shame ever since the day her daughter's baby had been born. Now she closed the door sharply behind him and said, "What you want, anyway?"

"I want to see Lili Belle."

"Hmm." She crossed her fat arms under the shelf-like bosom of her black crepe dress. "Lilian Belle is very tired, Benjamin," she said. "Got troubles of her own. What you wanting to see her for?"

"Mrs. Mosely, I won't stay long. I just wanted to see her a minute. It's important."

"Well, I'll tell her. But I don't know, I don't know."

"Thank you, ma'am."

He followed her across the small, mousy-smelling hallway into the almost totally dark sitting room. Against the shaded window he could make out the outline of an unlit lamp, double-globed and beaded. Mrs. Mosely stood like a mountain barring the rest of the view; she called into the room, "Back."

Lili Belle was in the shadows, sitting on a cane chair. She stirred a little and said, "You say something, Mama?"

"Back again to pester us."

"Who?"

"Him." She jerked a thumb behind her. "Ben Joe."

"Oh, my goodness. Benjy, honey, come in!" She stood up and ran to the windows to raise the shades. In her right hand was a bowl of soup, which she shifted awkwardly to her left hand when she tried to maneuver the shade. The room was suddenly light again. With the light a feeling of relief came to Ben Joe; this wasn't going to be as hard as he thought. He always forgot how easy Lili Belle made him feel the minute he saw her.

"It's okay, Mama," she was saying now. "You can go on now. Come on in, Benjy honey. I do apologize for sitting in the dark like this, but my eyes is strained."

"It's okay," Ben Joe said.

He looked at her closely, noticing how tired she looked. It was hard to tell how old she was. Nine years ago, when his father had first met her, she had been about twenty. Now she could be any age. Her face seemed never to have resolved itself but stayed as vague and unformed as when she had been a girl. Her hair was straggly and colorless, and she was never anything but homely, but she had an enormous, bony frame that made people look a second time when they passed her on the street. There was not an ounce of fat on her. When she walked, her bones seemed to swing loosely, and she never hit hard upon the earth or seemed, for all her boniness, to have any sharp corners to her. Yet he could see the strain lines beginning around her eyes and mouth, and the way the skin of her face had grown white and dry.

"You sit yourself," she was saying now. "Wait a minute . . ." She looked around among the straight-backed chairs, searching for the most comfortable. When she found it she pushed the bowl of soup into Ben Joe's hands and ran to pull it up. "If we'd of known," she said, "I'd of cleaned up house a little. How come they've not told us you were back?"

"Well, I only got here yesterday."

"Sit, now. Oh my, let me take that soup bowl off your hands. What you think of New York?"

"I like it all right." He sat down on the chair and stretched his feet out in front of him. On the table under the window, among the doilies and flower pots and bronzed baby shoes, sat a photograph of his father. It was taken when he still had his mustache, long before he had ever met Lili Belle, but he looked much the same as he had when he died – rumpled hair, black then with only the first touches of white, and crinkling gray eyes and a broad, easy smile. Except for Gram's bedroom, where Ben Joe's mother never set foot, this was probably the only place in the world that still had a picture of Phillip Hawkes. Ben Joe reached out and turned it a little in his direction, looking at it thoughtfully.

"You have to excuse Mama's being so rude," Lili Belle was saying. "She has gotten like that more and more. The other day this lodger of ours, he stopped to talk to me on account of wanting to know where the clean towels were kept, and Mama clunked him in the chest with the griddle-cake-flipper. Didn't hurt him none, but I had a whole heap of explaining to do."

"Was she right about your having some kind of trouble?" Ben Joe asked.

"I'd say she was. That's why I was sitting in the dark like a spook. Little Phillip is in the hospital with pneumonia and I was resting my eyes from sitting up with him so much. I don't know where he got it. Folks tell me I take *too* good care of him, so it can't of been that he got too cold. Though he is right much of a puddle-wader, that could've done it. I told him and told him. When it was serious and I had reason to be worried I was just *possessed* by the thought of those puddles. I had it in mind, in this dream I had one night, to take me a vacuum cleaner and go vacuum all the puddles up. But the worrying part is over now. Doctor says another ten days or two weeks and he'll be out."

"How long's he been in?" Ben Joe asked.

"Two weeks."

"How're you managing the bills?"

"I plan to make it up gradual. I been working at the mill part time since little Phil started school, but not a full day, because I like to be home when he needs me. Oh, Mama would take care of him – says she's ashamed he was ever born, but I notice she's right fond of him. But I'd rather it be me. I'll work full time till the bill's paid off and then go back half-days again."

"We've got some money in the savings account," Ben Joe said.

"No, honey, I don't want it."

"But we never even touch it. It's the money Dad saved up and Mama won't use it no matter what – says it's only for emergencies. You're right, you shouldn't work when little Phillip's at home."

"I wouldn't take it, Benjy. It bothers me to take what we *do* take offen you all. Your sister Jenny's been bringing it real regular."

"Been what?"

"*You* know – the once-a-month money. She's not missed a time."

"But I thought – Doesn't she mail it?"

"Why, no." Lili Belle stopped playing with the folds of her skirt and looked up at him. "Neither *one* of you's ever *mailed* it," she said. "What she said the first time she came was, she would bring it the same as you'd always done."

"For Pete's sake." Ben Joe sat forward in his chair with his elbows on his knees. "I wonder how she knew."

"Oh, girls're smarter than you think." She laughed, and then became quiet again and looked at her hands. "She's a real nice little girl," she said. "First time she came I was just merely polite, you know, figuring that what's your mama's is your mama's and I didn't want to seem to be trying to make friends of your mama's own daughter. But she was so friendly – came in and taught little Phil how to play this game about scissors cutting rock and rock covering paper, or something. Real good with children, she is."

"She is," Ben Joe said. He sat quietly for a minute, and then he cleared his throat and said, "Lili Belle?"

"Hmm?"

"I've got something I want to talk to you about."

"Well, I'm listening."

"I thought I should get it said, in case I don't come back to Sandhill for a good while again. I figured . . ."

He was silent.

"I'm right here listening," she said. Her face was gentle and interested; Ben Joe wondered if it would become angry by the time he was through talking. Did Lili Belle ever get angry?

"I've got this letter," he said miserably.

"This . . . ?"

"Letter. Letter." He touched his pocket, where the rim of the pink envelope showed. "This, um—"

"*Oh*, yes."

"Ma'am?"

"Letter."

"Yes. And I wanted, wanted to show it to you because—"

"Well, I seen it before, Benjy honey.

"I know you have. That's what I'm trying to—"

"No, I mean I seen it on *you* before." She laughed gently, startling him. "Sure. First time you came after your daddy died, I seen it. Little piece of pink in your pocket, just like now. You'd not been to see me for two whole months, and then you came by but never said nothing about the letter. I figured you had found it in your daddy's office and read it, all about how I was asking him to come back to me and little Phillip. I was afraid you'd come to taunt me with it."

"Why to *taunt* you?"

"Account of the spelling, of course."

"The what?"

"The spelling. I never spelled too good."

"Oh," he said. He could think of nothing else to say; he was too surprised. For a moment he sat staring at her blankly and then he had to smile back at her.

"When you never did mention it," she was saying, "I figured you had just brought it along that one time to show me you had it safe. To show me you had took it from his office after he died so that no one else could see it. That why you brought it, Ben Joe?"

"No, ma'am," he said.

"No?"

"No, I took that letter *before* he ever died. What I came to tell you is, I took it before he even *saw* it."

He was afraid to look up at her. When he finally did, when she had been silent so long that he *had* to look, he saw that she didn't seem shocked or angry but was just absorbing the news still, shaking her head a little and trying to fit all this in with what she already knew.

"Lili Belle, I am awfully sorry," he said. "It's bothered me for so long I couldn't see any way to get rid of it now but to tell you, and say how sorry I am."

"Well, that's all right, Ben Joe." She licked her lips nervously, still frowning off into space. "That's all right – it didn't make no difference, did it? Everything would've happened the same, I reckon, letter or no letter."

"But I—"

"You didn't do nothing *wrong*, Benjy. Why, it seems to me your family is kind of queer-like sometimes. Meaning no offense. It's not *natural* to come see me and all, not even to speak to me on the street, but you do, and I reckon it's even a little relief, maybe, having you do something on your mother's side like most would do."

"Well—" Ben Joe stopped, not certain what to say. "What bothered me," he said, "is that maybe Dad would have gone back to you soon as he got your letter. And then, who knows, not had that heart attack a week later. Old Gram, she's blamed herself forever for forgetting to refill the ice-cube trays. Says that's why he died – going downtown to get ice. Though Mom says he could have stepped next door if he'd been sober enough to think of it. But sometimes when Gram gets on those ice-cube trays I'm almost tempted to show her the pink envelope, to prove it's not she that's to blame."

"Well, it surely ain't you," Lili Belle said. She bent forward to rub her eyes, tiredly, and then leaned her head back again and smiled at him. "I don't guess my letter would of made any change in him one way or the other. If your mother'd said one *word* he'd have stayed with her, always would have. He was just wanting her to ask him. But she didn't. He waited two weeks, and I guess he would have waited that long if I'd sent *fourteen* letters, even. Then he came back to me, not even planning to but just drunk and tired, and I took him in."

"But you can't say for sure," Ben Joe said.

"What?"

"You can't say for sure your letter wouldn't have made him come back earlier, you can't say—"

"Benjy honey, don't you worry. Can't say *nothing* for sure, if it comes to that. Don't you worry."

Both of them were silent for a minute, Lili Belle rocking steadily in her chair and filling the silence with slow creaks. Then she sat up straight again and said, "*Well*, how long you going to be here?"

"I don't know yet. Not too much longer, I guess."

"I heard your older sister's in town."

"That's right."

"Well, it'll work out. Her husband'll come and get her, you just watch. She's a right pretty girl – I seen her downtown before – and *he'll* come claim her. You just wait."

"Well, maybe so."

"Uh, you know my brother? Freeman? Well, Freeman he—"

"I thought his name was Donald."

"No, he changed it. That's what I was about to tell you. He said he was sick of this town and sick of blue denim and wanted to be free, so he changed his name to Freeman and went to work in a diner in New York. He likes it right much, I hear. Sent us this picture postcard saying, 'This here New York is a right swinging town.' That's what he said, 'a right swinging town.' You being in New York reminded me of it."

Her head was against the back of her chair again, lolling wearily. There was no telling how many nights she had sat up with little Phillip.

"You're tired," Ben Joe said. "I'll be going, Lili Belle. Here's the letter."

He pulled out the pink envelope and put it in one of her hands. She took it listlessly, stopping her rocking to frown down at it.

"Oh, land," she said. "Land."

She didn't go on speaking, though Ben Joe waited. She dropped the letter in her lap and went on rocking.

"I'll find my own way out," he said finally. "And I'm going to take care of that hospital bill, Lili Belle. Soon as I get it from the bank."

"No, Benjy, I don't—"

She was up on her feet now, wanting to protest, but he pulled on his jacket and left hurriedly. "You tell little Phil hey!" he called back.

"Well—"

He ran down the porch steps and into the yard. The sky above the river had grown churned and dark, and a cold wind was rising. As he walked he stuck his hands deep into his trouser pockets and hunched up his shoulders against the cold.

8

WHEN HE HAD finished what he had to do at the bank, Ben
Joe headed toward Stacy's. It was a small, grim-looking café,
but he and his friends had almost lived there once, back when
they were in high school. They could meet up with almost
anyone they wanted to see there if they waited long enough.
Now, looking at the dirty gray front of the building while he
waited for the traffic light to change, Ben Joe wondered why
they had ever liked it. The picture window was dark and
smudged, cluttered with neon beer signs and hand-lettered
pizza posters. In front of it two weird-looking high school boys
slouched, watching the people who passed by. When Ben Joe
crossed the street and came closer to them, he stopped looking
in their direction and stared steadfastly at Stacy's doorknob in
order to avoid those amused eyes of theirs. But once inside it
was no better; clustered in the dimness, lit briefly by the
twirling rainbow from the jukebox, were more slouching boys
and more leather jackets. Occasionally he caught a glimpse of
a girl or two, with her hair piled in a fantastic frizzed mountain
on her head and her skirt well above her knees. It was only
after he had blinked a couple of times and strained his eyes
into the farthest corners that he found Joanne.

She was sitting at a booth with her red coat thrown back
behind her and a cup of coffee sitting on the table in front of
her. But the coffee was going unnoticed; Joanne stared out at
the empty dance floor with her mouth partly open and her
eyes thoughtful.

"Hi," Ben Joe said.

She started a little and looked up at him. "Oh, hi," she said.
She turned toward the cash register and called, "Stacy!"

Stacy was a fat blond woman who hated everyone under forty. No one knew why it was to her place that all the high school kids came. She bumbled toward them down the aisle, muttering something under her breath and slapping her round feet hard upon the floor at every step.

"*What*," she said.

"Ben Joe's here now."

"Hmm!" She stared at him blankly, with her eyes narrowed. "What you want?"

"Coffee. With double cream."

"With *what*?"

"Double cream."

"Double cream, hey. Double cream. My soul, double cream." She stamped off again, still muttering.

"Seven years gone by and she hasn't changed a mite," Joanne said. "How long's it been since you've come here, Ben Joe?"

"Oh, I don't know. Couple of years. Why?"

"I just wondered. Seems to me it used to be more lively."

"Mmm."

"Doesn't it to you? Seem that way?"

"I guess."

"On one of these tables there's a monument carved," she said. "It says, 'Memorial to Joanne, for her spirit.' Buddy Holler did that the day I walked out of chemistry class because it was boring."

Ben Joe smiled across the table at her. He wasn't listening to what she said; he was just glad to be having that cheerful voice of hers babble on. Before he had been walking too thin a line, losing sight of the division between Lili Belle's world and his mother's. Now there was Joanne to help. She was talking in an everyday voice about matter-of-fact things, and she was from home and reminding him that that was where he was from, too.

"Joanne," he said, "how well would you say you know Jenny?"

"Jenny our sister, you mean?"

"Yes."

She frowned. "Oh, I don't know. How old was she when I left – only eleven. Just barely getting a good start in life."

"You don't figure you know her very well?"

"No, not very well."

"Well, how about— What does she say in her letters to you?"

"Oh, *you* know." She grinned suddenly. "Just facts and figures – gotten much worse since you turned the money over to her."

"Does she say how she spends the money?"

"Sure."

"No, I mean does she tell you what bills she mails and what bills she takes in person? I mean . . ."

His coffee was set before him. He looked above the steam of it to Joanne's puzzled face.

"I'm not following," she said. "What do—"

"Well, does she say how the money is partitioned *up*, for instance? A certain amount to groceries, a certain amount for savings, and so on. Has she ever told you that?"

"Not even *Jenny* gets *that* specific," said Joanne. "What's the matter, Ben Joe?"

"Nothing. No, I just . . ."

He picked up his coffee and began drinking it, not meeting Joanne's eyes. She was giving him that amused little knowing smile again; he'd never find out how much she knew. Either she didn't know a thing or she was determined not to tell what she *did* know, and he'd never be able to find out which it was.

"I don't understand a soul in this world," he said.

"What makes you think you should? Especially girls. Think what a— Oh, hey, speaking of girls. Is that Shelley Domer?"

Ben Joe turned. Shelley was just coming in the door, dressed all in blue and carrying a coat over her arm. Behind her came a man Ben Joe didn't know.

"Who's he?" Joanne asked.

"I don't know."

"Sure looks familiar."

"Well, it might be Jack Horner. Shelley said the other night—"

"*John* Horner," Joanne said. "I remember all about him. Used to live just outside Sandhill, went to Murphy High School."

She put her chin in her hand and examined John Horner. So did Ben Joe, although he tried to look as if he were watching something else. He was surprised to see that Horner was a nice enough looking man, with a broad face and a mop of brown hair. For some reason, Ben Joe had pictured him as thin and sinister; he couldn't say why. Shelley was smiling up at him with that small, formal smile she always put on when she felt awkward, and when she saw Ben Joe she looked pleased and her smile broadened. Immediately she came over to their table, letting Horner follow if he wanted to.

"Hey, Ben Joe," she said. "Hey, Joanne. It's good to see you again."

"It's good to see *you*. Why don't you sit down?"

"Well, all right."

Shelley looked back and forth, first at the seat beside Joanne and then at the seat beside Ben Joe, and finally she chose the one beside Ben Joe and slid shyly into it. Opposite her, John Horner sat down by Joanne and began talking to her immediately, not waiting for an introduction to Ben Joe.

"You look kind of glum," Shelley said to Ben Joe.

"I do?"

"What you been doing that makes you look so glum?"

"Well, I don't know. What've *you* been doing?"

"Looking for a job. I didn't find one, though."

"Where'd you look?"

"Sesame Printery." She smiled, unexplainably, at her fingernails. "I worked there one summer proofreading, remember? And they're so low on work that Mr. Crown – that's the boss – he's just thinking *up* things to keep the typesetters busy. This morning they turned out five hundred labels reading 'Strawberry Jam,' one hundred labels reading 'Pickled Pigs' Feet,' though Mrs. Crown hates them and won't pickle any no matter *what* inducement Mr. Crown offers, and seven school-book covers saying, 'All cats look gray in the dark,' because that's little Sonny Crown's favorite quotation. This afternoon they'll print the Crowns' stationery. So I don't reckon they need any help."

Across the table, Horner was laughing at something Joanne had said. Shelley looked over at them and said, "I'd introduce you to John if he wasn't talking just now. But anyway, that's the John Horner I was telling you about. You like him?"

"Well, what I see of him I do," Ben Joe said.

"He and I are going roller-skating this afternoon. I just know I'll break my neck."

"Has he asked you yet?"

"Asked me what?"

"About marrying him."

"No, not yet."

"What you going to say?"

"Oh . . ."

"Come on, now," he said. He was teasing her, but she turned suddenly serious and began pleating the paper napkin beside his saucer. "Haven't decided yet?" he asked her more gently.

She shook her head

"You couldn't *drag* me in this place again," Joanne was saying to John. "It's all taken over by hoods, looks like. Used to be a real happy place, everybody dancing together—"

"Remember Barney Pocket?" John asked. "Remember how he used to make up dances all by himself? Lord, he was a funny guy. Put himself through college, later, calculating how soon people would die and then borrowing money from them. It worked, too."

"He walked to Newfoundland one summer," Joanne said. "On a dare."

Ben Joe cleared his throat. "Joanne," he said, "I think Gram expects us home for lunch."

"Okay, Ben Joe."

Shelley and John stood up to let them out. While Ben Joe was struggling into his jacket, Shelley edged closer and said, "You coming tomorrow?"

"Sure," Ben Joe said. "I'll be by at—"

"Hush!" She frowned toward where John was standing talking with Joanne and then turned back to Ben Joe. "Will you *hush*?"

The urge to tease came over him again. He grinned down at her and said, "Don't tell me he doesn't *know* I'm coming! Why, Shelley Domer, that amounts to outright two-timing. I swear if you're not—"

"I *mean* it, now!" Her face was white and miserable; Ben Joe immediately felt sorry. "He *is* a steady boy-friend, after all," she said. "I don't want to—"

"Okay, okay."

He reached around to help her with her coat, and then raised one hand in Horner's direction.

"See you," he said.

"So long."

When they were outside, Joanne stopped to button up her coat. "It's getting kind of chilly," she said. "Shelley hasn't changed much, has she?"

"I don't know."

"I mean, she's still sort of quiet and drifty. You always did alternate between two extremes, come to think of it – first a dreamy, drifty girl and then a shrieky, dancing one."

"Well."

"That all you got to say?"

He watched the traffic light patiently, not hearing her.

"What you got on your mind, Ben Joe?"

"I don't know. Joanne?"

"What?"

"Would you say about ten dollars a day is enough to pay for a stay in a hospital?"

"That depends on the circumstances."

"Well, I don't know the circumstances, really. It's just this friend of mine. I'm worried about how much money he'd need."

"Light's changed."

She pulled him impatiently into the street, but once they had crossed she walked more slowly, studying the question.

"It sounds like a fair guess," she said. "Yes, I'd say so."

"Well, I don't know," said Ben Joe. "I keep thinking it should be more, somehow."

"That's *your* problem," said Joanne.

9

OVERNIGHT THE WEATHER turned much colder. The wind howled and rattled at the bones of the house, and dry leaves scraped along the sidewalk. In the evening, when Ben Joe began dressing for his date with Shelley, his whole family pounced on him out of sheer boredom and wanted to know where he was going.

"Just out," he said.

He was in the living room, buttoning up the shirt Jenny had just ironed.

"I thought you might take me to see Jamie Dower tonight," Gram said.

"In *this* weather?"

"Well . . . it's Sunday. Good visiting time."

"I'll take you tomorrow," he said. "I don't know why we can't get synchronized on this Jamie Dower thing. If I'm ready to go you've got an iron-bound excuse *not* to, and now that I'm busy you're almost out in the car honking for me. Where's Susannah? I bet you anything she took my cuff links."

"She's in the attic," said Tessie. "Hunting squirrels."

"Oh."

"She took the only gun of mine that really shoots and she's been up there since suppertime. Got a whole soup can full of B-B's beside her."

"Funny way for a grown woman to spend her time. You notice if she's wearing my cuff links?"

"The squirrels have been nesting there," his mother said. "*Someone* has to get rid of them. Besides, your shirt has button cuffs."

"Oh. Well, then, it's the wrong shirt. I asked for the one with the French cuffs on it."

Jenny, sitting on the rug with a book, looked up and made a face at him. "Serve you right if I'd made you iron it yourself," she said.

"That one looks just as nice, Ben Joe."

"Okay, okay. How can she hunt squirrels in the dark?"

"She's got the extension lamp," Tessie said. "She's really mad at them."

"She'll never shoot one."

"Ben Joe, your shirt tail is out."

"I know it."

He jammed it into his trousers and went to the hall mirror to put his tie on. In the wavy glass he saw his face, sullen and heavy with the boredom of a long day at home. Behind him a part of his family was reflected, looking just as bored as he did. His mother sat in the rocking chair, absently glancing through a newspaper; her neck was made funny and crooked by a flaw in the mirror. Beside her sat Tessie, doing nothing at all but looking admiringly at her new shoes and occasionally wetting one finger and bending down to wipe at an imaginary scuff. The shoes were not reflected, but he had been asked to give an opinion of them so many times in the last day and a half that he thought he would be seeing them in his sleep forever – clumsy, too-white oxfords that were still new enough to look enormous on her feet. Also in the mirror were Jenny's legs, but not the rest of her. He thought even her legs looked bored.

He finished knotting his tie, made a ferocious face in the mirror to see if his teeth needed brushing, and went back into the living room for his jacket.

"I'm going," he said.

"Are you going to be anywhere near the drugstore?"

"Or the newsstand?"

"Nope," he said. "Not going anywhere near anything."

"Well, it's hard to believe when you're dressed up so handsome," Gram said. "Come kiss me good night."

He bent down and kissed her cheekbone, and then kissed the tops of Tessie's and his mother's head for good measure.

"I won't be late," he said.

"All right, Ben Joe."

At the doorway he turned to look at them again. He was in one of those faraway moods when everything he saw seemed to be inside a shining goldfish bowl, and he suddenly saw how closed-off his family looked. They went peacefully on with what they were doing; Ben Joe, having vanished, might as well not exist. When he stepped outside he gave the door an enormous slam, just to make himself exist a minute longer.

The wind bit at his face and his bare hands. It was very dark, without a moon, but he could see the white clouds swimming rapidly past the house tops. And before he had even reached the front gate, the cold had begun to seep in all over. He didn't care. He was glad to get out in the fresh air after the long, stuffy day, and he was glad to be going to Shelley's, although he couldn't say why. There were times when even Shelley's shyness and her slowness seemed to be exactly what he needed. And he would like the way she greeted him at the door, with her face so formal.

He hurried on, making his arms hang loosely instead of huddling them close to his body, because the cold air still felt good. A twig from one of the trees along the sidewalk stung across his face. He ducked and then turned in, whistling now, to climb the long steps to Shelley's house.

She answered almost as soon as he knocked. He saw the outline of her behind the mesh curtain, running in order to let him in quickly. The minute the door was open she tugged at his arm with both hands and said, "Get in, Ben Joe, aren't you *frozen?*"

He nodded, smiling at her, and stepped inside so that she could shut the door behind him.

"Come on in," she said, "come in. I declare, I think you're just frozen stiff and silent. Take off your coat, now. That's right."

She took the coat from him and smiled into his eyes. It had been a long time since he had seen her looking so pretty. Her hair was down, the way she had worn it when she was in high school, and it was well brushed and shining. There was something besides lipstick on her face – rouge, he thought –

103

that made her look excited and bright-eyed, and she was watching him with that half-scared expression.

"I sure am glad to see you," he said suddenly.

'Well, thank the Lord you've said something. I thought maybe you were going to be speechless all evening."

She took a hanger from the closet for his coat, and Ben Joe went into the living room. A fire had been lit in the fireplace, a tall fire that roared out and glinted on the bare wood floor. The thought of having to go out again, away from all this warmth, was depressing. But as soon as Shelley came into the living room he turned and said, "Do you want to go somewhere?"

"Oh, I don't care. What do you want to do?"

"Well, anything you want to."

"No, you say."

He spread his hands helplessly. "*You* say," he said.

"I really don't have a preference in this world, Ben Joe."

"You must have."

"Oh . . ." She put her hands together and stared into the fire. "I hate to be the one to say," she said finally.

The fire light kept moving and flickering on her face. And her hair just brushed the top of her collar. Something about her – the expectant way she stood, the dress-up navy dress with its spotless white collar – reminded him of a night he thought he had forgotten, back when his sisters were still very young. Joanne had thrown a barbecue party, with what seemed like millions of couples, and had suggested off-handedly that anyone in the family could have some barbecue with them if they wanted to. At the time Jenny was no more than eleven, but she was just beginning to notice boys and had started reading beauty magazines. The night of the barbecue the whole house reeked of some heavy-scented bath oil and no one knew why; but then down the stairs came Jenny, wearing a white puff-sleeved dress, with her hair perfectly combed and a thick envelope of perfume encircling her wherever she moved. She had come down and sat quietly on the lawn with the older couples, who were in sloppy Bermudas and T-shirts, and she hadn't spoken unless spoken to, but all evening she watched the party with that same happy, frightened look. He had wanted to cry for her, without knowing why – or at least hug her. He wanted to hug Shelley now, but she had awakened from her staring into the fire and was watching him.

"What're you thinking about?" she asked.

"I don't know."

"Well, I tell you. One thing I do know about New York is that when they have dates they like as not never set *foot* in a movie house or a skating rink. The girls just serve them cocktails in their apartments. So I have bought some bourbon, in case that's what you're used to doing. Is that all right?"

"It's a wonderful idea," Ben Joe said.

She ran out to the kitchen immediately; for some reason she didn't seem to be in slow motion tonight. Ben Joe sat down on the couch and relaxed happily against the cushions. The fire was slowly drawing the cold out of him, leaving him warm and comfortable. He could hear glasses tinkling in the kitchen.

"I've put you some ice and a little water," Shelley said when she came in again.

"That's perfect."

She had brought the bottle in on a tray, and next to it stood their two glasses, her own very pale. When Ben Joe picked his glass up, she watched his face carefully to see if he liked it, and smiled when he nodded to her.

"Just right," he said.

"I'm glad."

She picked up her own glass and, after turning over in her mind the problem of where to sit, chose a spot next to Ben Joe on the couch, settling there so delicately that her drink hardly wavered in its glass.

"Is it you that's going to talk?" she asked.

"Well, I don't know."

"I think it is."

"Why?"

"Oh . . ." She took a sip of her drink and began turning her glass around, smiling into it. "When you come in slow and smiling, likely something is on your mind. Also if you're too much the other way. And then me, I'm not in a real talky mood myself. So I figured it would be you to talk."

"Maybe so." He slid down, so that his feet were under the coffee table and his weight was upon the small of his back, and scratched the top of his head. "I'm thinking about it," he explained when she laughed.

"Well, tell me what you did with your day."

"My day. Lord. Nothing to speak of. It was Sunday. We all got the Sunday blues. Got them so bad that Susannah's up in the attic hunting squirrels with a B-B gun now. Nobody went out. Me, I slept and then I read the funny papers twice through, and then I finished a murder mystery and peeled potatoes for Gram. It's been a God-awful day, considering."

He sat up straighter and took a swallow of his drink.

"You know," he said, "except for an occasional Sunday, they don't make days like they used to. I mean, they don't make them *whole* any more. You noticed?"

He looked over at Shelley, but she only shook her head, puzzled.

"Oh, well, what I mean is, the days seem to come in pieces now. They used to be in blocks – all one solid color to them. Sometimes whole *weeks* would be in blocks. Someone could say, 'What's this week been like?' and right off the bat you could say, 'Oh, lousy. My father won't let me have the car because he caught me scratching off in front of Stacy's café the other day.' Or it would be a great week, for another reason just that clear-cut. It's not that way any more."

"Well . . ." Shelley said. She was trying, but in the end she gave up and said, "I reckon I never did notice that, Ben Joe."

"No, I guess not."

"You tell me about the pieces, then."

"All right."

He settled back again and thought a minute. "What I'm mainly wondering," he said, "is whether Mom ever looks at the bank records. I've never actually seen her do, it. She's real funny that way. Sometimes I think Jenny is the one who manages the family now, as if Mom weren't there. Jenny tells her what's going on but only to keep her informed, not to ask her for any decisions. So maybe she doesn't know anything about the bank books."

106

"What difference does it make if she does?" Shelley asked.

"Well, I took some money out when I shouldn't have. I don't know what she'd do if she knew. I'm worried about it."

He drained the last of his drink and then balanced the glass on his knee. It made a cold, dark ring in the fabric of his trousers. "I don't know why it's always so hard deciding which side I'm on," he said.

"Let me pour you another drink, Ben Joe."

"Also, I found out Joanne's asking for a divorce," Ben Joe said. He watched Shelley's hands as she poured his bourbon; they were long, thin hands that seemed uncertain about what they were touching. "She says she just *left* Gary, not even telling him about it. The lawyer's getting in touch with him now. Sometimes I'm hoping Gary'll say no, she can't have the divorce, and Joanne will leave Sandhill and go back and be happy in Kansas again. But most times I'm hoping she'll get divorced and stay with us. That Gary, I don't know whether I like him or not. Well, hell, I've never even *seen* him. Except in this blurred snapshot Joanne sent us of him holding Carol when she was just newborn. There was all kinds of excitement when Carol was born. The girls went around calling each other 'Aunt' – even Tessie – and Mom was 'Grandma' for I don't know how long. Then they forgot about it. But Gary sent out these birth announcements that say there's a new product on the market, giving the name of the manufacturers – that's the parents – and all."

"I think that's *nice*," Shelley said.

"Well. It just seems funny in our particular family, is all. Like that sentimental kind of letter he wrote us after Joanne called to say they were married. It began, 'Dear Mom,' in this unreadable handwriting, and Mom looked at the greeting and then at the closing to see what stranger was calling her Mom and she said, 'Who's Gary?' It wasn't till she'd read the letter that she figured it out. No, that's a nice idea but it doesn't fit, somehow, and I kind of hope he'll give Joanne the divorce." He sat up straight again and stared into the fire. "Why can't they all just let *me* take care of them? My sisters are so separate. I'd be happy to take care of them."

"I know," Shelley said comfortingly.

He smiled at her. She was sitting very straight and still, almost touching him, and listening completely to what he said. Anyone else he knew would be getting restless by now.

"*You* talk," he said.

"I got nothing to say, Ben Joe."

"Neither do I, seems like." He bent to untie his shoelaces and slip the shoes off. Then he swung his legs up and settled his feet on the coffee table. "Tomorrow we're going to see Jamie Dower," he said. "He's eighty-four. How do you reckon it would feel to be eighty-four? Do you think you'd *realize* you were that old? I don't realize I'm twenty-five. I keep thinking I'm about eighteen or so. I don't even know if Gram realizes how old *she is*. Somehow I think not, or she wouldn't still be making a fuss about bygone things. Still keeping up the old war with Mom. She never did like her much. Grandpa, now, he thought Mom was wonderful. Said she had backbone. First time she came to visit here before she and Dad got married, she came down to breakfast saying she was thirsty and Grandpa poured her a glass of water. Only it turned out not to be water but moonshine, that clear kind that comes out of a Mason jar. Mom was right surprised but she drank it anyway, without coughing, and Grandpa said, 'Honey, *you're* no Yankee,' and loved her like a daughter ever since. But Gram, she said all it proved was that she was no lady. Oh, hell, I'm getting off the subject. Whatever the subject was."

"It's all right," Shelley said. "Don't you worry, Ben Joe."

"Me? I'm not worried."

"Well. Anyway, it's all right."

She looked sad, and Ben Joe didn't know why. He didn't know what to do about it. He put one arm along the back of the couch behind her, not actually touching her but just protecting her, and looked at her face to see what was bothering her. There were lots of things he *might* do; he might say something funny and make her laugh, for instance. But for some reason he didn't. He pulled his hand in tighter, around the curve of her shoulder, and then leaned forward and kissed her cheek.

"Nothing's worrying me," he said.

She turned her face full toward him, and he put his other arm around her and kissed her mouth that was as familiar as if he had been kissing her only last night instead of almost seven years ago. Even the taste of her lipstick was the same – like strawberries. And she had the same way of hugging him; the minute she hugged him she stopped seeming scared and became soft and warm, first kissing him and then gently laying her cheek against his as if he were a child to be comforted. For a minute he relaxed against her, but then he began to feel a crick in his neck. He sat up straight again and cleared his throat.

"Um . . ." he said. He leaned forward a little, with his elbows on his knees. "I forgot about Horner," he said.

"What?"

"Horner. I forgot about him."

"Oh."

He lit a cigarette and puffed on it a few times before he looked at her again. "Have you got an ash tray?" he asked her.

"I'll get you one." She stood up and crossed to the desk. She was the kind of person who rumpled easily; her hair was fluffed now and her lipstick was a little blurred. When she came back with the ash tray she said, "We're not *engaged*, after all. I just go out with him some."

"Well, still."

"Of course, I *like* him and all . . ."

"Oh, sure. Sure, he looked like a nice person."

"He is. He's real nice, he really is."

"Where did you meet up with him?" he asked.

"At my aunt's house. She used to know his family."

"That's right. Joanne said he was from around Sandhill. I don't know where *she* met up with him."

"At a basketball game," said Shelley, "when Joanne was still in high school."

"How you know that?"

"Oh, John's told me *all* about his past." She settled back against the cushions, smiling a little now.

"His *past*? Does that include just meeting a girl at a basketball game? He must have been pretty thorough."

109

"Oh, no, he dated her a while. But he felt—" She stopped, and looked into her half-empty glass.

"He felt what?"

"Oh, now I've forgotten what I was going to say."

"Come on, Shelley."

She kept on staring at her drink, pressing the corners of her mouth down. Finally she said, "Well, I suppose he just met her at . . . at one of those ages when girls are in a sort of, um, wild stage. I mean, rebellious. That's what I mean. *Rebellious* stage."

Ben Joe sat up straighter.

"Now, Ben Joe, I'm sure he didn't mean to—"

"Who does he think he—"

"Ben Joe, *I know* he didn't mean to carry tales. He wouldn't do that."

"Oh, never mind." He sat back again. "She *was* kind of a *flirt* in high school," he said. "The way she dressed and all. I suppose if you just met her a couple of times you'd think she really *was* wild."

"But—" Shelley looked down in her drink again. "Well, yes, Ben Joe, I'm sure that's what he meant. You want another drink?"

"No."

"There's lots more."

"No. People who just look at them on the surface, *they've* got no right to say what my sisters are like."

"I know that."

"Okay."

She was still watching him, trying to tell if he was feeling better. He looked back at her blankly.

"Ben Joe," she said finally, "have you got a girl in New York?"

"Why?"

"Because I want to know."

"Not one steady girl. No."

She nodded, satisfied. "Anyway," she said, "I'm sorry I told you what I just did. I wouldn't have you worried for anything."

"I'm *not worried*!"

110

"All right."

She put her hands on his shoulders and he settled down next to her again, fitting his head beneath her chin. Against his back he could feel her hands patting him softly, so lightly he could hardly feel it.

"The trouble is," he said into her collarbone, "I'm reversible."

The words were muffled. She pulled back a little and looked down at him and said, "What?"

"I don't guess you're hardly *alive* if you're as reversible as I am. But the *ir*reversible people, they get someplace. Good or bad. Murder is irreversible, for that matter. Even if it's bad, you can tell you're getting somewhere definite. But me, I am reversible."

"You silly," Shelley said. "You talk like you're some kind of raincoat, Ben Joe. Don't get upset, now."

He was pulled in next to her again, and soothed with the same small pats. Gradually he closed his eyes and let the full weight of his head rest against her chest.

He heard Shelley's voice beginning above him, faraway and soft, saying, "You were the first person I ever wanted to ask me out. There'd been two other boys asked me out before, but I didn't like them and I've forgotten now where we ever went or what we did. One was that fat little Junior Gerby, who was shorter than me, and the other was Kenny Burke, who was so greasy and hoody back in those days. Though later on he changed. His mama says he's right nice now. She was always afraid he'd end up in Alcatraz. But when I started thinking about you asking me out, now that you weren't just a little boy to play roll-a-bat with any more, I'd pray every night for you to ask me. I'd say, 'Please, God, you let Ben Joe Hawkes ask me out and I will never ask for anything more as long as I live.' Though I knew at the time it was next to impossible. There were three other girls after you and all of them prettier than me, though you never noticed and were always playing baseball and fiddling with your microscope. I took to shoplifting lipsticks, even if I *did* have plenty allowance, and trying on all manner of different shades in front of the mirror. Then I figured God was mad at me for it and I buried all my lipsticks in the backyard, where they are to this day."

He moved his head a little, and she let him settle down again and then began stroking his hair with her hand. Above him the voice went on; he barely listened to the words but just concentrated on the sound, slow and murmuring above him.

"And then they announced how the Future Homemakers were going to have a supper at the Parnells' Restaurant out by the college and we could ask dates, and I asked you, although I was shaking so hard I had to lean against the wall while I was talking to you. When you said yes I got all happy, but then when it came time to go I was terrified and wished I'd never asked you. I was afraid I'd vomit at the dinner table. And I didn't know what to order. I could order spaghetti and get a big, long, endless strand of it and have to keep sucking it up from the plate just indefinitely. Or pizza, and misjudge how soon it had cooled, the way I always did, and take a hot bite and have to spit it out. Or chicken, and have it slide from under my knife and fork right across the table into somebody else's plate, like it had done once before."

"What did you order?" Ben Joe asked sleepily.

"A roast-beef sandwich. Only the meat was tough, and when I took a bite the whole slab of beef came out of the sandwich and hung from my teeth."

She was quiet a minute. Ben Joe stirred again, sitting up straighter so that his face was level with Shelley's. "I love you, Ben Joe," she said.

This time when he kissed her her mouth was softer, with that first stickiness of her lipstick gone, and he didn't care whether there was a crick in his neck or not now. He wanted to say he loved her back, but he couldn't because her mouth was in the way, and then when she drew back to nestle down next to his shoulder, he felt too warm and comfortable to say anything at all. He just sat still, letting her nuzzle a little place for her face between his neck and his shoulder. It was only when he knew that they were about to fall asleep that he spoke again, and then in the softest whisper, as if her family was still alive and gently watchful in other parts of the house.

"Shelley."

"What?"

"I better go home."

"It's early still."

"I know, but anyway."

"Well, all right."

They both stood up, Shelley patting her hair down as she rose. The minute Ben Joe was up he was awake again and felt almost sorry that he had mentioned going home. But he took the coat when she handed it to him and kissed the top of her head and said, "When can I come back?"

"Tuesday. You going to?"

"Yes."

She pulled the door open and a blast of cold air came in, taking both their breaths away.

"You hurry, now," she said. "You're going to freeze, Ben Joe!"

"Good night," he said.

"Night."

Then the door closed behind him, and all he could hear was the shrieking of the wind.

10

OUTSIDE IT WAS sheer blackness, rolling in around him with the wind. He walked down Shelley's steps slowly, pausing when he reached the street to button up the collar of his coat. But walking was too quiet; he wanted to run. And if no one had been within earshot he would have started singing, too, or laughing at nothing, because he felt happy and easy. But it was the hour just before bedtime, when everyone had something to do outdoors – walk the dog, or set out the milk bottles, or simply take a breath of fresh air in the yard before they shut themselves up in their houses for the night. So he ran silently; he doubled up his fists and tore down the sidewalk with the leaves rattling behind him and people occasionally pausing on their porches to turn and watch him run.

Someone came down a front walk and set a cat down outside the gate. It was a small cat of some nameless color, with its sling-eyes glowing, and when its owner turned to go inside, the cat hunched sullenly on the sidewalk as if it resented being put out for the night. It stared unblinkingly at Ben Joe. Ben Joe stooped down to pat it.

"There, there, cat," he said. His hand reached out for the cat almost blindly, aiming only for a blurred patch of darkness against the lighter background of the sidewalk. When he felt the cat's head under his hand he stroked it gently. "I'll take care of you," he said.

The cat was used to people; it began purring instantly and pressing its little head against Ben Joe's hand. Ben Joe picked it up and began walking again, hugging the cat next to his chest to keep it warm. He was afraid to run, for fear the cat would become frightened, but he was tired, anyway, and contented himself with walking fast.

Some of the houses were already dark; most of them still had soft yellow lights in the windows. He could see people moving around upstairs, pulling down shades or simply walking about their rooms in bathrobes. In one house a woman stood brushing her hair, and Ben Joe stopped to watch the dreamlike rhythm of it. Then the little cat stirred restlessly, and Ben Joe went on. The sky above the lights of the houses was a deep blue-black, but when he stepped out into the street and kept his eyes away from the lights it was pale and glowing, and stretched almost white behind the black skeletons of trees. He was almost running again, and the cat began mewing softly and squirming in his arms.

"Now, don't you worry, cat," Ben Joe said. "No call to worry."

He laughed, for no reason he could name. Laughing made his teeth cold. He closed his mouth and his teeth felt cold and dry against the inside of his lips.

"That you, Ben Joe?" someone called.

He turned; a dark figure was standing on the sidewalk.

"It's me," he said. "Who's that?"

"Jenny."

"Oh. What *you* doing out?"

"Nothing." She stepped off the sidewalk and walked over to him. "I went to bed early and just got myself all wound up in the bed sheets," she said. "Thought I'd have a walk and hot milk and then try going to bed all over again. What's that you got?"

"A cat. There's something I meant to talk to you about."

"Where'd you get him?" She bent forward to see the cat, and then touched it. All he could see of her was a pale face and the dark hollows where her eyes were. "Doesn't like being carried," she said.

"I'm keeping it warm. I wanted to ask you—"

"It doesn't *want* to be kept warm."

"It does too. Jenny, there's a sort of money matter I'd like to—"

"You better put it *down*, Ben Joe."

115

"He *likes* me, I tell you."

"Got his own little overcoat sewn right on him, doesn't he? What's he want to be kept warm for? No, when they squirm like that, Ben Joe . . ."

He gave in, knowing she was right, and bent to let the cat hop down and run away.

"It's much happier now," she said.

"*Jenny!*"

"Well, I'm listening."

He smiled suddenly, without knowing why. "Oh, never mind," he said. "Oh, what the hell, what the hell . . ."

"Well, good night, Ben Joe."

"Night."

He was off again, tearing along the cracked pavement and leaving Jenny far behind. He swung three times around the tree on his corner, the way he had always done for good luck when he was small. Then he clattered through the wire gate and up the walk to the porch. The bark from the tree had left his palm gritty: he rubbed his hand against the side of his coat as he climbed the steps. At the front door, dark now with only the softest yellow light glimmering through the round stained-glass window, he bumped smack into a girl and boy.

"Excuse me, excuse me," he said, and found himself smiling again. "I didn't see you. Funny house this is – they just never think of leaving the light on for you. They forget all about you, the minute you—"

He opened the screen door with a flourish, almost bumping into the couple, and with his hand on the knob of the inside door he turned back again.

"Excuse me," he said.

John Horner and Joanne were looking at him, their faces serious and lit very dimly by the pale-yellow light. Joanne's hand was clasped in John's, against John's chest, but it was forgotten now as they both stared at him.

"*Quite* all right," said John Horner.

The heat inside the house burned Ben Joe's cold face. As soon as he had slammed the door behind him he ripped off his overcoat and threw it on a chair in the hallway and began undoing his collar as he climbed the stairs.

116

"That you, Ben Joe?" his mother called.

"Yup."

"Come on into the living room and say hello, why don't you?"

"I can't," Ben Joe said.

He stopped on the stairs, hearing his mother's footsteps in the hallway, and turned to look down at her.

"Why can't you?" she said.

"I just can't. I just can't. I can't be bothered with that right now."

"You can't be—"

He climbed the rest of the stairs at a steady, slow pace. His tie trailed by one hand. It wasn't until he was in the upstairs hallway that he let the actual picture of the couple on the porch come back to him, and then all he did was stop and stare tiredly at the wallpaper. After a minute he turned and started doggedly down the hall toward his room.

"BEN JOE," GRAM said, "a promise is a promise. If you didn't want to see Jamie Dower you shouldn't have told me he was here."

Ben Joe pushed a rubbery piece of scrambled egg around his plate.

"You hear me, Ben Joe?"

"Yes'm."

"Well, you going to take me there or aren't you?"

"All I'm doing is being honest about it," he said. "I just honestly don't *feel* like going to the home, Gram. Never have liked going. That time I went to see Mrs. Gray with you I couldn't get it out of my mind again."

His grandmother poured him a second cup of coffee and then slammed the pot back on the stove. "Liking's got nothing to do with it," she said. "What's the matter with it, anyway? No, I don't enjoy thinking of my friends in an old folks' home, but this I *will* say: homes are a lot more cheerful nowadays. They don't *depress* the tar out of you."

"I don't care if they depress me. I just get confused in homes. I walk out of there all confused and I never can tell what time it is."

"What difference is the time of day? What difference does it make?"

"Well, the time of *day* doesn't make *any* difference, Gram. That's not what I'm talking about."

"You." She flounced into the chair opposite him and began pulling out her three bobby pins. "Now, it's got to be this morning that we go, Ben Joe, because I got to take Tessie to her drawing lesson this afternoon. Your mother's too busy. *Busy.*" She jabbed one of the bobby pins back in.

"What you need me along for? To go to the home, I mean. What good'll I do? You tell me a good reason, I'll be glad to come."

"I just want someone with me. Besides."

"What."

"Besides, I want you to remember how I tagged around after Jamie Dower when I was little. Then you'll see how it might seem a little forward for me to be going there alone today."

"I don't see why," Ben Joe said. "You're seventy-eight years old now, Gram."

"That's not too old to do things ladylike."

"All right, I'll go." He knew it was no use arguing; he shrugged resignedly and speared another piece of egg.

"You promise?"

"I promise. Give me a minute to finish my breakfast."

"Well, do you think I look all right?"

He looked at her carefully for the first time that morning. She was wearing a huge black turtleneck sweater, knitted in haste, and a wrap-around denim skirt, and on her feet were the usual black gym shoes. But there were a few small changes that he hadn't noticed: her face looked feverish with its dabs of rouge and the careful line of orange lipstick that ordinarily she never wore; and next to the worn little wedding band on her finger was a huge diamond engagement ring that was used only for church-going.

"You look fine," he said.

"I bet he won't recognize me."

"I bet he won't."

"Last time he saw me I was a little roly-poly fat girl with lollypop juice down my front. I bet he won't know what name to call me by, even."

"No, I bet he won't."

"Come *on*, Ben Joe."

He gulped down the last of his coffee and stood up. "Where are the keys?" he asked.

"On the wall, where they belong. Put your dishes in the sink, now. Jenny was raising the roosters about how you don't do your share of picking up around here."

"Oh, pick up, pick up." He stacked the dishes helter-skelter in the sink and then knelt to tie his shoe. "*Joanne* never picks up. I had to scrape pablum off the damn *toaster* this morning."

"That was Jane that fed Carol. Joanne's still in bed."

"No wonder," he said.

"No wonder what?"

"No wonder she's still in bed. Get your coat, Gram."

"I've got it right here." She picked up one of his father's old lab coats from the back of a chair and began putting it on. It came down almost to the top of her gym shoes, but she looked at it proudly and stuck her hands in the pockets.

"You going to be warm enough in that?" he asked.

"Course I am."

"Well, it's your lookout."

He followed her across the living room, which was still cluttered with all the things the family had been doing the night before. His heel crushed something; it was the flatiron from the Monopoly set. He scraped it off his shoe and kept going.

Outside it was bright and still. The wind was gone but it was still cold, and in shady places there was something that was either very heavy frost or light patches of snow. He turned on the windshield wipers in the car to get rid of the thin covering of frost.

"Now, I want you to be very polite to Jamie," his grandmother said.

"Am I ever *not* polite?"

"Sometimes. Sometimes. Or at least, absent-minded. So you watch it, Ben Joe. Jamie Dower is older even than I am. I used to think maybe someday he'd save my life."

"How would he do that?"

"Oh you know. Pull me out of the water or something. I'm just saying that to show how *much* older he is. Old enough to be kind of looked up to and admired, so's the only way he'd really notice me would be for me to die or something."

"All right," Ben Joe said. "I'll be polite."

She settled back, satisfied. But when they had pulled out into the street and were drawing closer to the home, the anxious expression came back to her face and she crossed her legs and began picking at the white rubber circle at the ankle of her gym shoes, a sure sign she was worrying.

"Maybe I should've brought him something," she said.

"I thought you were going to."

"No. No, ordinarily I would, would have brought something to pretty up his room or tempt his appetite. But Jamie never liked that kind of thing. When I was little I would walk to his house every day and bring him my dessert from lunchtime, but he never wanted it."

"Well, that was nearly seventy years ago. You want to stop at a florist's?"

"No thank you, Ben Joe."

She settled back again, still frowning. When they drew up in front of the home, which looked like just a larger sort of yellow brick family house, she remained in her seat and looked at it through the window pane without changing her expression or giving any sign that she was about to go in.

"Would you rather not go?" Ben Joe asked gently. "I could bring you back another time, if you want."

"No, no. I was just thinking, oughtn't to ever put brownish curtains in a yellow house. It's ugly." She swung her door open and got out, grunting a little as her feet hit the ground. "Don't know what they could have been thinking of," she said.

"We'll get inside where we don't have to look at it."

But she kept standing there, looking up at the home.

"You're going to stay right by me, aren't you, Benjy?" she asked.

"Course I am."

"They say," she said, beginning to walk slowly across the yard, "they say when people get old they take to reading the obituary column to see if their names're in it. Well, I'm not to that yet, but one thing I have noticed: I do hate going to the home for the aged, for fear I can't get out again. They might mistake me, you know. When I said I wasn't a patient, they might think I was just planning to escape."

Ben Joe took her by the elbow and began walking with her. "I'll watch out for you," he said. "Besides, they must have a

121

sort of roll book here. And your name's not on it. They couldn't keep you here."

"Oh, don't be so *reasonable*, Ben Joe." She made an exasperated face and pinched the arm that she was hanging onto. "You're just like your mother. So reasonable. Just like her."

"I am not."

"Well, no, but you surely are an annoyance."

"If you're not more polite I'm going to leave you here," Ben Joe said. "And sneak up and put your name on the roll book just to make sure you stay." He gave her a small pat on the back.

The front door of the home was huge and heavy. Ben Joe pulled it open and they stepped inside, into suffocating heat and the smell of furniture polish. The flowered brown rug they stood on was deep and made everything seem too quiet; it stretched for what seemed like miles across a huge sort of social room. There were easy chairs arranged next to the walls, and in them sat a few old people talking or playing checkers or staring into space. In the center of the room hung a great tarnished chandelier that Ben Joe could almost have reached on tiptoe. He stared past it at the old people, but his grandmother looked fixedly at the chandelier, never letting her eyes move from it.

"Can I help you?" a nurse said. She had come up soundlessly on her thick-soled shoes, and now she faced them with her arms folded across the cardboard white of her uniform and her face strangely young and cheerful.

"We've come to visit a Mr. Dower," Ben Joe said.

"Algernon Hector James Dower the Third," said his grandmother, still looking intently at the chandelier.

"You members of his family?"

"Raised together."

"Well, he's not feeling too good. He's a bed patient. If you'll only stay a few minutes . . ."

"We'll be quiet," said Ben Joe.

"Follow me, then."

She led them through the social room, toward an elevator around the corner. As they passed the other patients there was a whispering and a stirring, and everyone stared at them. "Mr. Dower," the nurse told them. They nodded and kept staring. The nurse turned back to Ben Joe and his grandmother and gave them a sudden, reassuring smile; when she smiled, her nose wrinkled like a child's and the spattering of freckles stood out in a little brown band across her face.

"If you'll just step in here," she said.

The elevator smelled dark and soapy. It was so small that it made Ben Joe nervous, and he could see that his grandmother was beginning to get that lost look on her face and was twisting her engagement ring. He smiled at her, and she cleared her throat and smiled back.

"Here we are," the nurse said cheerfully.

The door slid open. Gram bounded out like a young goat, with a suprising little kick of her heels, and looked back at the nurse.

"My, I wish *our* people were as spry as *you* are!" the nurse said.

Gram smiled.

"Arc those – those are very, um, sensible shoes you're wearing," the nurse went on pleasantly. "They must be—"

"I get them at Pearson's Sport Shop," Gram said.

"Ah, I see. Down this corridor, please."

The corridor was very long and silent. It was hard to imagine that such an average-looking house could hold it all. The walls were covered with a heavy brown paper that had columns of palm leaves up and down it, and the doors were of some dark wood. At the next to last door, which was slightly open, the nurse stopped and tapped lightly with her fingernails.

"Mr. Dower?" she called.

She peeked in, all smiles, and said, "We have company, Mr. Dower."

Then she looked backed at Ben Joe and Gram and said, "You can come in. Don't stay long, now. I'll be out here when you want to go down again."

They tiptoed in, Gram ahead of Ben Joe. Jamie Dower was lying in a spotless white iron bed, with his white hair fluffed out around his polished little face. His eyes were as alert as when Ben Joe had first seen him, but his breathing was worse; even when he was lying flat now, there was that squeaky kittenish sound that had been there when he'd climbed the hill.

"Oh, young man," he said, recognizing Ben Joe.

"Hello, Mr. Dower."

"Who is—"

Gram stepped forward. She had her hands folded primly in front of her and she looked very small and uncertain. For a long time she looked at Jamie Dower, taking in every change she must have seen in him. Then she dropped her hands and became brisk and lively, the way she always did at a sickbed. "I look familiar?" she asked him. She flounced over to sit on the edge of the chair beside his bed and smiled brightly at him. "I look like anyone you know, Jamie Dower?"

"A doctor—"

"Oh, no, no." She twisted out of the white lab coat impatiently and flung it behind her. "Now?" she asked. "Well, ma'am . . ."

"*I'm* Bethany Jane *Chrisawn*!" she caroled out loudly. The nurse came swiftly to the doorway and put one finger to her lips, but Gram was watching only Jamie Dower. "*Now* you remember?"

"Bethany . . ." He raised himself up on one elbow and stared at Gram puzzledly. For a minute Ben Joe held his breath; then the old man's face slowly cleared and he said, "Bethany! Bethy Jay *Chrisawn*, that's who!"

Ben Joe breathed again, and Gram nodded smugly.

"Bethy *Jay*!" the old man roared.

"Mr. Dower, *please*," the nurse said.

"Well, I'll be," said Jamie Dower. He lay back down and shook his head as he stared at her. "Bethy," he said, "you surely have changed some."

Gram turned around and beamed at Ben Joe. "I told you," she said. "Didn't I? Before we even left the house I said to Ben Joe, I said, 'I bet he won't recognize me.' This is Ben Joe Hawkes, Jamie. My grandson. He's the one told me you were here."

"I'm going," the nurse called across to Ben Joe, barely mouthing the words. She trilled the fingers of one hand at him, gave him a warning look, and vanished.

"Never thought you'd still be alive," Jamie said.

"Why, I'll be! I'm younger'n *you* are."

"Well, I know that. I know."

He tried to sit up higher, and Gram reached behind him to pull the pillows up.

"You're looking good, Jamie," she said.

"That's funny. View of the fact that I'm dying."

"Oh, now, *you're* not dying."

"Don't argue, Bethy Jay. Your word against the doctor's and I'll take the doctor's any day. Yes sir, I'm dying and I come to die where I was born at, like any good man should. Not that I'd *recognize* the damn place."

"Language, Jamie. You're right, town has changed some."

"Sure has. This your grandson, hey? You got married?"

"Well, of *course* I got married. What'd you think?" She sat up straighter and glared at him. "I married Lemuel Hawkes, that's who."

"Lemuel *Hawkes*?"

"Why, sure."

"That kind of chubby guy whose voice wasn't changed?"

"Well, by the time I *married* him it was changed," Gram said. "Good *heavens*, Jamie."

"When I knew, when I knew—" He laughed, and the laugh ended in a wheezy little cough. "When I knew him he was sending away for all kinds of creams and secret remedies, that's what. He had this kind of black syrup made by the Indians, you're supposed to put it on your throat and lie out in the moonlight with it, and it was guaranteed to give a manly vibrance to your voice. A 'manly vibrance,' that's the exact words. Only his mother found him lying under the clothesline and all she could see was something dark and wet all over his neck, oh, God—" He choked and choked again and still laughed, with his little wheezing breaths pulling him almost to a sitting position.

"When *I* knew him," Gram said firmly, "he sang bass in the Baptist choir. Had his own business, and—"

"Did he have a little sort of pot above his belt? With his navel sitting on it like a button on a mountain? Oh, God—"

and he was off again, laughing delicately this time so as not to choke.

"*And*," Gram said, "I married him and had four girls and a boy and all of them healthy. Lemuel he died after the children were grown on account of having influenza, but the children are all alive to this day excepting Phillip, who passed on due to a combination of circumstances. And he left behind him seven children, Joanne Ben Joe Susannah Lisa Jane Jenny and Tessie and a wife and a granddaughter Carol who is just as—"

"Let me say mine," the old man said. He struggled up higher against the pillows and folded his hands across the sheet. "While making bed linens in New Jersey I married my secretary though of good family and not just an every*day* secretary, mind you, and to my grief she died having Samuel our son—"

"You're not married any more?"

"Don't interrupt me. You always were one to interrupt me. I raised him honest and respectful and first he kept books—"

"A *bookie*?"

"A book*keeper*, for our company and gradually rose to an even higher position than I ever had. He has now got a wife and six healthy children Donald Sandra Mara Alex Abigail and uh, uh, Suzanne and one of them—"

"*I* got a grandchild named Susannah," Gram said.

"*One* of them, I say—"

"How's she spell it?"

"*One* of them went to *Europe*!" the old man shouted joyfully.

"Is that so!"

"Summer before last, she went."

"*My* Susannah is spelled kind of like 'Savannah,' Georgia," said Gram. "Only it's *Sus*annah."

"Well, mine's not. It was Sandra that went to Europe. She got to see the Pope."

"The Pope!" Gram's mouth fell open. "Why, Jamie Dower, you haven't gone and become a—"

"Oh, no. Oh, no. But she went with this touring group, her and her aunt, and the itinerary said they could have an

126

audience with the Pope. The family came to me and asked what I thought of it; they ask me about everything important. And I said, 'Sandra, honey,' I said, 'I'll tell you what to do. You go visit the Pope and then right after that, the very same day, you go see a *Protestant* minister too. And encourage him in his work and all.' Only it turned out the touring group had to move on before she could track down a Protestant. She was heart*broken* about not keeping her promise."

"Did she sell the clothes the Pope blessed her in?" Gram asked.

"Oh, yes. Excepting her shoes. I think it's good to keep *some*thing he blessed her in, just in case, you know."

"Ma'am," the nurse said, "remember what I said about keeping it short, now. If you could be thinking about drawing your visit to a close . . ."

She was standing in the doorway with her hands pressed neatly together in front of her, and when they looked up she smiled. Ben Joe, leaning silently upon the window sill, nodded at her. When she was gone he turned back to look out at the view, but Gram and Jamie kept on staring blankly at the place where she had been. Their faces seemed crushed and pale. Finally Gram forced her bright smile again and began anxiously working her dry little hands together.

"Um, Jamie," she said. "Do you remember the time your cousin Otis bought a wild horse?"

"Horse?"

"I was thinking about it while watching a Western the other night. He bought this wild horse that couldn't *no*body tame and rode off on it practically upside-down, the horse was bucking so bad, but he was waving his scarf and shouting all the same, with your mother and your aunt on the porch watching after him and crying and wringing their hands. And after dark he came back safe and sound and singing, with the horse so polite, and dismounted into the sunken garden and broke his leg in two places. Oh, law, I reckon I never *will* forget—"

"You know," said Jamie, "I just can't recall it."

"Well, it came to me out of the blue, sort of."

He nodded, and for a minute there were only the kitten squeaks of his breathing.

"Then I reckon you remember Grandfather Dower getting religion," he said finally.

"Not offhand I don't."

"Sure you do. Along came this revivalist by the name of Hezekiah Jacob Lee, preaching how nothing material is real and things of the spirit is all that counts. He only stayed for some three days of preaching, but Grandfather Dower, he latched right on. Gave up his swaggering ways and his collecting of old American saloon songs and went around acting unfit to live with. And one day, after Hezekiah Jacob Lee had been gone about a month, Great-Aunt Kazi got stung by a bee on the wrist knob and naturally she went to Grandfather, him being a doctor, and he stamped his foot and shouted, 'Don't bother *me* with your material matters; put mud on it, woman!' when suddenly he frowned and his eyes kind of opened and he said to her, Why,' he says, '*why* do you reckon Hezekiah Jacob Lee went off and left me holding the bag this way?' And what a party there was *that* night, with alcohol floating on the garden path—"

"I declare," Gram said, "it rings a bell, sort of. I just vaguely do remember."

They were quiet again, thinking. Jamie Dower drew the edge of his sheet between his small, brittle fingers.

"About all that's left now is Arabella," said Gram.

"Arabella."

"Your cousin, the fat one. Auntie Adams's little girl."

"Oh, her."

"I don't see her much," Gram said. "She was always kind of a prissy girl."

"She was. She was at that. She went to study in Virginia, I remember, before I'd even left home. We heard from her regular but stopped reading her letters."

"It was on account of her mother, I believe," Gram said. "She was the same way. Told Arabella to watch out for germs in public places. Every letter Arabella sent us after that sounded like something from a health inspector. All these long detail-ly descriptions of every— You remember that?

128

Auntie Adams finally wrote back and said she would take Arabella's word for it, but I don't recall that Arabella paid her any mind."

"How about her brother Willie?" Jamie asked.

"Oh, he was prissy too. That whole *section* of the family was prissy."

"No, I mean, what is he doing now?"

"Oh. Well, he's dead. He died about a year ago."

"I didn't know that."

"And of course Auntie Adams is dead. She died."

"I remember someone telling me."

"All that's left now," said Gram, "is Arabella."

They both stared at a place in Jamie's blanket. Behind them the door cracked open softly and the nurse poked her head in and said, "About time to be saying our good-bys now."

"Do you remember," Jamie said suddenly, "do you remember that funny old L-shaped bench that sat on your front porch?"

"What color was it?"

"Green. Dark green. Forest green, I think they call it. Us kids used to sit all together on it in the summer afternoons and eat fresh peaches out of a baskety box. Remember?"

"Well, no."

"I do. I do. You-all were having Hulda Ballew as your maid then, and is was she that set the peaches out for us to dice up small with sharp kitchen knives and eat in little bitty bites, the boys to poke a bite on the tip of a knife to some girl they liked and she to bite it off, dainty like, on summer afternoons. You got to remember that."

"Well, I don't," Gram said. "I remember Hulda Ballew, but no green bench comes to mind."

"You got to remember."

"Ma'am," the nurse said.

Something in her voice made Gram know it was time to give up. Her shoulders sagged and she fell silent, but she kept staring at the blanket.

"Say bye to our guests, Mr. Dower."

"I'm coming," said Gram. "We'll come back, Jamie Dower. If you want us."

"That'll be right nice, Beth. Funny thing," he said, looking at her suddenly. "You were such a *fat* little girl."

Gram patted his hand on the sheet and then stood up and left the room, so suddenly that she took all of them by surprise.

"Well, good-by," said Ben Joe.

"Good-by, young man."

"You take a nice little nap now," the nurse said. She pulled the venetian blinds shut and then tiptoed out of the room behind Ben Joe, closing the door behind her. "He's not well at all," she whispered as they walked down the hall. "I don't know how he lasted this long, or managed to get here all by himself."

"Hush," Ben Joe said. They were approaching Gram, who stood waiting by the elevator. The nurse nodded without surprise and clamped her mouth shut.

When they were out in the car again Ben Joe said, "Put on your coat, Gram, you'll catch cold."

"All right, Ben Joe."

"You want me to turn the heat on?"

"Oh, no."

He started the motor but let it idle while he watched her, trying to think whether there was something to say or whether there was even any need for anything to be said. Her face, with its clown's coating of rouge, told him nothing. When he kept on watching her, she folded her arms across her chest and turned away, so that she was looking out of the window toward the home. Ben Joe let the car roll out into the street again.

"That house," Gram said, looking back at the home, · "wasn't even *here* when Jamie Dower was born."

"I know."

"It wasn't even here when we were growing up, did you know *that*? They hadn't laid the first brick yet. They hadn't even dug the foundation yet. There were only trees here, trees and brambly bushes with those little seedy blackberries on them that aren't fit for pies, even—"

"I know. I know."

She grew silent. He didn't know what her face looked like now. And he didn't try to find out, either. He just looked straight ahead at the road they drove on, and kept quiet.

12

ON THE WALL behind the silverware drawer in the kitchen was a combination blackboard and bulletin board, frayed at the edges now from so many years of use. Ben Joe stood leaning against the refrigerator with a tomato in his hand and studied the board very carefully, narrowing his eyes. First the blackboard part. Jenny's great swooping handwriting took up half the board:

Eggs
Lavoris
Contact lense fluid

Who in this family wore contact lenses? He frowned and shook his head; he felt like a stranger. Under Jenny's list his grandmother had written, in straight little angry letters:

Chewing gum

And then came Tessie's writing, round and grade-schoolish, filling up the rest of the board right down to the bottom:

What shall we do about it? I will think of somthing. What I want to know is, how do you think?

He switched the tomato to his left hand and picked up the piece of chalk that hung by a string from the board. With his mouth clamped tight from concentrating, he bent forward, inserted an "e" in "somthing," and then stepped back to look at it. After a minute he underlined the "e" twice and then dropped the chalk and reread the whole message. Something about it still confused him.

His eyes moved over to the bulletin-board part. In the old days it had been crowded with the children's drawings, ranging from kindergarten-level pictures of houses with smoking chimneys up to the tiny complicated landscapes Ben Joe had done in upper grade school. Now only one of them was left – a drawing done by Jenny, when she was six, of a circle superimposed on a furry cylinder, which she had said was the Lone Ranger and Silver seen from above. Other than that, there were only two yellowed scraps of paper. The first was one of the few reminders of his father that had been allowed to remain; it was a note written by Susannah, back when her writing was as uncertain as Tessie's, saying:

> Mama, the last five times that Gram has gone to a church supper and you've gone to a Legal Women Voters' supper both at the same time Daddy has fed us as follows: (1) popcorn (2) grilled cheese sandwiches (3) fudge (4) popcorn (5) ice cream, please talk to him.

Ben Joe frowned again, considered changing the comma to a semicolon, but eventually let it go for some reason and turned to the next piece of paper. This was his own, in crooked, preschool capitals, and he could not remember when or for what reason he had written it. It said:

Song By
    Benjamin Josiah Hawkes

What shall we do with the trunk-ed sailor
Is a matter worth disgusting.
Everybody's pinto is agoing to heaven
Heaven, in the morning.

It had a tune, his mother had told him, something like the scissors-mender's chant, all on one note, except that the last word in each line was several notes lower. They said he used to sing it at the beach, but he had no memory of it now.

He looked down at his tomato. There was a bite in it, although he hadn't noticed he had taken one. He considered storming into the den and accusing Tessie of spit-backing, which was a habit she had developed after biting into chocolates that turned out to be caramel-filled; but on second thoughts he decided he might have taken a bite after all. There was no telling. He had been confused and absent-minded all day; he attributed it to the visit at the home for the aged, but just knowing the reason didn't help him any. All he could think of that might help was to isolate himself in the kitchen for a while after supper and stare at the bulletin board, where years arranged themselves one on top of the other in layers before his eyes. Sometimes that helped. Sometimes it didn't, too. He sighed, took another bite from his tomato, and began rereading the blackboard.

Eggs
Lavoris . . .

"What are *you* doing here?" Jenny asked.

"Why?"

"I thought you were just going out to get a snack. You missed the last half of the program."

"Oh. Okay."

He moved aside to let her get into the refrigerator.

"Ben Joe . . ."

"*What*," he said. Every time she interrupted him he had to go back to the very top of the blackboard and begin reading all over again.

"Never mind," she said.

"Well, go *on*, now that you've interrupted me."

"I just wanted to know where the ice water is. I'm getting some for Gram. What's the matter with you to-night?"

"I don't know. I went with Gram to the old folks' home." He jammed his hands into his pockets and with the toe of his sneaker he began tracing patterns in the linoleum. There was no sense in going back to reading the blackboard until Jenny was out of the room again.

She had found the ice water. She poured it into an orange-juice glass and put the jar back in the refrigerator.

"Hey, I wonder . . ." she said suddenly.

But Ben Joe, off on another track now, interrupted her. "Who in this family wears contact lenses?" he asked.

"Contact— Oh, you're talking about the list. Susannah does."

"How come I didn't know?"

"You weren't here," Jenny said.

"Oh."

"She got them with her first pay check from the library, after she switched jobs."

"I never heard about it."

"You weren't *here*, I said." She picked up the glass of water and started out again. At the door she stopped. "What I was just wondering," she said, "was it this morning you went to the home? With Gram?"

"Yes."

"Well, why don't you come out into the living room? Gram just heard an old friend of hers died. She says she only saw him this morning, so that must be who it is. That Mr. Dower."

"He's dead?"

"That's what she said."

"But he can't be. We only saw him this morning."

"Doesn't stop him from being dead, does it? Why do people always—"

"Ah, no," said Ben Joe. He shook his head gently and turned his back to the bulletin board. (What good would it do him now?) There was no reason for him to feel so sad, but he did, anyway, and he just kept staring at a corner of the kitchen cabinet while Jenny watched him curiously.

"Why don't you come talk to Gram?" she asked him.

"Well . . ."

"Come on."

She backed against the door to open it and let Ben Joe pass through ahead of her. "All I ever know to do is get people water," she said, "I know when *I'm* sad *I* don't want water, and I don't guess others do, either, but it's all I know to do."

"Well, I'm sure she'd like it," Ben Joe said.

"Maybe so."

In the living room he found his grandmother upright on the couch, sitting very stiffly with her hands in her lap and her eyes dry. Around her was clustered most of the family, some sitting next to her and some on chairs around the room.

"Only this morning," she was saying. "Only this morning." She caught sight of Ben Joe and called out, "Wasn't it, Ben Joe? Wasn't it only this morning?"

"Yes," said Ben Joe.

"There. Ben Joe can tell you." She turned to nod at the others and then, realizing that Ben Joe hadn't yet heard the whole story, she looked his way again. "I called the home," she said. "I wanted to tell him about something I'd forgotten. This evening I was just hunting under the bed for Carol's hair brush and suddenly it came to me, so clear: Jamie's mustache cup."

"His what?" Ben Joe asked.

"Mustache cup. Mustache cup. You know, Jamie Dower was the only man I ever knew who really did use a mustache cup. That was something wonderful, when I was twelve. He got it just the last year he was home, on account of this lovely mustache he was growing. He was kind of a dandy, Jamie Dower. *Always* was. But it was a beautiful mustache, I have to say. Ben *Joe* knows. You tell them, Ben Joe."

"Well . . ." Ben Joe said. The picture of Jamie's face was before him, small and white and clean-shaven.

"Ben Joe knows," Gram said to the rest of them. She smiled down at her hands. "I know it's a small thing, but I suddenly thought of that mustache cup, white with pink rosebuds, it was, and I just had to tell him about it. So I called the home, and after a right long spell of hemming and hawing they told me. They said he had passed on just an hour ago. I didn't let on how it hit me. I just said I hoped he'd had a peaceful passing, and hung up." Her mouth shook for a minute, and the first tear slid down the dry paper of her cheek. "But it was only this *morning* . . ." she said.

A glass of water was poked suddenly under her chin. Gram drew back and blinked at it through her tears. Her eyes traveled slowly from the glass itself to the poker-stiff arm that held it and above that to Jenny's face, sober and embarrassed.

135

"Why, thank you," she said. She took the glass, looked at it a minute, and then smiled at Jenny and drank until the glass was empty. "There is nothing like clear water," she told Jenny formally.

Ben Joe looked around at the rest of the family. His mother was in the easy chair, looking worried; Tessie was on the arm of the chair, and the twins and Susannah were sitting around their grandmother on the couch. All of them were unusually quiet. When the silence had gone unbroken for at least a full minute, his mother cleared her throat and said, "We'll have to send a nice wreath of flowers, Gram."

"He wouldn't like it," Gram said. "Used to get angry when I brought him my dessert."

"Your— Well, anyway. It'd be a nice gesture to send a small wreath, just to show—"

"I will *not* send him *flowers*!" Gram said.

Ellen Hawkes was quiet a moment, figuring this out. Finally she said, "Well, some people prefer the money to go to a worthy cause instead. Maybe to the missionary league of his church, if he has one—"

"I tell you, no, Ellen. He never could accept a gift graciously. My mother said accepting gifts graciously is the true test of a gentleman, but I don't go along with that. Jamie Dower was a gentleman all the way through. He just didn't like gifts, is all."

"But that was some seventy *years* ago, Gram—"

"No point discussing it," said Ben Joe. "We don't send flowers."

Gram began crying again. The girls fluttered and crowded in around her and Jenny backed toward the door, in case she had to get more ice water. Ellen Hawkes clicked her tongue.

"What's going on?" Joanne said.

She was standing in the doorway dressed to go out and carrying a coat over her arm. Everyone looked up except Gram, who had just been handed Ben Joe's handkerchief and was now blowing her nose in it.

"Gram's lost an old friend," Susannah said.

"Oh, no." She came quickly over to the couch and knelt down in front of her grandmother. "Who was it?"

136

"Jamie Dower," said Gram, "and I can't send him flowers."

"Well, of course you can. What's the matter with this family? Mom, since when have we got so poor we can't send—"

"My God," her mother said. She stood up and left the room, not sharply but with a slow kind of weariness.

"It's not the money," Ben Joe said. "It's that Jamie never could accept a gift graciously."

"Oh, I see." She nodded and began gently stroking Gram's shoulder.

"If you see," her mother said from the doorway, "will you please explain it to *me*?"

"Well, it makes sense."

"Not to me it doesn't. Does it to you, Ben Joe?"

"Well, yes," said Ben Joe.

His mother vanished into the hallway.

"What *doesn't* make sense," Ben Joe said, "is why it makes you unhappy not sending him flowers. If you know he'd be happier not getting them."

"Because I *want* to send them, that's why," his grandmother said. "I always did want to give him flowers."

She began crying into her handkerchief, and the other girls moved over so that Joanne could sit beside her and hug her. "I know, I know," she said soothingly. "Now, I tell you what do, Gram. You just buy some flowers and give them to someone you like. Prettiest flowers you can find. And then you tell yourself you wouldn't have done it if Jamie Dower hadn't died. That way you solve the whole thing, right?"

"Well, maybe," Gram said.

The doorbell rang. Joanne gave Gram a brisk pat on the shoulder and stood up. "Don't bother," she told Ben Joe. "I'll get it. It's my date."

"What?"

But she didn't answer; she was already out of the room. Gram refolded the handkerchief to a dry place and then suddenly, in the middle of the process, stopped and looked up at Ben Joe. "What'd she say?" she asked.

"She said it was her date."

"Did she mean her appointment? Or did she mean her date?"

"Her date, is what she said."

All of them fell silent, listening. A young man laughed in the front hallway. Ben Joe could read in Gram's face the slow transition from grief to indignation.

"Why, *she* can't do that!" she said. "Joanne?"

The two voices ran on, ignoring her.

"*Joanne*!" Gram said.

Joanne reappeared, still carrying her coat over her arm.

"Who's that you got with you?" Gram asked.

"John Horner, Gram. Come on in, John."

John Horner appeared next to her, soundlessly. He still had his broad, open smile and he didn't seem to think it strange to be greeted by a whole silent, staring family grouped around a weeping old woman. He nodded to all of them in general and lifted a hand toward Ben Joe, whom he recognized.

"This is my grandmother," said Joanne. "And Ben Joe, and Susannah, and Jane, Lisa, Jenny, and Tessie. This is John Horner."

"How do you do?" John Horner said. He was addressing mainly Gram, as the oldest member of the family, but Gram just sat up straighter and stared narrowly at him.

"I wish I'd of married Jamie Dower," she said.

"Ma'am?"

"Gram has just heard that a friend passed away," Joanne began. Her voice was the old high-school Joanne's, soft and bubbling. She stood very close to John Horner while she talked to him. Under cover of Joanne's voice Gram went on muttering to the others.

"If I'd of married Jamie," she said, "I would of had a different family. On account of different genes mingling. They wouldn't all have gone and done queer things, or acted so—"

"Hush, Gram," Susannah said.

"Ben Joe?" Joanne called.

"What."

"John was asking you something."

"Excuse me?"

"I was just asking," said John, "aren't you the one that's at Columbia?"

"That's right."

"I was there for a while. Took a business course. Mrs. Hawkes, ma'am, I'm sorry to hear about your friend's passing."

Gram frowned. "Well," she said ungraciously. She thought a minute and then added, "Troubles always descend lots at a time, seems like."

"They do," said John. He came further into the room to sit on the arm of the rocker, and Joanne moved over to stand beside him. "My old man had a saying. My old man used to say, 'It never rains but it—' "

"Who is your daddy?" Gram asked suddenly.

"Jacob Hart Horner, ma'am."

"Jacob Hart Horner. That so."

"Yes'm."

"Oh. I know him."

"Do you really?" He smiled politely.

"*Yes*, I know him."

"Ah."

Gram nodded a while, considering.

"What you think he'd say if he saw you here?" she asked.

The silence before her question had been long enough so that John was just beginning to consider the conversation over. He froze now, in the act of turning toward Joanne, and looked back at Gram blankly.

"Ma'am?" he said. "What's that?"

"If he saw you here. If Jacob Hart Horner saw you here. What you think he'd say?"

"If he saw me *here*?"

"*Yes*, here."

"I don't—"

"Saw you taking Joanne out. Joanne Hawkes *Bentley* out. What you think he'd say?"

"Well, nothing, I don't guess."

"Nothing." She nodded again, with her eyes fixed veiled and thoughtful upon the floor. "No, I don't guess he would," she said finally. "*I* remember Jacob Hart Horner. Remember him well. Came here in his teens, he did, and took up with my boy Phillip. He was supposed to be working, but he didn't do much of *that*. Lived off little Sylvester Grant and my boy

Phillip. I never *will* forget, one time he called his folks long distance from this very house and me sitting in the same room listening to him. I reckon they wanted to know had he got a steady job and he said yes, he was working in the chicken cannery. There was a chicken cannery then, down by the river near the blue-denim factory, but I never saw *him* near it. And I reckon they wanted to know what he did there, because he started talking about carrying grain – said that was his job. Now, I don't know what his folks were like and I don't *want* to know, but let me just ask you this: what kind of intelligence do you suppose they had, to believe a body could get a job carrying grain in a factory that deals with dead chickens?"

"Well, now, I don't know," John Horner said. He was laughing, and didn't seem to be insulted.

"There's bad blood there," Gram said. She looked at him a while, at the friendly face with the dark eyes made slits by laughter, and then she blew her nose and looked down into her lap. "I am getting old," she said.

The room grew silent. John looked over at Joanne soberly, and she clutched her coat more tightly to her and started toward the door.

"Gram," she said, "I hope you feel better."

"Well. New things come up. A minute ago Jamie Dower slipped from my mind altogether for a second."

"Sure. It's always that way. You'll—"

"What I was meaning to bring up a minute ago," Gram began, "what I wanted to say . . ."

She stopped and looked over at Ben Joe.

"Um," he said. He took his hands out of his pockets and walked over to where John was standing beside Joanne.

"What's the matter?" Joanne asked.

"Well, I was just wondering." He looked at her face, with its blank brown eyes, and then changed his mind and directed the question toward John. "What I think Gram was trying to say," he said, ". . . well, hell with it, what *I'm* trying to say is, it doesn't look to me like a good idea for you to be going out, Joanne." But he was still facing John; it was to John's more open eyes that he said it.

140

"Why *not*," John said, turning it into a challenge instead of a question.

"Well, it's a small town. That's one reason."

"Small town, what's *that* got to do with it? Listen, boy, you and your family got to stop hanging on to your sister this way. Got to start—"

"But she's still *married*, damn it!"

His mother, coming in on the tail end of the sentence, stopped in the doorway and looked at Ben Joe.

"What?" she said.

Ben Joe turned to her. "Mom, I'm asking you, now. Do you think Joanne ought to go out on a date?"

His mother frowned. "Well," she said finally, "I don't know. If it's just an old friend of hers, I don't see the harm in her getting out of the house for a while. It's up to Joanne, after all. None of *our* business."

"But he's *not* just an old *friend*!"

"What is he, then?"

There was a silence. Everyone looked at him.

"Frankly," John said finally, "I don't see how—"

"No, listen. Please *listen*!"

"We're listening, Ben Joe," said his mother.

"No, you're not. You never are. Look, I was just worrying if people would *talk*."

"What would they talk about?"

He sat down, realized immediately the disadvantage at which this put him when everyone else was standing, and stood up again.

"Joanne," he said, "don't you see my point?"

"No," Joanne said.

"John? *You* do."

"I'm sorry, I don't," said John.

"*You* talk, don't you?" Ben Joe said. He took a step closer to him. "Don't you?"

John blinked his eyes at him.

"Look," Ben Joe said. He was facing all of them now, with his arms straight by his sides and his fists clenched. "All I'm trying to do is stop one more of those amazing damned things that go on in this family and everyone takes for granted,

141

pretends things are still all right and the world's still right-side up. The most amazing things go on in this family, the most *amazing* things, that no one *else* would *allow*, and this family just keeps on—"

"Just what sort of amazing things are you talking about?" his mother asked. She was looking at him straight on and sternly, with her eyes just slits. "This family's just like any other family, Ben Joe. There's nothing going on here that—"

"Oh, *no?*"

"No."

He slitted his eyes back at her.

"Just to give you a for-instance," he said, "I don't know if you all can dredge far enough back in your memories or not, but I can recall a time when Dad and the sheriff were out all one night in their pajamas—"

"That is *enough*," his mother said.

"—pajamas, chasing down to Dillon, South Carolina, because Joanne had run off with a total stranger that came here selling clear plastic raincoats one autumn afternoon, run off to get married as soon as he asked her, which as near as we could figure it was three seconds after she had opened the front door to his ringing, and Dad was frantically chasing down every highway to Dillon and finally found them at seven-thirty in the morning waiting to fill out a marriage license. And he brought her back and everyone just said, 'Well, let her sleep.'"

"It's true!" Gram said. "It's true. I remember it all!"

"What else could we have done?" his mother asked the clock.

"Which was fine, except didn't they wonder even what *led* to it, or *why*, or try to do something to help her? No, and at supper they all told jokes and passed the biscuits and there was Joanne with a new trick, a piece of plastic that looked just exactly like vomit – she'd bought it at the magic store – and she was retching and then throwing the plastic on the floor, and she squealed, 'Ooh, wouldn't my vomit go good on the living room *rug*!' and you all laughed and ran with her to the living room and life went on, and on, while—"

Joanne stepped up, and for a minute he thought she was

going to hit him, but instead she pushed her coat in his face, choking him with the force of it, leaving him in a forest-green darkness that smelled of wool and spice perfume. He could feel the bones of her hands pressing through the wool to his face, and above the uproar John Horner was shouting, "Stop it, *stop* it!" but the coat was still being pushed against his face.

"Anybody home?" someone called.

There was a long, deep silence.

The coat fell away from Ben Joe's face and hung, crumpled, around his shoulders. He blinked his eyes several times. Everyone in the room was looking toward the door, with their faces blank, staring at the tallest man Ben Joe had ever seen. He was bony and freckled with a long, friendly face, and though his overcoat hung on him badly, there was something very easy and graceful about the way he was standing.

"I would have called," he said cheerfully, "but then if I had, you probably would be gone when I got here. And I would have waited for you to answer the door, but a man can't wait forever. Can he?" he asked, and grinned at Ben Joe.

People were coming out of their surprise now, opening their mouths to speak, but the stranger had moved rapidly into the center of the room with his hands still in his pockets and he said, "I knew the house. Know it anywhere. Though that glider has *got* to be new. I didn't know that. You people are—" he looked around at them, still cheerfully— "Gram, Ben Joe, Mom, uh . . . Jenny? and a man I don't know with, of course, Joanne—"

"You go away," Joanne said softly.

"But I only just got here."

"I'm telling you, Gary . . ."

But before the name was out of her mouth, Ben Joe knew. He suddenly recognized the hair, flaming red and pushed carelessly back from his forehead exactly like Carol's, and the familiar-looking eyes that had stared out of the dim snapshot. He stood gaping at the three of them – Joanne and Gary and John – in a brightly tensed, three-cornered group in the center of the room.

"I'm leaving," he said.

"Ben Joe!" his mother called.

143

"I don't care, I don't care, I'm *leaving*!"

And he shoved the coat back in Joanne's face. It fell to the floor, but she let it stay there and didn't look his way. Jenny was in his path; he pushed her aside without even knowing it and flew through the hallway and out the door. Then he was outside. He was in the dark wind, with the cold already slapping at his face.

13

SHELLEY'S FACE WAS small and white; her hair was a mass of sausage-shaped curlers, shrouded under a heavy black net. She stood behind her screen door and looked out to where Ben Joe stood on the porch, under the yellow outside light, and to Ben Joe it seemed as if she was suddenly considering every detail of him, weighing him in the back of her faraway mind. With one hand she reached up vaguely to touch her curlers, obeying that part of her that wondered always, no matter what, whether she was fit to be seen. But it was only the most absent-minded gesture. Her eyes were still fixed on him, and she frowned a little and bent forward to see him more clearly.

"It's me," Ben Joe said.

"I know."

She kept watching him. The two of them seemed to be standing between the two ticks of a clock, in a dead silence of time where there was no need to hurry about anything; as long as she stayed silent and watchful they were frozen stock-still between that clock's ticking. Then she gave up, not finished with whatever it was she was trying to do but just giving up in the middle of it, and, clutching her quilted bathrobe more tightly about her, opened the door for him.

"I've been walking for hours," he said.

She nodded. Nothing seemed to surprise her. When he stepped inside she held up both hands, in a gesture like a doll's in a toy-shop window, to take the light sweater he was wearing, and he shucked it off and handed it to her.

"I know you weren't expecting company," he told her as she turned to hang up his sweater. "You can go on and do whatever you were doing before. I won't mind."

145

She didn't answer. The hangers in the closet tinkled flatly as she rummaged among them, and when she lifted one from the rod another fell with it, making a blurred explosive sound as it landed on a floor full of old rubbers and high-heeled galoshes. She ignored it; her eyes concentrated upon what suddenly seemed, to Ben Joe, the impossibly complicated task of getting his sweater upon the hanger. What was wrong with Shelley? Her fingers fumbled tightly at the collar of the sweater, taking hours to make it lie straight around the hook of the hanger. If it had been any other night, Ben Joe would have gone on in, would have left her in the hallway and headed for the living-room sofa. But tonight he felt uneasy. He wanted to tread as delicately as possible so that she would turn out to be glad he came. So he stood clenching his cold aching hands together and waiting hopefully for Shelley to finish this interminable business of getting his sweater up, and he never even looked toward the living room.

"I reckon you'll want some bourbon," she said.

"No."

"It'll do you good, if you're cold."

She headed toward the kitchen, making only the softest whispering noise across the floor in her bare feet. After a minute Ben Joe followed her. If she took so long to hang a sweater up, how long would she spend making a drink? And he really didn't want one; he felt awkward and foolish stumbling in here like this, and he didn't want to make it worse by accepting anything.

"I'm sorry I came without warning," he said.

"It's all right."

"I should have called first."

"It's all *right*, Ben Joe."

She stood on tiptoe to reach a liquor bottle from the cupboard, and Ben Joe leaned against the kitchen sink. He was surprised at how messy everything was; ordinarily Shelley was almost old-maidishly tidy. He could remember her spreading peanut butter on a piece of bread and then washing the knife and putting it and the peanut butter away even before she finished making the sandwich. And she had some sort of phobia about seeing that all the cannisters were neatly aligned along the counter and all the measuring spoons hung in order on the wall according to their sizes. But tonight the place was in chaos. Dishes and leftovers littered the counter; a recently washed sweater was balled up in the dish drainer and a shower cap was flung over the towel rack. He looked around at Shelley, trying to figure out what sort of mood she must be in. In her pale flowered bathrobe, a little too small for her, she looked wire-thin and brittle. But the shyness was gone, so much forgotten that she seemed not at all embarrassed at being caught in her bathrobe. In place of the shyness was a sort of heavy sullenness that he hadn't often seen in her before, that made her face look fuller and the lower lines of her cheeks sag. Her eyebrows had lost the high, uncertain arch they usually had and sat straight over blank eyes, and she was poking out her mouth in a way that made it seem like a pouting child's mouth. When she poured the drink she did it heavily, with finality.

"Have you got something on your mind?" Ben Joe asked.

She stopped, looked at the bottle, and then reached for another glass and poured a drink for herself.

"If you do," he said, "I wish you'd tell me. I hate this ferreting things out of people. I ask what's wrong and they say nothing, and then I say *please* to tell me and they say no, really, it's nothing, and I say well, I can just *feel* something's wrong. And by then we both hate each other. I keep thinking of everything bad I've done in the last ten years, things you wouldn't even begin to know, but somehow I start thinking maybe you've found out—"

"Oh, Ben Joe," Shelley said tiredly.

She handed him his drink and then picked up her own and headed for the living room. Behind her Ben Joe walked slowly, dragging his feet and watching the back of Shelley's head. The curlers bobbed up and down cheerfully, but her shoulders were slumped and careless. When they entered the living room, Shelley chose a seat in the wicker chair by the fireplace and Ben Joe had to sit alone on the couch opposite her. He felt exposed and defenseless, with all that bare expanse of couch at either side of him.

147

"I would do anything to help," he said. "But I don't know what's wrong."

Shelley raised her eyebrows slightly, as if what he was saying was a curious little toy he had handed her and she wanted to act polite about it. He had forgotten that she could be this way. He had seen her angry only a few times in his life – once or twice when he had dated other girls, and then one memorable time when she had taken three months to knit him a sweater in high school and then found he had grown two inches while she was busy knitting. Each time that she had been angry, the change in her had surprised him all over again. She became suddenly cool and haughty, and she left him feeling bewildered. Tonight no matter how hard he looked at her, no matter how patiently he waited for her to speak, she was unchangingly cool and blank-faced, sitting aloof in her solitary wicker chair. He sighed and took a long drink of the straight warm bourbon. He thought about the bourbon winding slowly to his stomach; with his head cocked, he seemed to be listening to it, noting carefully which part of him it was burning now. Shelley was turned into a carefully shut-out inanimate object on the other side of the room. A tune began in his head, hummed nonchalantly by that sexless, anonymous voice that lived inside him and always spoke words as he read them and thoughts as he thought them.

"So I guess I won't be coming tomorrow night," he said absently. Shelley's fingernail, tapping rhythmically against her glass, was suddenly stilled. "I've got to go back to New York."

The fingernail resumed its tapping. Ben Joe watched a specific place on the coffee table, a corner where the dust had gathered between the table top and the raised rim of it in a tiny triangle. He suddenly thought, without meaning to or wanting to, that tomorrow night when he was rattling northward on the rickety little train, this table corner would be exactly the same, would exist solid and untouched no matter where he was. Shelley would wash and neatly stack her dishes, and Gram would roar songs at the top of her lungs while she polished the silver, and everything – the solid little coffee table, the narrow polished windows, the hundreds of curtained front doors, all this still, unchanging world of women – would stay the same while he rushed on through darkness across the garishly lit industrial plains of New Jersey and into the early-morning stillness of New York. He leaned forward, resting his chin on his hand, and stared at the floor.

"Every place I go," he said, "I miss another place."

Shelley was silent.

"I don't know why," he said, just as if she'd asked. "When I am away from Sandhill, sometimes the picture of it comes drifting toward me – just the picture of it, like some sunny little island I have got to get back to. And there's my family. Most of the time I seem to see them sort of like a bunch of picnickers in a nineteenth-century painting, sitting around in the grass with their picnic baskets and their pretty dresses and parasols, and floating past on that island. I think, I've got to get back. I think, they need me there and I have got to get back to them. But when I go back, they laugh at me and rumple my hair and ask why I'm such a worrier. And I can't tell them why. There's nothing I can tell them. Pretty soon I leave again, on account of seeing myself so weak and speechless and worried. I get to thinking about something I just miss like hell in *another* town, like this tree on a street in Atlanta that has a real electric socket in it, right in the trunk, or the trolley cars in Philadelphia making that faraway lonesome sound as they pass down an empty street in the rain, through old torn-down slum buildings with nothing but a wall-papered sheet of brick and a set of stone steps left standing . . ."

Shelley was staring at him now, with her forehead wrinkled, trying to understand and not succeeding. When he saw that he wasn't making sense he stopped, and spread his hands helplessly.

"Oh, well," he said.

"No, I'm listening."

"Well." He paused, trying to arrange his words better, but finally he gave up. "Nothing," he said. "So you *go* to Atlanta, and you *see* the damn electric socket, and you *go* to Philadelphia and you *see* the damn trolley cars. So what? They only turn out to be an electric socket and a trolley car, in the long run. Nothing to keep you occupied longer than five minutes, either one of them. Then, in the middle of being loose and strong and on my own, wherever I am, along through my mind floats this island of a town with my family on it, still smiling on the lawn beside their picnic baskets . . ."

Shelley nodded several times slowly, as if she understood. He couldn't tell if she really did or not. He thought probably she didn't, but what mattered more than that right now was whether she was still in that black mood of hers and whether she would tell him why. He looked across at her steadily; her face returned to its original blankness and she stared back at him.

"So you're going back to New York," she said.

"I guess."

She was silent again. He began twirling the bourbon around in his glass, watching it slosh up and leave its oily trail along the sides.

"So you just come," she said, "and then you leave."

"Well, that's what I've just been explaining to—"

"You're not fair, Ben Joe Hawkes."

He looked up; Shelley's eyes were narrowed at him and she was angry. As soon as he looked at her she reached one hand up to her curlers again and then began pulling them down, with hasty, fumbling fingers, ripping them out and tossing them into her lap, where her other hand was clenched so hard that the knuckles were white. In spite of all his worries, in spite of being concerned at her anger and sad at the way this whole night had been, a part of Ben Joe wondered detachedly why she was taking her curlers out and why she was choosing this moment to do it. He watched, fascinated. Her hair without the curlers remained still in little sausage shapes around her head, and since she had no comb handy, she began raking her fingers through the curls in order to loosen them. But all the while her face seemed unaware of what was going on, as if this business with her hair was just a nervous habit.

"You come and then you leave," she repeated, "just like that. You're not fair. The trouble with you, Ben Joe Hawkes, is you don't *think*. You're a kind enough person when you think about it, but that's not often, and most of the time you—"

"Don't think about what?" he asked.

"Your coming and your going."

"Shelley, for God's sake."

"And then on *top* of all that, there's your sister."

He stopped in the middle of putting his drink on the table and looked up. There was something nightmarish about this. It was like one of those dreams in which he was playing the leading role in a play on opening night and had no idea what the play was.

"My sister," he said.

"*Yes*, your sister."

"Which one?"

"Benjamin Hawkes, don't you joke with me."

"Well, but what *sister*?"

"What sister my foot. How can you—"

"I have six," Ben Joe said patiently. He took another breath to go on and then suddenly, realizing what she meant, let his breath out again and sank back. Once more John Horner and Joanne stood looking at him on the porch steps, stood defensively close together in the Hawkes's living room, and Ben Joe shook his head at his own stupidity. There was something about Joanne; the minute she met a man, that man seemed to belong to her. Even John Horner, whom Shelley had so definitely identified as her own, was associated in Ben Joe's mind only with Joanne now that he had seen the two of them together. He had seen them first, after all, the night that Shelley had seemed to forget about John Horner completely. It was too confusing; he shook his head and said, "Lord, I'm stupid."

"Why?" Shelley asked curiously. She seemed to have expected more of a fight, and now she was temporarily taken aback.

"Joanne, you meant."

"Well, of course." She put both hands together in her lap and stared down at them. "Mrs. Murphy told me," she said. "Well, if it hadn't of been her, it'd been someone else. This town knows everything. I know she's your sister, Ben Joe, but I tell you she's just wild. With a husband and a baby, even,

151

she's wild. She's wild and no-count and after anyone who'll pay a little attention to her. Anyone can tell you that. Doesn't take a detective to figure it out. It's just you that won't listen. You don't hear facts too good if it's your own precious sister they concern."

"I hear them," Ben Joe said. He sat there, not looking at her, twisting his hands aimlessly between his knees.

"Oh, I didn't mean to go mud-slinging . . ." Shelley said suddenly. For the first time that evening Ben Joe saw the beginnings of tears in her eyes. She looked up shinily, with her mouth blurred and shaky, and stared hard at a point just above his head to keep from blinking the tears onto her cheeks. Shelley was the kind of girl who cried often, and from years of experience he had learned that with her the best thing was to be cheerful and brisk and to pay as little attention to the tears as possible. The little anonymous voice in his head picked up the tune again and went cheerfully da-da-deeing along. He kept his eyes upon an empty knickknack shelf in the corner behind Shelley's chair.

"Anyway," he said finally. He kept his voice pleasant and reasonable. "At least we've got to why you're angry with me."

"Why?" Shelley asked, and bit her lip hard and went on staring above him.

"Well, you were with me and therefore John went out with Joanne. It was black magic. Once in college I was in love with a coquette. She had a cute little pony tail that bobbed on the back of her head every time she took a step, and I thought she was wonderful. I would go for whole weeks without even looking at other girls, not even looking at one that I just saw on the campus somewhere, because I thought that then she wouldn't look at another boy. Sometimes it amazes me how superstitious I am. In the end, of course, she ran away and got married to this tuba player from Ditch 29, Arkansas—"

"You are just as lighthearted as a bird," Shelley said. "I declare, every time a body gets sad, it's a fact that someone'll come along all cheerful and tell them *their* problems, which aren't a bit more related—"

152

"I'm sorry," Ben Joe said. "I thought it was related. I'm sorry."

He began twisting his hands between his knees again, still not looking at her. When it seemed safe to start speaking again, when he was fairly sure that he hadn't sent her off into a real crying fit, he said, "All I meant was, that's why I'm to blame. Because it was me you were with. If you're superstitious too, of course. But I surely didn't mean to send John Horner off to my sister. God knows I—"

One of Shelley's tears must have escaped. She was too far away and the room was too dim for him to tell for sure, but he saw her hand flicker up to her cheek and then back to her lap again.

"Oh, well," he said, "you're probably not superstitious at all. It's probably nothing to do with that. But I'm trying to think what I've done and I can't come *up* with anything—"

"Oh, you silly," Shelley said. She hunched forward and began crying in earnest now, without trying to hide it any more, burying her face in her brittle white hands.

"Well," Ben Joe said for no reason. He searched hurriedly through his pockets, but there wasn't a handkerchief. On the mantel he spied a purse, a black leather clutch purse with a clasp, that always reminded him of old ladies. He rose and went to it just at the moment when the tune started up in his head again, but this time not even the little voice could drown out the whispery choking sounds behind him. He rushed through the contents of the purse – glasses, keys, coin purse, lipstick, arranged neatly inside – and found beneath them an unused Kleenex. Shaking the folds out of it as he went, he crossed over to Shelley and stuck the Kleenex in her hand.

"The way you talk," she said in a thick voice as she took the Kleenex, "you haven't done a thing in the world and are just asking what you did wrong to humor me, like. Well, I'll tell you what you've done." She blew her nose lightly. Ben Joe, standing over her, felt as if she might be Tessie or Carol. He wanted to say, "Come on now, blow hard. You'll never breathe again if you blow *that* way," but he resisted the urge and only waited silently for her to continue. "You just come to me when you want comforting," she said, "without ever thinking, without giving it any thought. My own mama told me that, although she thought the world of you. Like when things got bad at home you would drop over to get comforted and then leave, bam, no thought to it, and when it came time for the Pom-Pom prom you asked Dare Georges, who I *will* say was as *flighty* as the day is long, her and that little majorette suit she wore everywhere but church—"

"Oh, Shelley," Ben Joe said wearily, "try .and stick to the subject, will you?"

She blew her nose and nodded at the floor. When Shelley cried she became almost ugly, with that translucent skin of hers suddenly mottled and blurred. As if she were thinking of this now, she passed one hand across her face and then through her uncombed hair, and she sat up straighter.

"It's worse this time," she said. "Worse than the times before, I mean. Because this time I had a steady boyfriend, who was getting serious, and then along you came and superstition *nothing*, it's plain fact I had to tell John Sunday night was out because of you. Well, I know it's my fault going out with you. And I know I shouldn't be crying if I turned him down for you, but he's *someone*, isn't he? Someone that'll stay, and think about me sometimes, and let me have a kitchen with pots and pans?"

She had worked herself up to a good crying session again. Her voice was shaky and her chin wobbled. Sometimes Ben Joe thought girls must actually enjoy crying, the way they kept dwelling on what made them sad. He reached down for her drink, which stood almost untouched beside her chair, and bent over her with it.

"Take a good drink," he said.

"No."

"Come on."

He held it to her mouth and she took a swallow and tried to smile. Her face was puffy, with her eyes sleepy little slits, like a child's, and her mouth smooth and swollen. He thought there must be something about tonight that made it right for crying. First Gram, and then Shelley, and in a way even he felt like crying now.

"One more drink," he said.

She drank obediently.

"You want a cigarette?"

She pressed her lips together stubbornly and shook her head. "No, thank you," she said. "They give me halitosis."

"Oh. Okay."

He took one for himself and lit it. It was the first he had had all day and it tasted bad, but he kept puffing hard and not looking at her.

"Well, it's really me to blame," Shelley said, as if they were in the middle of an unfinished conversation. "It's me. For years, now, I haven't let anyone sweep under my feet."

"Under your—"

"So that I wouldn't be an old maid. I worry too much about having someone to settle down with, but I can't help it. Back home, when my family was alive, I would come in from work every day at the same time and climb the front steps of where we all lived thinking, 'It's five-ten just like it was yesterday and the day before, and just like then I am climbing these steps with no one but the family to greet me and the family to spend my evening with playing parcheesi and no man to care if I *ever* get home.' And I'd come in and head up the stairs toward my room and Mama would call from the parlor, she'd say, 'That you, Shelley?' and I'd say, 'It's me.' I'd climb the rest of the stairs and go toward my room and then out of Phoebe's room Phoebe would call, 'That you, Shelley?' and I'd say, 'It's me—'"

"Shelley, I don't think we're really getting anywhere with this," Ben Joe said.

"I'm explaining something, Ben Joe. I'm explaining. I'd go to my room and change to my house clothes, and I'd hang up my work dress neatly and I'd take my stockings to the bathroom and wash them out and hang them over the shower rail. Then I'd go back to my room and rearrange my underwear drawer, which I'd rearranged the week before, or I'd mend something or work a double crostic. At suppertime there'd be two questions for me. Daddy always said, 'You have a good day, Shelley?' and I said, 'Yes, Daddy,' and Mama'd say, 'You going to be doing anything special tonight?' and I'd say, 'I don't guess so, Mama.' Which was true and which went on and on, so sometimes I think I could

155

have just sent a tape recording home from work with my same old answers on it and done as well—"

"Well, what are you telling me for?"

"I'm explaining why I'm mad at you."

"You're still mad?" he asked.

"Course I am."

"Oh, look now. Look, *don't* be mad at me."

"You come, you go," she said doggedly.

"I don't either."

"You don't?"

"Well, I won't," he said. He had a desperate, sinking feeling; there swam into his mind again the picture of himself on the train and Shelley behind in Sandhill calmly washing dishes as if he'd never been there.

"I don't believe you'll *ever* change, Ben Joe," she said.

"Shelley, *I* won't come and go. I won't go on not thinking. Look, you come with me. You come to New York."

"Oh, now, wouldn't *that* give people—"

"No, I mean it. We could . . . hell, get married. You hear? Come on, Shelley."

She stopped looking at her hands and stared at him. "I beg your pardon?" she said.

"We could . . ." The words in his mouth sounded absurd, like another line from the unknown play in his nightmare. He hesitated, and then went on. "Get married," he said.

"Why, Ben Joe, *that* wasn't what I was after. I wasn't asking—"

"No, I mean it, Shelley. I mean it. Don't be mad any more. You come with me on the train tomorrow and we'll be married in New York when we get there. You want to? Just pack a bag, and Jeremy will be our best man . . ."

She was beginning to believe him. She was sitting up in the chair with her mouth a little open and her face half excited and half doubtful still, trying to search underneath his words to see how much he meant them.

"Sure," he said. "Oh, hell, who wants to go away and leave you with the dishes—"

"The what?"

"And come back like, I don't know, Jamie Dower maybe,

156

with no one to recognize him but a girl, and even she went on and married someone else—"

"Ben Joe," Shelley said, "I'm not following you too well, but if you mean what you say—"

"Of course I do," Ben Joe said. And he did; he was becoming excited now, watching her face eagerly to see that she was convinced and not angry any more. "Do you want to, Shelley? I'll meet you at the station for the early-evening train tomorrow. Do you want to?"

"Well, I reckon so," Shelley said slowly. "I just don't know . . ." For the first time that evening she really smiled, even with her eyes, and she rose and crossed over to where he stood. "You won't be sorry?"

"No, I won't be sorry."

"All right," she said.

"Will *you*? Be sorry, I mean. Will you?"

"Oh, no. Didn't I always tell you that, even back in high school?"

"I guess so," he said.

"Seems like you are always loving the people that fly away from you, Ben Joe, and flying away from the people that love you. But if you've decided, this once, to do something the other way, I'll be happy to agree. I'll meet you at the station, then."

She reached up and kissed him and he smiled down at her, relieved.

"What time is it?" he asked.

"About one."

"Lord. Shelley, if it's all right with you, I want to sleep on your couch. I can't face going home right yet, and I'll be out of here before morning."

She looked a little doubtful, but then after a minute she nodded. "Won't do any harm, I guess," she said. "But it's bumpy."

"That's all right."

"Phoebe used to sleep there sometimes. She was a little bit sway-backed, and she said there was a poking-up spring on that couch that would support the curve in her back."

She gave his cheek a pat and then turned and went quickly

over to the hall closet. From the top shelf she took a crazy quilt, permanently dingy from years of use.

"This ought to keep you warm," she said as she walked back to the couch. "You just hold this end, now, and I'll wrap you up in it. That's warmer than just having it over the top of you. Here."

He kicked off his shoes and then took the end of the quilt she handed him. Shelley walked around him in a circle, winding the blanket about him like a cocoon. When she was done she stood looking him over and then nodded to herself.

"You'll be fine in that," she said. "The lamp's above your head, and if you need anything you just call. Good night, Ben Joe."

"Good night."

He stood there by the couch, wrapped tightly in his quilt, until she had smiled for the last time and climbed the stairs to her room. When her bare feet padded gently across the floor above his head he laboriously unwound himself again and tucked the quilt around the foot of the couch. Then he took one of the throw cushions and placed it at the head for a pillow. He did these things with the special businesslike air that he always adopted when he didn't want to be bothered with thinking; if he let himself think tonight he would never get to sleep at all. So he sat on the couch and worked his feet down under the quilt methodically, concentrating solely upon the mechanical business of getting settled. And once he was in bed he made his mind into nothing but a blank, faceless blackboard, bare of everything that might remind him of the restless puzzling at the back of his mind.

14

IT WAS NOT yet morning when Ben Joe passed through the gate in front of his house again. The night was at the stage when the air seemed to be made up of millions of teeming dust specks, and although he could see everything, the outlines were fuzzy and the objects were flat and dim, like a barely tinted photograph. Ahead of him his house loomed, blank-faced. If he were passing by in a car at this hour, he would look at the house for a second and envy the people inside it, picturing them gently asleep in silent darkness. Even now he envied them, in a way. His eyes were gritty from a bad night and he thought of his sisters in their clean white beds beneath neatly curtained windows, most probably sound asleep and dreamless. But because he was no mere stranger passing by, he paused at the gate, and stared harder at the house than any stranger would have. It was such a locked-looking house, and so importantly secretive. In the daylight, especially in summer daylight, the house passed off those secrets carelessly and took on an open, joyous look; the screen door banged innumerable times and the girls in pastel dresses passed out lemonade to the young men lounging on the porch railing, and bumblebees buzzed among the overgrown hollyhocks beside the steps. But now, with those voices stilled and the porch deserted and all the windows black and closed against the winter darkness, who knew how many secrets lay inside? Who knew, from that self-important, tightly shut front door, what had gone on tonight and what new decisions his sleeping sisters had arrived at? He hesitated with his hand upon the gate and found himself swinging between loving that house and hating it, between rushing into the sleepy darkness of it and turning away and shrugging off its claim on him forever. Then the gate squeaked a little, and he pushed harder against it and walked on up the sidewalk to the front steps.

His feet on the cement made a gritty, too-clear sound; except for a few aimless chirpings in the trees around the house it was the only sound he heard. When he began climbing the steps his footsteps seemed dogged and heavy, and he thought again of how unreasonably tired he was. He had awakened often during the night, always with a sense of having forgotten something or left something undone, and even his sleep had been restless and strewn with brightly colored fragments of dreams. Now his head swam with just the effort of climbing the porch steps. Instead of going directly into the house, he turned toward the porch glider and let himself sink slowly down on it, to rest a minute and look out across the yard.

The cold of the metal glider soaked sharply through his trousers. He shivered and hugged his arms across his chest, and after a while his body became used to the cold and relaxed once more. The glider whined back and forth, making a lonesome, sleepy sound that sank into him as clearly as the sound of his footsteps had. If he were asleep now, safe inside his house in a warm, deep bed, and it were someone else upon this glider, those slow, gentle creaks would lull him into a deeper and deeper sleep. He would turn a little on his pillow and pull the blankets up closer around his ears, and the sound of the glider penetrating into his dreams would gradually build pictures in his mind of warm summer evenings and soft radio music drifting across green lawns . . .

He stood up sharply, feeling his eyes begin to mist over with sleep. If he were found asleep here in the morning, wouldn't they laugh then? Neighbors on their way to work would stop and look over the gate at him and smile. One sister would find him and would call the others delightedly, and they would all come out and laugh to see funny old Ben Joe torturing himself on a cold tin glider. Ben Joe the worrier. He would wake up to come in and have a sheepish breakfast among their little jokes, or he could sit huffishly out here and be even funnier. No, he didn't want to take a chance on falling asleep in the glider.

He sighed and crossed the wooden floor toward the front door. The backs of his legs were cold and stiff, like metal themselves, and there was a sore place in his side where Phoebe's favorite couch spring had poked him. As he was turning the key in the door he decided the only thing to do was go to his own bed. Tomorrow – or today – was going to be hectic enough and he might as well get rested up for it. The lock clicked open and he went through the complicated process of getting inside the house, ordinarily an automatic one but now, in his dreamlike state, as sharp in his mind as a slow-motion movie: press down the thumb latch, pull back hard on the door until it clicked, then abruptly press downward and inward upon the door until it gave and swung open, creaking a little and brushing across the hall carpet with a soft *sssh*. He stepped inside, pushing the front door shut behind him. There was a close, dusty smell in the hallway that rushed to meet him instantly, and for a minute he paused to adjust to the sudden darkness and warmth. He could see almost nothing. A pale flash on the wall identified the mirror; that was all. There was a deeper silence here than outdoors, but also there was the feeling that people were in the area. He no longer felt that he was by himself, even though there was no definite sound to prove it.

He headed blindly across the hall toward the stairs. As he passed the living room he looked through the wide archway of it and saw that the room was lighter, lit gray-white by the long bay windows. On the couch was a long, dark shape that stirred slightly as Ben Joe watched, and to satisfy his own curiosity, he changed direction and headed toward the couch. At his feet there was a sharp *ping;* a saucepan full of what looked like popcorn had been in his path. But the figure on the couch didn't move again, and after holding his breath for a minute, Ben Joe went on. He stopped at the head of the couch and stooped over, squinting his eyes in the attempt to see through the dusty dimness. It looked like Gary. His expression was hard to see, but Ben Joe could make out his pale face emerging from the depths of two feather pillows. His mouth was open but he was not snoring, only breathing gently and regularly in little even sighs. And his hair, drained of all its flaming color by the night, stuck out in sharp spikes against his pillows. Ben Joe watched him for a minute, considering the blandness of people asleep. Not even dreams or fits of restlessness seemed to bother Gary; he was peaceful and relaxed. Ben Joe shook his head and then, after putting away the thought of waking Gary up and asking him what had happened that evening, he turned back toward the hallway again.

Halfway up the stairs a sudden picture crossed his mind. He saw millions of houses, viewed from an airplane, and every couch in every tiny house was occupied by someone from yet another house. Everyone was shuffled around helter-skelter – Ben Joe on Shelley's couch, Gary on Ben Joe's couch, and God knew who on Gary's couch. The picture came to him sharply and without his willing it, and before it faded, it had nearly made him smile.

The upstairs hall was almost black; no windows opened onto it. He felt his way past the circle of tall white doors, all of them closed and with only the murmuring sounds of sleep behind them. Then he was in his own room, where his bed was a welcoming white blur with the covers turned neatly down and waiting for him. From the bedside stand he picked up his alarm clock and tilted it toward the light from the window, frowning as he tried to see where the hands stood. Five-thirty. That gave him at least another hour, and maybe more if only the girls would rise quietly for a change. The shade on his window was raised and a square of pale white shone through it onto the rug; he pulled the shade down to the sill so that the sun wouldn't waken him. Then he undressed, doing it slowly and methodically and hanging his clothes neatly in the closet so that he could go to sleep with the feeling that everything had been attended to in an orderly fashion. His socks he put in the small laundry hamper behind the door, making sure to lower the lid again without a sound. All his sisters slept lightly – downright night birds they were, and prone to wandering around at all hours – and right now there wasn't a one of them he wanted to see. He tiptoed to his bed and lay down, still in his underwear, and reached for his blankets gingerly so as not to creak the springs. The top sheet against his skin was cold and smooth and he felt immediately protected, and more ready for sleep than he had been under the rough, mothball-smelling quilt at Shelley's. He pulled the sheet up under his chin and closed his eyes, feeling them bum beneath the lids.

Wanting to be quiet kept him from changing his position. Gradually he grew stiff and tense, and his face muscles wouldn't loosen up, but he was afraid to move around. Why hadn't he got into bed on his stomach? He *knew* he couldn't sleep on his back. Carefully he turned on his side, trying to make his body light on the mattress and tightening his jaw with the effort. Now he was facing the center of the room, away from the wall. He could see all the dim objects he had grown up with and a white rim of pillow case besides (his right eye was half hidden in the pillow), and he couldn't *not* see them because his eyes wouldn't close. They kept springing open again. They looked around the room continually and searched out the smallest thing to stare at, while the rest of his body ached with tiredness and a headache began just above the back of his neck.

His room seemed to be made up of layers, the more recent layers never completely obliterating the earlier ones. Of the first layer only the peeling decals on the closet door remained – rabbits and ducks in polka-dotted clothes, left over from that time when he had been a small child. Then the layer from his early boyhood: a small red shoe bag, still in use, with a different symbol of the Wild West on each pocket, a dusty collection of horse books on the bottom shelf of the bookcase. And after that his later boyhood, most in evidence: a striped masculine wallpaper pattern, brown curtains, a microscope, the *National Geographics*. He tried closing his eyes again and thought about how each layer had become less distinct progressively; the top layer was flat and impersonal, consisting only of a grownup's clothes in the closet and a grownup's alarm clock on the stand, while the bottom layers were bright and vivid and always made him remember things, in striking detail, that had happened years and years before. He turned to the other side, grimacing at a creak in the springs, and faced the one picture on the wall: a black-and-white photograph of himself and Joanne on tricycles, in look-alike playsuits, with a younger, out-of-date mother between them in a mannish shoulder-padded suit and black lipstick. There had been another picture, with the cleaner square on the wall left to prove it, of his father in slacks on the mowed lawn with his hand on a teenaged Ben Joe's shoulder; but during the bad years Ben Joe had burned it, not knowing what else he was supposed to do.

He pushed his eyes shut; they popped open again. He turned on his back and looked at the ceiling and switched the room upside-down, picturing the furniture hanging from the ceiling and the light fixture sticking straight up from a bare and peeling plaster floor. To go out of the room, he must reach up an unusual height to the white china doorknob, and when the door was opened he must step over a two-foot threshold of striped wallpaper onto the chandeliered floor of the hallway . . .

The door opened. The crack of black at one side of it widened and widened until a girl's face appeared in it, a small oval that could have been any of them except that a sort of space helmet of lace above it identified the face as Jenny's. She didn't speak out but crept very stealthily toward his bed without so much as creaking the floor. To Ben Joe, lying there watching her from under heavy, aching eyelids, she seemed very funny all of a sudden – cautious and bent forward like a nearsighted old woman.

"Ben Joe?" she whispered.

He didn't answer.

"Ben *Joe*."

Her whisper was piercing; she must have seen the slits of his half-open eyes. Ben Joe stirred slowly and then muttered something, making his voice purposely sleepy-sounding.

"Come on," she said patiently. "*You're* not asleep."

She came to the foot of his bed, hugging her bathrobe around her, and sat down with a bounce that he was sure would wake the whole household. He sighed and drew his knees up.

"I'm *almost* asleep," he said.

"You're not."

164

She settled herself down more securely, tucking her feet up under her to keep them warm. Her face was lively and wide awake.

"How come you're up?" he asked.

"I don't know. Well, for one thing, I was wondering where you were."

"I'm all right," he said.

"Well, I was just wondering."

He lowered his knees and swung his feet to the other side of the bed so she would be more comfortable, and smiled at her, but all he could think of to say was "I'm all right" again.

"I know." She rested her chin in one hand and looked at him seriously. "Where'd you go?"

"Just out."

"Oh."

He paused a minute, and then finally gave in and said, "What happened to Gary?"

"He's sleeping on the couch."

"I know, but what happened to him? To him and Joanne?"

"Nothing, I guess." She began stirring around restlessly and after a minute she rose and pulled the window shade up. "Joanne said she was committed to a date and was darn well going to keep her commitments," she said. She was leaning her elbows on the window sill now; her whisper came back cool and sharp, resounding off the pane. "And even though that Horner guy said he thought it'd be better to take a rain check, she said no and went out real quick, leaving Gary kind of empty-handed-looking and Gram crying into the sofa cushions and wishing she'd married Jamie Dower—"

"What happened when she got back?" Ben Joe broke in.

"Joanne? I don't know. I don't think her date came inside with her when he brought her home again—"

"Thank God for small gifts," he said.

"Well, but she and Gary didn't talk too much. She just went on to bed after a few minutes. I reckon she's counting on getting it settled in the morning. While she was on her date, Gary stayed home and taught us how to make a French omelet. You take—"

"Jenny, I'm getting awful sleepy."

Jenny went on looking out the window, her face cheerful and her mouth pursed silently to whistle. "You should see Lisa," she said after a minute. "She's out walking under the clothesline. Can't get to sleep, I guess."

"Oh, Lord."

"Well, it's no wonder she had to go all the way outside, considering she shares a room with Jane. Can't make a sound in there. Step on a dust ball in your bare feet and Jane's wide awake wanting to know what that crunching sound was."

"Well, tell Lisa to come in," Ben Joe said. "Makes me nervous."

"You'd be more nervous if she did come in."

"No, I wouldn't."

"Oh, she'll come soon of her own accord, anyway. Don't worry about it."

"Well, all right," said Ben Joe. But he frowned and picked at the tufts on his bed spread. He never could have the feeling that the whole family was under one roof and taken care of; one always had to be out wandering around somewhere beyond his jurisdiction.

"You try and get some sleep, now," Jenny was saying. She straightened up and left the window, heading toward the door and tying the sash of her bathrobe as she walked. When she reached the hallway she turned back and said, "Night."

"Night."

"See you in the morning."

"If morning *comes*," Ben Joe said.

She smiled suddenly and closed the door on him with a gentle click. Ben Joe turned over on his side, facing the wall. He closed his eyes and found that this time they stayed closed, although the muscles of his face were still drawn tight. Against his cheek the pillow was cool and slightly rough. Every time he breathed, the pillow brushed his skin with a soft, crisp sound and it made itself into a rhythm, plunging him farther and farther down until he found himself in the black, teetering world of half-sleep.

His father was sitting at the sunlit breakfast table. His mustache was gone and his face was as lined and leathery as it had been the day he died, although Ben Joe himself was only a small boy sitting at the table beside him. Why wasn't he dreaming the ages correctly? Either his father should be a mustached, smooth-faced young man or Ben Joe should be at least old enough for high school. He pulled his mind up from the deep water of his dream and opened his eyes. He must get all this arranged right. No, he thought suddenly, he had to stop the dream altogether. He thought about flat, green things – leaves, chalk boards, lawns seen from a distance – to make his mind blank again. The face of his father stayed in one corner, twinkling and deeply lined.

He closed his eyes and gave in, sinking back into the stream of the dream. His father, frozen in one position at the breakfast table, became animated again, like a movie that has been stopped and then started at the same place. He was telling a story, one that they all knew by heart. Only he told it in that anonymous voice inside Ben Joe's head instead of his own deep booming one; Ben Joe's mind, searching frantically, was unable to recapture even the vaguest semblance of his father's voice. But the story came to him perfectly, word for word:

"When I was young, and liked to go places, my Uncle Jed said he'd take me to the Farmers' Market in Raleigh. *You* remember Uncle Jed. He was the one could walk barefoot on broken glass without feeling it and went on farming even after the family got their money. Well, sir, this was back in the days when the farmers went to market the night before and all slept on the ground in blankets so as to be up at five. And that's how I saw my first silly-minded boy.

"Not that I haven't seen plenty since.

"Big as an ox, he was, and kind of round-eyed, and hung his head like he knew he was silly and was damned ashamed of it, too. And well he might be. For soon's we all got to bed this boy began saying, 'What time's it, Pa?'

"And his pa would say, growly-like, 'Bout ten o'clock, Quality.'

"Quality Jones, that's what his name was.

"Name like that would make anybody silly-minded.

"And then Quality would say, 'What time's it *now*, Pa?'

"And his pa'd say, 'Little after ten, Quality.'

167

"Well, sir, this went on for maybe two hours. Farmers are patient men. They got to be. Got to see those seeds come up week by week, fraction by fraction, and sweat it out for some days not knowing yet is it weeds or vegetables making all that greeny look. So they kept quiet – just sort of muttered around a little. And when Quality started snoring, there was this little relaxing kind of sigh, like a breeze through a cornfield, all over the Farmers' Market.

"What good's a clock to a man in bed? What good?

"But that wasn't the half of it. For soon's Quality started snoring, his pa raised up on one elbow and looked over at him and he says, 'Quality, son?'

"'Huh, Pa?' says Quality, all sleepy-like.

"'You all right?' his pa asks.

"And Quality says, 'Yes, Pa.'

"That's the way it was all night. A fellow didn't have time to get his eyes shut properly before it'd be, 'You want to pee, son?', 'You want a drink of water, Quality?' Lord, I never will forget.

"After about two hours of this, my Uncle Jed he stood up and grabbed his army blanket and he shouted, to the whole market place he shouted, 'Folks,' he says, 'if morning ever comes, I hope you get to meet this Quality!'

"And everyone laughed, but Uncle Jed paid them no mind. He grabbed my blanket right up from under me and said, 'Come on, boy, we're going home,' and that sure enough is where we went.

"I never went back to that market place. Folks say it is still going, only modern now, but every time I think about it, it seems like the only way I can see it is at nighttime still, with Quality still on his crazy quilt, and all those men still waiting, waiting still, for morning to be coming. Yes, sir. Yes, sir."

His father smiled, and leaned back to look around at his family. In his sleep Ben Joe smiled too. (He was proud of himself; he'd dreamed it all correctly from beginning to end.) And there was the contented murmuring of the family settling back in their chairs in the sunlight. It was their favorite story. It belonged to them; their father always told it after a night like this one, when he said the women in this family thought night was only a darker kind of daytime, just as good as any time for wandering and for talking. Ben Joe leaned back in his chair exactly the way his father did, and looked around and smiled at his family smiling.

His mother said, "The *least* you could do is try to keep it a secret from the *children*."

(How had that got in? That was from another time; that was from years later.)

A man said, "Feel the calluses on my hand."

Ben Joe sat on an unfamiliar porch beside his mother. His mother was very angry. He looked down at the old man, way below him on the ground, reaching his hand to Ben Joe.

"Feel the *calluses*," the old man said. "I've worked and worked."

"Don't do it," his mother said.

He looked at his mother and then at the old man. He bent down toward the man's upturned, lined face and then he touched the man's hand, and quick as a wink the hand gripped his, vice-like, and hauled him off the porch and down to blackness.

"*Mother!*" he screamed.

But his mother's hand, reaching for him, gripped him harder, yanked him until his shoulder snapped. He was torn from the blackness back toward the porch but too far, and too hard, and now he was in greenness and falling even faster.

"Wake up," a voice said.

He awoke and he was on the glider, only it was the wrong color. In front of him stood his mother, looking out thoughtfully across the lawn with her arms folded. When he opened his eyes the eyelids creaked and groaned and scraped like the heavy tops of old attic trunks, and at the sound his mother turned and glanced down at him.

"You've been dreaming about your father," she said.

"I haven't," said Ben Joe.

"Ben Joe, *please*. Wake *up*."

He opened his eyes for the second time; this time he knew without a doubt that he was really awake. At the foot of his bed stood his mother, with a faded corduroy bathrobe tossed hastily around her. She was bent over a little the way Jenny had been earlier, and she was watching him with kind, worried eyes.

"What?" he said.

"You had a bad dream, I guess," she said. "You screamed 'Mother!' I thought – Where's your pillow?"

"Oh . . . on the floor," said Ben Joe. He watched dazedly as she reached down to pick it up for him.

"Is something wrong?" she asked. She had stepped closer now, and he could see the deep lines around her mouth and the anxious twisting motion of her hands upon the cord of her bathrobe.

"I'm all right," he said. "You go back to bed now. I'll be fine."

"If you'd like for me to sit with you awhile—"

"No, no. You go back to bed. Please.

She stayed another minute, looking down at him anxiously, but he made his face smooth and cheerful and eventually she sighed and straightened up again.

"Well, all right," she said. "But if there's anything I can get you, now—"

"Good night, Mom."

"Good night."

He thought she would never leave. Finally she turned and went absently to the door, and after looking back at him one more time she was gone. He tried to unstiffen his muscles. His legs were rigid and cold, and he couldn't relax them for more than a second before they stiffened again. But gradually, as the dream faded piece by piece and image by image from his memory, his body relaxed again. All that was left was a faintly sad feeling because he was afraid he had been rude to his mother. In this house there was only one recognized cure for nightmares; you rushed to the dreamer's room and offered him Postum and pleasant conversation. Only with Ben Joe that always seemed to make it worse. Probably that was what his mother was telling the others now. He could hear her voice in the hall, murmuring along against a background of other voices, low and questioning. When was night going to end?

He lay back tensely, and with great determination he began naming all the places he had ever been. Even one-night stays

170

in hotels. He pictured every single place (though the hotels tended to merge into a single dreary prototype) in his mind's eye, exactly as it would look at this very hour. His New York apartment, with Jeremy curled up like a bear in the pale light from the dirty window. The camp cabin he had slept in when he was ten, with half-finished lanyards dangling from all the nails on the wall. The boat he had stayed on one summer in Maine with his uncle, where the sunlight came to pick up the colors in the Hudson Bay blankets at something like five o'clock in the morning. Only no, it was winter now. He'd forgotten. Maine would be icy and gray with only the bleak Nova Scotia lobster boats moored in the tiny harbor. Maybe not even they would be there; he'd never seen it in the winter.

He reached back, turned his pillow over to the other side, and let his head fall back into the coolness of it. At the back of his mind the little voice began prodding him, pushing him into the next subject. Shelley. He frowned at the ceiling, turning the idea of Shelley every possible way and trying to think how all this had come about. He pictured himself walking to the train station and meeting Shelley, taking her to New York and surprising the daylights out of Jeremy and the few other friends he had. Writing home and announcing he was married. It sounded to him like one of those wild little what-if thoughts that was always wandering through his head – nothing logical or concrete but only a little tale to pass the time. But when he forced himself to believe it, when he went over all the plain facts of it like actually buying Shelley's ticket, he began to believe it. He sat up straighter now, tenser than ever. He caught himself in the act of sitting up and tried to lie back down, but his eyes were doing their springing-open act again; it was no use.

The clock said six forty-five. He stood up and stumbled toward the closet, not caring now *how* much racket he made. From the hangers he pulled down a white shirt and an old pair of slacks and piled himself into them hurriedly. He didn't want to stay in this room another minute.

Again the door opened. He heard the creak.

"What now?" he said, with his back to the door. He threaded his belt through the loops.

"Ben Joe?" Tessie said.

"Yes."

She padded over in her bare feet to stand beside him. In her too-long bathrobe and rumpled hair, she looked no older than Carol, and so cross and sleepy that Ben Joe felt sorry for her.

"Ben Joe," she said, "is it time to get up yet?"

"I think we could say so."

"I'm so *glad*," she said.

She turned around and walked out again. Out in the hallway Gram started singing, just a little more softly than usual, as she came down the stairs from her attic room:

"If you don't love me, love whom you please.
Throw your arms round me, give my heart ease . . ."

The shower in the bathroom was turned on. One of the twins opened the door of their bedroom and shouted out, "Susannah, does milk chocolate remind you of Chicago?"

"Of what?" Susannah said. It sounded as if she were in her closet.

" 'Chicago,' I said."

"I've never *been* to Chicago."

"I've been thinking about it all night," said the twin. "Milk chocolate reminds me of Chicago."

"You've never been to Chicago either."

"Well."

Someone downstairs started playing the piano. Ben Joe got down on his hands and knees beside his bed and began fishing under it for his shoes with an unstrung tennis racket.

172

15

"GARY," BEN JOE said. "Hey, Gary. Wake up, will you?"

He hated to wake people up. His grandmother had told him after breakfast that it wasn't good for people to sleep late and especially not in the middle of the living room, and that it was his job to see that Gary got up, but Ben Joe had put it off all morning. Now it was almost eleven; he had spent the last half-hour whistling very loudly in other parts of the house and kicking the furniture in the hallway, but Gary was still peacefully asleep with his mouth open.

"You're worse than Joanne," Ben Joe said to the freckled face. "*Gary?*"

Gary opened his eyes, opaquely blue, and stared up at Ben Joe. "Hmm?" he said.

Ben Joe was instantly embarrassed, caught peering at the privacy of a man's face asleep.

"Uh, would you like some breakfast?"

"That wouldn't be half bad," Gary said. It was amazing how quickly he came alive. He sat straight up and swung his incredibly long, pajamaed legs off the couch and scratched his head.

"What time is it?" he asked.

"About eleven."

"Oh, Lord."

He reached for the faded blue bathrobe at the foot of the couch and stood up to put it on. "It's a disgrace," he said, grinning happily. "I should've been up hours ago. What goes *on* in this house at night? All night long it sounded like mice above my head, just scurrying around as busy as you please. They went to bed so early and I thought it was a peace-loving family. And then I find out they didn't go to bed at all, seems like, just adjourned upstairs to carry on where they'd left off before, slamming doors and visiting back and forth. Me, I've always thought sleep was a wonderful invention. Not that being awake isn't nice too, of course. But when I get up in the morning I think, boy, only fourteen more hours and I can be back to sleep again. I like to see the covers turned down and waiting and the pillows puffed up so I can hop right in. And I never dream, because it distracts my mind from pure sleeping, so to speak . . ."

He was dipping his arms into his robe and tying it and then folding up the bed clothes as he talked, stopping every now and then to gesture widely with one arm. There was something fascinating about that constant flow of speech. He was the way he had been the night before – big and graceful and always in the center of the room, chattering happily away in a steady stream that left his listeners virtually speechless. Even Ben Joe, who had been an incurable talker as a small boy and had once lost a family bet that he could keep totally silent for fifteen minutes straight, could find no place to break in.

"Not that I'm complaining," Gary was saying. "I just think it's worth commenting on, is all. For years now I've been wondering at Joanne, wondering where she got her habits. You'll have to admit they're kind of odd. She's the only mother I know of that used to keep waking the *baby* all the time, instead of the baby waking her. And making milk shakes in the Waring blender at two a.m. Now, where, I'd think, as I'd wake up and hear her whistling and the blender going and the dishes clattering, *where* did she learn to live like that? Well, I'm mighty glad to meet your family, Ben Joe. It's good to see you."

He stuck out one long, bony hand and Ben Joe, taken off guard, stared at it a minute and then shook it.

"Uh, how about that breakfast?" he asked.

"Sure thing."

"I'll get it."

Ben Joe fled. He was glad to get out to the kitchen; Gary was much better than he had pictured him, but at the same time he felt inadequate around him. He couldn't welcome him

174

or say he was glad to see him or make one small response to all that puppy-dog friendliness because Gary was too busy talking to hear. Where had Joanne ever met him? He dropped an egg in the frying pan and stared out the window, trying to remember, but it seemed to him that Joanne had never said. She had simply announced that she was married. Well, Joanne never *was* one to tell much of her personal life. Her letters were full of things like how much wool cost in Kansas nowadays and what movies they had seen and how crabby Carol's pediatrician was. Everyone in the family wrote like that when they were away; it was probably because of Jenny's being the official letter writer. What *else* could you answer to a letter of Jenny's except the price of wool in Kansas? Still, he wondered where Joanne had met Gary. He cracked the second egg into the frying pan and went to the refrigerator for orange juice.

Gary appeared the instant his breakfast was ready, rubbing his hands together. He was dressed in a plaid shirt that clashed with his hair and a pair of corduroy slacks and he looked exuberant.

"Boy oh boy," he said, "I just love a big breakfast. They tell you what we had before bed last night? Pizza. A great big pizza with all *kinds* of stuff on – You seen Joanne?"

"She went out," Ben Joe said. "Downtown, I think." He cleared his throat. "I was just wondering where you and Joanne ever met up with each other."

"Oh, she was dating a buddy of mine. This was when I was in the Marines, back east. She was one of those gals that flits around a lot. Danced with practically everyone at this dance and I was one of them. Keeping her *with* me, now, that was harder than just dancing one dance with her. And she didn't like it that in civilian life I'm a salesman. Said salesmen always smiled even when they didn't want to, so how could she trust me. That's what she kept harping on, how could she trust me. And, besides, she thought I had no manners. You ever seen Joanne's feet?"

"What?"

"Her feet. You ever seen them?"

"Well, of course," Ben Joe said. "She's always barefoot."

Gary nodded and shoveled half a fried egg in his mouth. "That's why," he said with his mouth full. "Why they look like they do, I mean. The rest of her is kind of slim, but her feet are wide and smooth and brown like a gypsy's maybe, or a peasant's. You see her barefoot and *you'll* know what I mean. I always liked her feet. First time she ever met my mother she had little bare sandals on and her hair piled high and I was so proud of her I said, 'Mama, this is Joanne Hawkes. See her peasant feet?'

"And after we were alone again, you should have seen the row. She kept saying, 'I've never been so embarrassed in my life before; see my peasant feet, see my peasant feet?' and kicked me in the shin with one of them peasant feet so hard I can still feel it if I think on it awhile. That's why she said I was bad-mannered. That and this door-opening business. I believe in opening a car door for a girl when she gets *in*, mind you. But when she gets *out*, well, she just sits and sits all useless in the car while you get out and plod all the way around to the other side . . ."

He held his hand out toward the cream pitcher and Ben Joe, mesmerized, placed it in his hand while he kept staring at Gary's face.

"*So*," Gary said, "I went off on a fishing boat named the *Sagacity* one weekend with a fellow from Norfolk. Figured there wasn't any use staying around right then. Joanne said she didn't trust me far as she could throw a tractor and then went and accepted five dates for that weekend. *Five*, mind you. There was this about Joanne back then: seems she liked drawing people to her. Once she got them, she sort of forgot what she was planning to do with them, like. But if you drew *away*, she'd be out to draw you to her again. So when she heard I had left she got them to radio the *Sagacity* to come in again. Saturday, it was. They kept calling the *Sagacity* but the catch was this: it was a borrowed boat and me and my buddy, who was the captain, thought its name was the *Saga City*. We didn't connect them, you see. Makes a difference. So the man told Joanne there wasn't an answer and he didn't know what could be the trouble, and she started crying and all, and by the time the mess was straightened out we were on dry land again and Joanne had her arms around my neck and said she'd marry me. That was quite some day," he said.

Ben Joe nodded, with his mouth open. Gary laid his fork down and rocked back easily on the kitchen chair.

"So we got married and all, and of course Carol came along. You get to see that first picture we took of her?"

"It's somewhere around the house right now," Ben Joe said.

"Well, I'm glad. It's a real good picture, I think. I was hoping you all thought so too. I always wondered why your mama didn't come when Carol was born, or one of your sisters maybe. Almost a custom, you might say. But no one came."

"Well, anyway, we were glad to hear about it," Ben Joe said.

"That so?" Gary looked happy.

"Um . . ." said Ben Joe. He bent forward to lean his elbows on the table. There was a long string of questions he wanted to ask, like why was Joanne here now and why was Gary himself here, but he would hate to see that happy face of Gary's get a closed, offended look. In the tiny silence he heard the front door open and a pair of high heels walk in, with little, soft baby steps beside them. He looked up at Gary to see if he had heard too, but Gary was musing along on some path of his own. The high heels climbed the stairs, and Ben Joe in his mind followed their journey to Joanne's bedroom.

"I'd like to have a lot more children," Gary said unexpectedly. "Dozens. I like kids. Joanne takes too good care of just the one. She needs a whole group of them. She's always saying how Carol's got to be secure-feeling, got to have no wonders about being loved or not. But this way she just makes Carol nervous – follows her around reading psychology books. Wants to know what her nightmares are about. I say let her alone – kids grow up all right. But that's just *like* Joanne. She got in this Little Theater play once back in Kansas and had a whole bunch of lines to learn and got all worried about it. So did she just take a deep breath and start learning them? No sir. The night before the play opened I asked her did she know her lines and she said no not yet but she *had* got

177

almost all the way through this book called *How to Develop a Super-Power Memory*. If that isn't just like her . . ."

He smiled into his plate and then clasped both hands behind his neck and stared at the ceiling.

"She was like that about *me* once," he said. "Followed me around reading books about marriage. But when Carol came along she got sidetracked, sort of. It happens. So if she was too busy with Carol I'd just go bowling with the boys or watch TV maybe. And Joanne'd start feeling bad – say it was her fault and she was making the house cold for me. First time she said that was in a heat wave. You couldn't hardly see for the little squiggly lines of heat in the air. '*Cold*?' I says. '*Cold*? Honey, you make this house cold and I'll love you forever for it,' but Joanne, she didn't think it was funny. Carol was crawling across the table in rubber pants and Joanne picked her up and spanked her for no reason and then started crying and saying history was repeating itself. Huh. You believe in history repeating itself, Ben Joe?"

"Well, not exactly," Ben Joe said.

"No, I mean it, now. Do you?"

"No," said Ben Joe. "I can't believe history's going anywhere at all, much less repeating itself."

Gary lit a slightly bent Chesterfield that he had pulled from his shirt pocket. He was enjoying himself now – as wrapped up in his story as if he were watching it unfold right there on the kitchen ceiling, he never even looked at Ben Joe.

"Course she meant *you*-all's history," he said, "which is so confusing I never *have* got it straight and don't intend to. Hardly worth it at this late date. But whatever it was, it's got no bearing on us and Joanne's house wasn't a cold one, no. But Joanne, she gets *i*-deas. And up and left one day. Well, I don't know why. But here I am, come to get her. I always say," he said, looking suddenly at Ben Joe, "no sense acting like you don't miss a person if you do. Never get 'em back pretending you wouldn't have them if they crawled."

"I hope you do," Ben Joe said suddenly. "Get her back, I mean."

"Thank you, sir. Thank you. It's a right nice house you have here. You born in this house?"

"Yes."

178

"I figured so. I always have wanted to come visit you all. Joanne, she sometimes talks about this place when she's rested and just sort of letting her mind drift. Tells about all the things that go on here just in one day. It's right fascinating to listen to. Tells about your daddy, and how his one aim in life was to go to Nashville, Tennessee, and watch real country-music singers, the way some people want to go to Paris, only he never did get there—"

"I'd forgotten that," Ben Joe said.

"Oh, Joanne didn't. She was full of things. I know about the time when your mamma and daddy were just married, and he bet her that she'd drop out first on a fifteen-mile hike to, to . . ."

"Burniston," said Ben Joe.

"Burniston, that's it. Only neither one of them dropped out, they both made it, but what really got your daddy peeved was that the whole town of Sandhill followed behind them for curiosity's sake, and none of *them* dropped out, either . . . O, ho . . ." He threw his head back, with his mouth wide and smiling for pure joy, so that Ben Joe had to smile back at him. "And how you are the only boy in Sandhill that they made a special town law for, forbidding you to whistle in the residential sections because it was so awful-sounding. And Susannah's cracker sandwiches, made with two pieces of bread and then a cracker in between—"

"Joanne told you all *that*?"

"She did."

Ben Joe was quiet for a minute. For the first time he actually pictured Joanne married, telling a person what she had noticed in a lifetime and giving someone bits of her mind that none of them had even known she had. What bits, he wondered, would he give Shelley (if there were any to give)? And how did one go about it? Would he just lie back and say what came into his mind the minute it came, removing that filter that was always there and that strained the useless thoughts and the secret thoughts from being made known? But how could *that* be any gift to her? He frowned, and marked the tablecloth over and over with his thumbnail.

"I'll do the dishes," Gary said.

There were some things Ben Joe didn't want to tell; he didn't care if she *was* his wife. He wouldn't want to tell all about his family, for instance, the way Joanne had done. Or about the little aimless curled-in-on-themselves things he was always wondering, like if you were an ant, how big would the rust on a frying pan look and could you actually see the molecules going around; and why was it that a sunlit train going through a tunnel did not retain the sunlight for a minute, the way the world did just at twilight, so that it was a little trainful of sunshine speeding through the dark like a lit-up aquarium – useless things that a child might think and that Ben Joe had never seemed to grow out of. What would Shelley say to him if she knew all that?

"Did you hear me?" Gary said. "I said, I'll do the dishes."

Ben Joe pulled his thoughts together. "No," he said, "Gram gets mad if we do them. She says that the only thinking time she has is when she's doing the dishes."

"You sure?"

"Sure."

"Well, then . . ."

For the first time that Ben Joe knew of, someone managed to interrupt Gary. It was Gram, bellowing from somewhere near the front of the house:

"*Soft* as the *voices of a-angels . . .*"

"What on earth," Gary said.

He scraped his chair back and stood up to head for the sound, with Ben Joe trailing aimlessly after him. They found Gram in the den, standing in the middle of the floor with her head thrown back and her arms spread like a scarecrow's, roaring at the top of her lungs:

"*Whisp*ering ho-o-ope
Da da *da* da da . . ."

In front of her, Carol sat in her rocking chair and rocked like mad. Her little feet stuck out in front of her; her head was ducked so that she could throw her weight forward.

"You're not *listening*," Gram told her. She dropped her arms and beamed at Gary and Ben Joe. "I'm teaching her 'Whispering Hope.'"

"What for?" asked Ben Joe.

"What *for*? *Every* little girl should know something like that. So she can stand up in a lacy little pinafore like the one she's got on now – that's what reminded me of it – and perform before refreshments are served on Sunday afternoons when callers come. All your *sisters* know how to do it. Joanne used to recite Longfellow's 'My Lost Youth' and then Susannah would sing 'Whispering—'"

"*I* don't remember that," Ben Joe said.

"Well, we never actually did it in front of guests. Your mother wouldn't allow it. But we had our own private tea parties, sort of."

"Well, I'm leaving," Ben Joe said.

But behind him, as he left, Gary was saying, "That's a *great* idea. Do you know 'My Heart Belongs to Daddy'? I'd like—"

Ben Joe climbed the stairs two at a time and crossed the hall to Joanne's door.

"Joanne?" he called.

"Who is it? That you, Ben Joe?"

"Yes. Can I come in?"

"Sure, I guess so."

He opened the door. Joanne was at the door of her closet, looking at herself in the full-length mirror that hung there. She had on one of the gypsy-red dresses that she used to wear in high school and that had been left behind in her closet because it had faded at the seams. Faded or not, it was still a brighter shade of red than Ben Joe had been used to seeing lately. He blinked his eyes, and Joanne laughed and turned around to face him.

"I found it hanging here," she said. "I'd forgotten I had it. Do you remember when I used to wear this?"

"Of course I do," Ben Joe said. "You wore it up till the time you left home."

"I'd forgotten all about it."

She spun once more in front of the mirror and then stopped

smiling and sat down abruptly on the bed with her shoulders sagging.

"Did you want something?" she asked.

"Well . . . no."

"Is Gary up?"

"Yes."

He took his hands out of his pockets and crossed to sit in the platform rocker opposite her.

"How do you like him?" she asked.

"Oh, fine."

There seemed to be no words that would fill in the silence. He got up again and wandered aimlessly around the room. At the bureau he stopped and began looking through a silver catch-all tray under the mirror, full of odds and ends like rolled-up postage stamps and paper clips and pieces of lint.

"Hey," he said, "here's my nail clippers."

"Take them."

"I can prove they're mine. See this little license tag on the chain? I got it from a cereal company when I was about twelve. It has the year on it and the—"

"*Take* it, for *goodness*' sakes."

She lit a Salem and threw the match in the direction of the window. With the nail clippers in his pocket Ben Joe wandered back to his seat, still with nothing to say.

"I've been looking all over for them," he said finally. "Also there's a dent in the file part, where Jenny bit it when she was only—"

"Ben *Joe!*"

"What?"

"Nothing," she said after a minute.

"Well, what'd you say 'Ben Joe' for?"

"No reason."

"It seems kind of funny," he said, "just to scream 'Ben Joe!' at the top of your lungs as a way of making small talk. Why, I could think of a better topic than *that* if I—"

"Are you *trying* to irritate me?"

"Well, maybe so." He examined his fingernails. "Yes," he said after a minute, "I liked him fine. I did. Gary, I mean."

"You did?"

"Yes."

He looked up, saw that she was waiting for him to go on, and went back to frowning at his fingernails. "Came all the way here for you," he said finally. "That's something."

Joanne blew out an enormous cloud of smoke and nodded. She seemed still to be waiting for him to say more, but there was nothing else he could think of to say. When she saw that he was through speaking, she went over and sat down at her dressing table, still not speaking. She put her cigarette in the groove of a glass ash tray and began unpinning her knot of hair.

"If I could just get *organized*," she said. "I never have believed in going backwards instead of forwards."

Ben Joe looked up at her. He knew suddenly, without her telling him, what she had decided she was going to do about Gary. He could tell by her face, half happy and half embarrassed at having to announce that she was as reversible as anyone. He could almost read what she was thinking, and how she was trying to figure out the best way to say it gracefully.

Her hair fell to her neck in a little puff. She put the bobby pins in a china coaster, and picked up a comb and began pulling it through her hair. The red dress made her different, Ben Joe thought. It turned her into exactly the same old Joanne, right down to the swinging hair that she tossed with a little teasing movement of her neck. And this could be any day seven years ago: Ben Joe in the chair watching her get ready to go out, funny old fussy Ben Joe telling her she really should start coming in earlier; and Joanne thin and quick and vaguely dissatisfied in front of her oval mirror. Any minute one of the children would come in (they were still called "the children" back then, not "the girls") to watch, too. Going out was something exciting and mysterious then, something only Ben Joe and Joanne and Susannah were allowed to do; and the others always liked coming to watch the preparations. He felt suddenly sad, thinking about them – as if instead of merely growing up and still being right here they had died, and he was only now realizing it. He pictured all the children in a circle on the floor, newly bathed and ready for bed (it would have to be evening, then), all looking in the mirror to see the miraculous things Joanne did to her face. Joanne would be talking rapidly, teasing the children behind her and giving that saucy smile as she stared at her mascara in the glass – "Oh, it's only old Kim Laurence I'm going out with. I think I'll just stay home and let the baby go instead. You hear that, Tessie?" She would turn around and make a little face at Tessie, only three years old and already half asleep in the lap of a twin. "And won't Kim Laurence be surprised when his date comes rolling toward him in a baby carriage?" Or: "I'll tell you who I'm seeing tonight – it's Quality Jones. Quality Jones, and he's taking me to a New York night club and he's such *a fascinating* conversationalist. All he says is, 'What time is it, Joanne?' and I say, 'If morning ever comes, Quality, I'll be happy to tell you.'"

The image of the real Joanne, seven years older, glimmered in the mirror. Ben Joe bent his head and laid his index fingers across his eyelids, just lightly enough to cool them, but the muscles of his throat stayed hot and aching with all those tears held back, pressing forward for no reason he could name.

"Headache?" the face in the mirror asked.

Ben Joe nodded silently.

"I'll get you an aspirin." She stood up and started for the door. When she was directly in front of him she stopped there – looking down at him, he guessed – but she didn't say anything and after a minute she went on out.

She was gone long enough for him to be sitting up straight and whistling a little tune under his breath before she entered again.

"Soft as the voices of *a*-angels . . ."

he whistled. Downstairs Gram's voice, coming loudly and only a little indistinctly through three closed doors, tramped along with him.

"Here," Joanne said. She handed him an aspirin and a glass of water.

"Thank you," he said cheerfully.

184

He swallowed the pill with one gulp of water and set the glass down on the floor beside his chair. There was a frown on his face now; he sat with his hands clasped tightly together and tried to think of a way to help Joanne say what she wanted to.

"Um, if by any chance you changed your mind about leaving Kansas . . ." he said.

He paused, waiting without realizing it for Joanne to interrupt, but she didn't.

"If just by chance you did," he said finally, "I don't know that I would call it going backwards instead of forwards. Sometimes it's not the same place when a person goes back to it, or not the same . . ."

That little inner mind of his, always scrutinizing him as if it were a separate individual from him, winced. Ben Joe nodded and tipped his hat to it; the separate mind returned his bow and withdrew.

"Not the same person," he finished.

"Oh," Joanne said. She was looking down at her hands, acting as if this were a brand-new idea that would have to be given time to soak in.

"I don't know," she said finally. Her voice was relieved, and lighthearted. "That is something to think about, I guess . . ."

Ben Joe stood up. "Thank you for the aspirin," he said.

"That's all right. Bye."

"Good-by."

He bowed again, this time for real, and left, clicking the door gently shut behind him.

16

BEN JOE CAME downstairs as slowly and quietly as possible; his feet instinctively veered away from the centers of the steps, where the slightest pressure always brought forth a creaking noise. In his left hand was his suitcase, held high and away from his body so that it wouldn't bang against anything. His right hand was on the polished stair railing. His whole face seemed to be concentrated on the sleek wood of it and the thin film of wax that clung a little to his skin. He lifted his hand and rubbed his thumb and fingers together, frowning down, and then abruptly dropped his hand to his side and descended to the next step. As yet he had not made a single sound. He could go all the way downstairs and out the front door without anyone's ever knowing it if he wanted to. But he wasn't sure he wanted to. If he left without saying good-by, could he really feel he had left for good? He switched the suitcase to his other hand and began descending more rapidly, still frowning at how silly he would feel to announce so suddenly that he was leaving. In the back of his mind he knew he would never leave the house without telling anyone; yet his feet still moved cautiously and he still held the suitcase carefully away from the railing.

Once in the downstairs hall, he moved quickly across the half-lit area between the stairs and the front door. There was a square of warm yellow light on the rug, cast through the wide archway of the living room, and the murmuring voices of his sisters were as clear as if they were out in the hall also, but nobody noticed when he crossed the yellow square. At the front door he stopped, setting his suitcase by his feet, and stood there a minute and then turned back and entered the yellow square again.

"Mom?" he said at the living-room doorway.

"Mmm." She didn't look up. She was sitting on the couch, sipping her after-supper Tom Collins and leafing through a *Ladies' Home Journal*. Beside her Gram was reading Carol a chapter out of *Winnie-the-Pooh*, although Carol wasn't listening, and on the other side of the room Jenny and Tessie and the twins were arguing over a game of gin rummy. The other two were out somewhere – Susannah with the school phys-ed instructor and Joanne with Gary, showing him her home town before they went back to Kansas in the morning. But those who were still at home looked so calm and cheerful, sitting in their lamp-lit room, that Ben Joe almost wished he could stay with them and forget the suitcase at the front door.

"Hey, Mom," he said.

"What is it?" She looked up, holding one finger in the magazine to mark her place. "Oh, Ben Joe. Why don't you come on in?"

" 'Many happy returns of Eeyore's birthday,' " Gram was saying in her bright, reading-aloud voice. Carol sniffed and bent down to touch the bunny ears on one of her slippers, and Gram glared at her. "I said, 'Many happy returns of—' "

"I'm going back to school," Ben Joe said.

" 'Eeyore's birthday,' " Gram went on, no longer looking at the book but just finishing the sentence automatically. "Where you say you're going, Ben Joe?"

"To school," he said.

"You mean, *tonight* you're going?"

"Yes'm."

His mother folded the page over and then closed the magazine. "Well, I don't see—" she began.

"I just suddenly remembered this test I've got, Mom. I really have to go. I'm going to catch that early train . . ."

His sisters turned around from their card game and looked at him.

"Where's your suitcase?" Jane asked.

"Out in the hall. I just stopped in to say good-by."

"Well, I should hope *so*," said his mother. "Why didn't you tell us earlier? Now I don't know what to do about those shirts of yours that are still in the laundry—"

"Don't worry about it. You can send them to me later." He felt awkward, just as he knew he would, standing empty-handed in the doorway with everyone staring at him. His grandmother was the first one to stand up. She came toward him briskly, her arms outstretched to hug him good-by, and he smiled at her and went to meet her halfway.

"If you'd only told us, I could've made some cookies," she said.

"No, I don't need—"

"Or at least some sandwiches. You want me to whip you up some sandwiches, Ben Joe?"

"I haven't got time," he said.

The rest of the family was clustered around him now; Carol had her arms about one of his knees as if he were a tree she was about to climb. Behind his sisters stood his mother, with her face no longer surprised but back to its practical, thoughtful expression.

"I suppose it's about time," she said. "Looked as if you'd *forgotten* school."

"We'll drive you to the station," said Lisa.

"No, thank you, I've got plenty of time."

"But you just said you *didn't* have—"

"No, really. I feel like walking. Come kiss me good-by, everyone."

There was a succession of soft, cool cheeks laid against his. His grandmother held Carol up and she kissed him loudly on the chin, leaving a little wet place that he wiped off absent-mindedly with the cuff of his sleeve.

"Look, Mom," he said, when his mother stepped forward to hug him, "you tell Joanne good-by for me, okay? And Susannah. Tell Joanne I'm sorry to leave without—"

"Of course I will," she said automatically. "Try to get some sleep on the train, Ben Joe."

Gram kissed him again, with her usual angry vigor, and said, "Don't buy a thing on the train if you can help it, Benjy. You never know how much they're going to upcharge. Me, now, I have some idea, because I used to be a good friend of Simon McCarroll that sold cigarettes and Baby Ruths on the train from here to Raleigh some twenty years back. He used to say

188

to me, 'Bethy Jay,' he says, 'you'll never know how they upcharge on these here trains,' and I'd answer back, I'd say—" She stopped, staring off into space. It was her habit, when saying good-bys, to lead the conversation in another direction and ignore the fact that anyone was leaving. Taking advantage of her pause, Ben Joe's mother patted him on the shoulder and became brisk and cheerful, just as she always did at such times.

"I know you'll have a good trip, Ben Joe," she said.

"You got enough money?" Jenny asked.

"I think so. Jenny, you tell Susannah to take good care of my guitar, will you?"

"I will. Bye, Ben Joe."

"Good-by."

His sisters smiled and began turning back to their gin-rummy game. His mother led the way to the front door.

"You'll tell her too, won't you?" he said to her. "Tell her it's a good guitar, and a good hourglass and all. Don't let her go forgetting—"

"Oh, Ben Joe." She laughed and pulled the door open for him. "Everything'll take care of itself."

"Maybe."

"Everything works out on its own, with no effects from what anyone does . . ."

He bent to pick up his suitcase and smiled at her. "Good-by, Mom," he said.

"Good-by, Ben Joe. I want you to do well on that test."

He started out across the porch, and the door closed behind him.

When he was across the street from his house he turned and looked back at it. It sat silently in the twilight, with the bay windows lit yellow by the lamps inside and the irregular little stained-glass and rose windows glowing here and there against the vague white clapboards. When he was far away from home, and picturing what it looked like, this wasn't the way he saw it at all. He saw it as it had been when he was small – a giant of a place, with children playing on the sunlit lawn and yellow flowers growing in two straight lines along the walk. Now, as he looked at the house, he tried to make the real picture stay in his memory. If he remembered it only as it looked right now, would he miss it as much? He couldn't tell. He stood there for maybe five minutes, but he couldn't make the house register on his mind at all. It might be any other house on the block; it might be anyone's.

He turned again and set off for the station. The night was growing rapidly darker, and his eyes seemed wide and cool in his head from straining to see. Occasionally he met people going alone or in twos on after-supper errands, and because it was not really pitch-dark yet, almost all of them spoke cheerfully or at least nodded to Ben Joe whether they knew him or not. Ben Joe smiled back at them. To the older women, walking their dogs or talking to friends on front walks, he gave a deep nod that was almost a bow, just as his father had done before him. Two children playing hopscotch on white-chalked lines that they could barely see stepped aside to let him pass. He walked between the lines gingerly so as not to mess them up, and didn't speak until the smaller one, the boy, said hello.

"Hello," said Ben Joe.

"Hello," the little boy said again.

"Hello," Ben Joe called back.

"Hello—"

"You *hush* now," his sister whispered.

"Oh," the little boy said sadly. Ben Joe turned right on Main Street, smiling.

People were gathering sparsely around the glittering little movie house, and he could see dressed-up couples eating opposite each other in the small restaurant he passed. Just before he crossed to head down the gravel road to the station, a huge, red-faced old man in earmuffs stopped beside him and said, "You Dr. Hawkes's son?"

"Yes," Ben Joe said.

"Going away?"

"Yes."

"Funny thing," the man said, shaking his head. "I outlived my doctor. I outlived my doctor, whaddaya know."

It was what he always said. Ben Joe smiled, and when the light changed, he crossed the street.

The gravel road was just a path of grayish-white under his

feet, but he could see well enough to walk without difficulty. Even so, he went very slowly. He stared ahead, to where the station house, with its orange windows, sat beside the railroad tracks. The tracks were mere silver ribbons now, gleaming under tall, curved lamps. All around there was nothing but darkness, marked occasionally by the dark, shining back of some parked car. Ben Joe shivered. He suddenly plunked his suitcase at his feet and after a minute sat on it, folding his arms, staring at the station house and still shivering so hard that he had to clamp his teeth together. He didn't know what he wanted; he didn't know whether he wanted Shelley to meet him there or never to show up at all. If she was there, what would he say? Would he be glad to see her? If she wasn't there, he would climb on the train and leave and then it would be *he* who was the injured party; something would at last be clearly settled and he could turn his back on it forever. He looked at the blank orange windows, still far away, as if they could by some sign let him know if she was there and tell him what to do about it. No sign appeared. A new idea came: he could wait a while, till after his train had left, and then surreptitiously catch a local to Raleigh and take the later train from there. But what good would that do? The picture arose in his mind of chains of future wakeful nights spent wondering whether he should have gone into the station or not. He rose, picked up his suitcase again, and continued on down the hill.

It was warm and bright inside, and the waiting room smelled of cigar smoke and pulp magazines. Nearest Ben Joe was a group of businessmen, all very noisy and active, who mulled around in a tight little circle calling out nick-names and switching their brief cases to their left hands as they leaned forward to greet someone.

"Excuse me," Ben Joe said.

They remained cheerfully in his path, too solid and fat to be sidled past. He changed directions, veering to the right of them and continuing down the next aisle. A small Negro man and his family stood there; the man, dressed stiffly and correctly for the trip north, was counting a small pile of wrinkled dollar bills. His wife and children strained forward, watching anxiously; the man wet his lips and fumbled through the bills.

"Excuse me," Ben Joe said.

The husband moved aside, still counting. With his suitcase held high and tight to his body so as not to bump anyone, Ben Joe edged past them and came into the center of the waiting room. He looked around quickly, for the first time since he had entered the station. His eyes skimmed over two sailors and a group of soldiers and an old woman with a lumber jacket on; then he saw Shelley.

She was sitting in the far corner, next to the door that led out to the tracks. At her feet were two suitcases and a red net grocery bag. Ben Joe let out his breath, not realizing until then that he had been holding it, but he didn't go over to her right away. He just stood there, holding onto the handle of his suitcase with both hands in front of him as if he were a child with a book satchel. He suddenly *felt* like a child, like a tiny, long-ago Ben Joe poised outside a crowded living room, knowing that sooner or later he must take that one step to the inside of the room and meet the people there, but hanging back anyway. He shifted the suitcase to one side. At that moment Shelley looked up at him, away from the tips of her new high-heeled shoes and toward the center of the waiting room, where she found, purely by accident, the silent, watchful face of Ben Joe. Ben Joe forced himself to life again. He crossed the floor, his face heavy and self-conscious under Shelley's grave stare.

"Hello," he said when he reached her.

"Hello."

Her dress was one he had not seen before – a waistless, pleated beige thing – and she had a round feathered hat and gloves the same color. So much beige, with her dark blond hair and her pale face, made her look all of one piece, like a tan statue carved from a single rock. Her face seemed tighter and more strained than usual, and her eyes were squinched up from the bright lights.

"Ben Joe?" she asked.

He sat down quickly in the seat opposite her and said, "What?"

For a minute she was silent, concentrating on lining up the

pointed toes of her shoes exactly even with each other. In the space of her silence Ben Joe heard the whispery sound of the train, rushing now across the bridge at Dublin Cat River and drawing nearer every second. Men outside ran back and forth calling orders; a boy pushed a baggage cart through the door and drenched them for a second in the cold, sharp air from outside. Ben Joe hunched forward and said, "What is it, Shelley? What've you got to tell me?"

"I came by taxi," she said after a moment.

"What?"

"I said, taxi. I came by taxi."

"Oh. Taxi."

He stood up, with his hands in his pockets. Outside the whistle blew, louder and closer this time. The two sailors had risen by now and were moving toward the door.

"I got my ticket," Shelley said. "And I've got, wait a minute . . ." She dug through the beige pocketbook beside her and came up with a navy-blue checkbook. "Travelers' checks," she said. "I don't want my money stolen. We didn't talk about it, but, Ben Joe, I want you to know I am going to get a job and all, so money won't be any—"

The train was roaring in now. It had a steamy, streamlined sound and it clattered to a stop so noisily that Shelley's words were lost. All Ben Joe could hear was the steaming and the shouts and above all that the garbled, rasping voice of the loud-speaker. Shelley was looking up at him with her eyes glass-clear and waiting, and he knew by her face she must have asked a question.

"What'd you say?" he asked when the train had stopped.

"I said, I wondered, do you still want me to come?"

She started lining up the toes of her shoes again. All he could see of her face were her pale lashes, lying in two semicircles against her cheeks, and the tip of her nose. When the shoes were as exactly even as they could get she looked up again, and it seemed to him suddenly that he could see himself through her eyes for a minute – Ben Joe Hawkes, pacing in front of her with his hands in his pockets, setting out in pure thoughtlessness toward his own narrow world while she looked hopefully up at him.

"Course I still want you," he said finally.

She smiled and at once began bustling around, checking in her purse for her ticket, leaping up to push all her baggage out into the middle of the floor and then stand frowning at it.

"We'll *never* get it all in," she said. "I tried to take just necessities and save the rest to be shipped, but—"

"Come on." He grabbed her two suitcases and left her to carry the grocery bag, which seemed to be filled with hair curlers and Kleenex, and his own, lighter suitcase. When she had picked them up, he held the door open for her, and they followed the straggling soldiers out into the cold night air, across the platform and up the clanging steps to the railroad car.

"Passengers to New York and Boston take the car to the right!" the conductor sang out cheerfully. He put one hand under Shelley's elbow to boost her up the steps. "Watch it there, lady, watch it—"

A thin white cloud of steam came out of Ben Joe's mouth every time he breathed. Ahead of them the soldiers paused, looking over the seats in the car, and Ben Joe was left half inside and half out, with his arms rigidly close to his body to keep himself warm. He looked at the back of Shelley's head. A few wisps of blond hair were straggling out from under her felt hat, and he couldn't stop staring at them. They looked so real; he could see each tiny hair. In that moment he almost threw down the suitcases and turned around to run, but then the soldiers found their seats and they could go on down the aisle.

The car was full of smoke and much too hot. They maneuvered their baggage past dusty seats where all they could see of the passengers were the tops of their heads, and then toward the end the car became more empty. Shelley ducked into the first vacant seat, but Ben Joe touched her shoulder.

"Keep going," he said. "There're two seats facing each other at the back."

She nodded, and got up again and continued down the aisle ahead of him. It seemed strangely silent here after the noise outside. All he could hear were the rustlings of newspapers and their own footsteps, and his voice sounded too loud in his ears.

194

At the last seat they stopped. Ben Joe put their luggage up on the rack, and then he took Shelley's coat and folded it carefully and put it on top of the luggage.

"Sit down," he told her.

She sat, obediently, and moved over to the window. When Ben Joe had put his own coat away he sat down opposite her, rubbing the backs of his hands against his knees to get them warm again.

"Are you comfortable?" he asked.

Shelley nodded. Her face had lost that strained look, and she seemed serene and unworried now. With one gloved finger she wiped the steam from the window and began staring out, watching the scattered people who stood in the lamplight outside.

"Mrs. Fogarty is seeing someone off," she said after a minute. "*You* remember Mrs. Fogarty; she's got that husband in the nursing home in Parten and every year she gives him a birthday party, with nothing but wild rice and birthday cake to eat because that's the only two things he likes. She mustn't of seen us. If she had she wouldn't still be here; she'd be running off to tell—"

She stopped and turned back to him, placing the palms of her hands together. "What did your family say?" she asked.

"I didn't tell them."

"Well, when *will* you tell them?"

"I don't know."

She frowned. "Won't it bother you, having to tell them we did this so sneaky-like?"

"They won't care," he said.

"Well. I still can't believe we're really going through with this, somehow."

Ben Joe stopped rubbing his hands. "You mean more than usual you can't?" he asked.

"What?"

"You mean it's harder to believe than it usually is?"

"I don't follow your meaning," she said. "It's not usual for me to get married."

"Well, I know, but . . ." He gave up and settled back in his seat again, but Shelley was still watching him puzzledly.

"What I meant," he said, "is it harder for you to believe a thing now than it was a week ago?"

"Well, no."

He nodded, not entirely satisfied. What if marrying Shelley meant that she would end up just like him, unable to realize a thing's happening or a moment's passing? What if it were like a contagious disease, so that soon she would be wandering around in a daze and incapable of putting her finger on any given thing and saying, that is that? He looked over at her, frightened now. Shelley smiled at him. Her lipstick was soft and worn away, with only the outlines of her lips a bright pink still, and her lashes were white at the tips. He smiled back, and relaxed against the cushions.

"When we get there," he said, "we'll look for an apartment to settle down in."

She smiled happily. "I tell you one thing," she said. "I always have read a lot of homemaking magazines and I have picked up all kinds of advice from them. You take a piece of driftwood, for instance, and you spray it with gold-colored—"

The train started up. It gave a little jerk and then hummed slowly out of the station and into the dark, and the tiny lights of the town began flickering past the black window.

"I bought me a white dress," Shelley was saying. "I know it's silly but I wanted to. Do you think it's silly?"

"No. No, I think it's fine."

"Even if we just go to a J.P., I wanted to wear white. And it won't *bother* me about going to a J.P. . . . ."

The Petersoll barbecue house, flashing its neon-lit, curly-tailed pig, swam across the windowpane. In its place came the drive-in movie screen, where Ava Gardner loomed so close to the camera that only her purple, smiling mouth and half-closed eyes fitted on the screen. Then she vanished too. Across from Ben Joe, in her corner between the wall and the back of her seat, Shelley yawned and closed her eyes.

"Trains always make me sleepy," she said.

Ben Joe put his feet up on the seat beside her and leaned back, watching her face. Her skin seemed paper-thin and too white. Every now and then her blue-veined eyelids fluttered a little, not quite opening, and the corner of her mouth twitched. He watched her intently, even though his own eyes were growing heavy with the sleepy rhythm of the train. What was she thinking, back behind the darkness of her eyelids?

Behind his own eyelids the future rolled out like a long, deep rug, as real as the past or the present ever was. He knew for a certainty the exact look of amazement on Jeremy's face, the exact look of anxiety that would be in Shelley's eyes when they reached New York. And the flustered wedding that would embarrass him to pieces, and the careful little apartment where Shelley would always be waiting for him, like his own little piece of Sandhill transplanted, and asking what was wrong if he acted different from the husbands in the homemaking magazines but loving him anyway, in spite of all that. And then years on top of years, with Shelley growing older and smaller, looking the way her mother had, knowing by then all his habits and all his smallest secrets and at night, when his nightmares came, waking him and crooning to him until he drifted back to sleep, away from the thin, warm arms. And they might even have a baby, a boy with round blue eyes and small, struggling feet that she would cover in the night, crooning to him too. Ben Joe would watch, as he watched tonight, keeping guard and making up for all the hurried unthinking things that he had ever done. He shifted in his seat then, frowning; what future was ever a certainty? Who knew how many other people, myriads of people that he had met and loved before, might lie beneath the surface of the single smooth-faced person he loved now?

"Ticket, please," the conductor said.

Ben Joe handed him his ticket and then reached forward and gently took Shelley's ticket from her purse. The conductor tore one section off each, swaying above Ben Joe.

"Won't have to change," he said.

Ben Joe took his suit jacket off and folded it up on the seat beside him. He put his feet back on the opposite seat and slouched down as low as he could get, with his hands across his stomach, so that he could rest without going all the way to sleep. But his eyes kept wanting to sleep; he opened them wide and shook his mind awake. Shelley turned to face the aisle, and he fastened his eyes determinedly upon her, still keeping guard. His eyes drooped shut, and his head swayed back against the seat.

In that instant before sleep, with his mind loose and spinning, he saw Shelley and his son like two white dancing figures at the far end of his mind. They were suspended a minute, still and obedient, before his watching eyes and then they danced off again and he let them go; he knew he had to let them. One part of them was faraway and closed to him, as unreachable as his own sisters, as blank-faced as the white house he was born in. Even his wife and son were that way. Even Ben Joe Hawkes.

His head tipped sideways as he slept, with the yellow of his hair fluffed against the dusty plush. The conductor walked through, whistling, and the train went rattling along its tracks.

penguin.co.uk/vintage